Ties of Bargains

TARA GRAYCE

TIES
OF
BARGAINS

TETHERED HEARTS

TIES OF BARGAINS

LCCN: 2025900397

ISBN: 978-1-943442-70-6

To all my Dutch and Frisian ancestors who crossed the ocean and started a new life in the USA (though some took a side trip through Canada first). Especially my great-great grandpa Harmen whose name I borrowed for this book.

And to Miss Kisses, for being an even crazier dog than this book could possibly capture.

N
W
E
S
Court of Ice
Wilderness Court
Court of Artisans
Goblin Court
Court of Stone
Court of Mists
Court of Islands
Harvest Court
Court of Sand
Warlord Zaya
Court of Grass
Faerie Market
Great Library
Court of Revels
Tanglewood
King Oberon & Queen Titania's Court
Queen Mab's Court
Court of Knowledge
Court of Dreams
Court of Jungles
Court of Seas
Queen Hippolyta's Court
Swamp Court
Fae Realm
Court of Swordmaidens

Chapter One

His brother was dying, his father was bargaining with the *feeënvolk*, and Harmen, heir to the Duchy of Tulpenland, was going for a walk. After all, appearances must be kept.

Harm strolled out the door of the royal palace onto the brick road stretching between the building behind him and the canal before him.

The canal bustled, from the trading boats with their bottoms laden with goods and their high gunnels rising only just above the water to the passenger boats packed with people traveling around the city of Tulpenwerf. Even a few barges trundled along the waterway, laden with farm goods and farmers, distinctive in their wooden shoes. A few of the captains and crew members lifted hands in a wave to Harm.

Harm acknowledged with waves of his own, even as he drew deep breaths of the scents of water and fish, fresh air and sun-heated bricks. The walk was supposed to clear his head, but it was also a chance to be seen. His family might be falling apart, but the people on these streets must only see their prince bearing up under this burden with all the fortitude expected of him.

With that in mind, Harm's blond hair was neatly tied back at the nape of his neck and his beard meticulously trimmed. His black jacket hugged his shoulders over a crisp white shirt and gray trousers. He looked nothing like the rumpled, unwashed person he'd been an hour ago when the palace steward had awakened him from his night-long vigil by his brother's bedside.

A brief walk. That was all he'd allow himself. By then, hopefully, his father would have returned from bargaining with the *feeënvolk* for good or ill.

Harm plastered an empty smile on his face as he set out along the canal, lengthening his stride to stretch his long legs. He tipped his head to those he passed, wishing them good morning as they wished him the same in return. Stranger or neighbor alike, it was impossible to walk the canals of Tulpenwerf without being thoroughly greeted.

The tall red brick rowhouses on either side of the canal towered above him, crowded against each other as they leaned slightly over the canal. Their roofs glinted in a variety of tiles, from orange red to charcoal gray. Pots by the doors overflowed with various flowers, including tulips, adding bright spots of color amid all the red brick and red clay tiles.

Harm crossed a bridge and turned down a street that bordered an even smaller canal. Shops lined the street with quarters above for the shop owners. One shop advertised cheese while numerous restaurants lined the street from the pubs with beer on tap even at this time of morning to eating houses serving breakfast.

He chose one he hadn't patronized lately and took a seat on one of the chairs set at small tables crowded next to the canal.

Within moments, the proprietor hurried to Harm's table, giving a slight bow. "Heer Harmen. It is my pleasure to serve you this morning. How is Heer Gijs?"

"He is hanging in there." Harm flashed a tight smile. He wasn't going to lie, but he couldn't tell the truth either.

His little brother was near to death. A week ago, he'd been fine. But now, the best physicians in Tulpenland could do nothing but keep him comfortable while his fever raged and his body wasted away. Only magic could save him now.

Thus the reason Harm's father, Duke Johannes, had gone to the tulip fields last night, hoping to find a *fee* frolicking through the spring blooms.

It was a risk. The *feeënvolk* might not help. Or they'd snatch him back to their own realm instead of bargaining.

But the *feeënvolk* were their last hope to save Gijs.

Harm couldn't tell this restaurant proprietor any of that. The last thing the people needed to hear was that their ruler had been reduced to such desperate straits that he risked a bargain with the *feeënvolk*. The situation was bad enough with King Hendrik, the king of the neighboring kingdom of Suskeny, rattling his sabers. The people did not need to know that they might lose their king during a time of such tensions.

"He is in our thoughts." The man nodded somberly, pausing a beat before he asked, "What would you have this morning?"

Harm ordered his usual breakfast, buttered bread, a side of cheese, and milk to drink. As he waited for his food, he stared at the canal without seeing, absently returning the greetings of those who passed by.

What would he do if his father didn't succeed in bargaining for a healing potion from the *feeënvolk?* Worse, what if his father simply never returned? Harm would become the duke, his brother would still be dying, and his duchy would still be facing the threat of King Hendrik's posturing.

When his plate of food was placed before him, Harm dug in with a nod of thanks to the proprietor. While he would normally linger, he ate quickly and paid the proprietor, who didn't even resist the payment. There was no such thing as groveling to the duke or his son by offering free food. No, here in Tulpenland, business was business. No one refused payment, and everyone squeezed each coin for all it was worth.

Once he finished, Harm hurried back the way he'd come to the royal palace instead of taking a longer walk along the Ronddwalende River, the water source for the canals that provided such a vital network of trade and defense.

As Harm climbed the palace's front step, a guard opened one of the double doors for him. Harm nodded, then continued inside.

The front foyer was tiled in blue and white up to the

chair rail, then papered in blue to the ceiling. A broad, dark-stained wooden staircase wound upward.

Stijn, the palace's steward, halted at the base of the stairs. "Welcome back, Heer Harmen."

"Has my father returned?" Harm scrubbed his boots on the front mat. One didn't track mud through the palace. Cleanliness was one of the most lauded virtues here in Tulpenland.

"Yes, he has. He is with Heer Gijs." Stijn gestured toward the stairs.

"*Bedankt.*" Harm tried to put all his gratefulness into the word as he dashed for the stairs, taking them two at a time.

At the top, Harm raced down the corridor at a pace that wasn't becoming for the heir to a duchy, but he didn't care. Around him, the walls were clad in plaster and wood paneling, covering the brick and creating a cozier feel. Cerulean rugs covered the floor from wall-to-wall while plates of blue-and-white pottery decorated the walls.

He skidded to a halt and stumbled into his brother's room.

On the bed, fifteen-year-old Gijs lay pale and thin beneath the sheet, his blond hair dark with sweat against the white pillow. Vlek, his orange-and-white fluffy kooikerhondje curled next to his legs, the puppy resting his snout on his paws as he kept watch over his master.

Father sat on the chair next to the bed, lines grooving into his face while gray threaded his blond hair.

The seconds ticked with agonizing speed as Harm waited…*waited*…for his brother's chest to rise.

The sheet moved with a shudder as Gijs sucked in another breath.

Harm released his own breath, sagging against the doorframe. His brother still lived.

Father slowly lifted his head, something in his gaze as lifeless and hopeless as it had been before he left. "Harm."

Harm's stomach sank even as he forced himself to move farther into the room. "You didn't find the *feeënvolk.*"

It wasn't a question. Surely only that would create the look of agony currently twisting his father's features.

"No, I found them." Weariness and something like despair weighted his father's tone.

Harm fumbled for the second chair and slumped onto it. "Then what happened? Are they going to cure Gijs?"

Father made a noise almost like a sob in the back of his throat before he dropped his head into his hands. His shoulders shook for a moment before pained words —his voice deep and rough—groaned out of him. "I'm an awful father. At least Doetje isn't here to see this."

On the bed, Vlek whined and crawled a few inches forward, as if the dog sensed the added distress in the room and wanted to comfort Father too.

Harm's throat closed at the mention of his mother's name. Fifteen years ago, Mother had died birthing Gijs.

"You're just trying to save him." Harm gaped at his

father, shifting uncomfortably at the sight of so much emotion. Emotions were things experienced in private. Not so much in a stiff upper lip kind of way. More in the sense that life was crazy enough as it was; there was no reason to get ruffled by it.

When Father lifted his head, his blue eyes were nearly as gray as his hair. "A life for a life. That was the bargain they offered. I thought they were asking for *my* life. So I agreed. Of course I agreed! What father wouldn't sacrifice his life for his son! But it wasn't me they wanted."

Harm opened his mouth to ask, but he snapped his jaw shut to swallow as a weight settled into his toes. "They wanted me."

"I sacrificed one son's life for the other. I didn't mean to do it—but it's done, and it can't be undone." Father dropped his head back into his hands, digging his fingers into his hair. "I've traded you to the *feeënvolk.*"

Harm swallowed again, breathing deeply through his nose as he let the words settle.

He'd been bargained to the *feeënvolk*. They'd take him away to their realm where he would become a plaything, tortured for entertainment until he died. If he was especially lucky. His fate could be even worse than that if he wasn't.

Harm released a breath slowly, forcing himself to think only of the practical. His father was currently gripped with enough emotion for the two of them. "It's all right, Father. I would gladly trade my life to save Gijs."

After all, this was the unspoken pact he and Father had shared from the day Gijs had been born. Mother had given her life to bring Gijs into the world. Harm and Father were willing to sacrifice the same to save him now.

Father's shaking stilled, though he didn't raise his head.

Harm clenched his fists at his sides. "I'm thankful it's me. I'm young. I'm strong. And I will escape."

When Father raised his head this time, the utter despair twisting his face had lessened, a glimmer of hope in the wetness of his eyes. "You don't know what you'll face. The *feeënvolk…*"

"Are cruel and malicious. I know." Harm didn't let his face show anything but a hard determination. "But I will survive, and I will come home. I give you my word."

His word might not be as magically binding as a bargain with the *feeënvolk*, but a man's word wasn't given lightly. Harm would keep that promise or die trying.

Father gave a shuddering sigh, swiped a hand over his face, and leaned against the back of the chair once again, more collected and himself than he had been a moment ago.

Good. Now they could talk this through without pesky emotions messing up the logic.

"When will the *fee* come to heal Gijs and take me away?" Harm gestured to Gijs.

The movement drew Vlek's attention, and the dog lifted his head, his tail swishing over the sheet.

Harm rested a hand on Vlek's head, giving the dog a scratch behind his ears.

Father turned his face away from Harm to face Gijs, as if he needed the reminder of why he was doing this. "The *fee* said to be at the circle in the tulip fields at midnight tonight."

Tonight. So little time to say farewell and prepare to be snatched away by the *feeënvolk*.

Harm nodded, swallowing down the lump of panic so that it twisted deep inside his chest but didn't so much as flicker on his face.

Perhaps it was just as well. Gijs needed that cure as soon as possible, and the dread of being taken away would be worse than simply facing whatever came.

Chapter Two

With his pack weighing heavily on his shoulders, Harm paced beside the strangely circular patch of pure white tulips in the field several miles up the Ronddwalende River from the city of Tulpenwerf. The full moon beamed overhead, its silver light glistening in the dewdrops on the tulip blooms. Near the river, the squat silhouette of a windmill broke the otherwise flat landscape, its blades still in the breezeless night.

The mucky black dirt squelched beneath Harm's tall leather boots, and he still wore his good black coat, white shirt, and gray trousers. He was likely overdressed, but he was the heir of Tulpenland. He couldn't walk into the realm of the *feeënvolk* looking scruffy.

His father marched back and forth a few paces away while a handful of guards waited with the barge docked beside the riverbank. They were far enough that they wouldn't overhear or see, but close enough that Father could get to them quickly if things went wrong.

So far, the only thing going wrong was that the *fee* was late.

Father halted and glared at the tulip circle. "It's well after midnight." His tone indicated that he found it quite insulting.

Punctuality came above cleanliness and thriftiness for virtues. Bad enough that a *fee* was coming to take Harm away. It was a nearly unforgivable affront that the *fee* would be late doing it.

Harm huffed and rubbed his hands over his arms. At this time of spring, the night held a chill. "What do we do if they don't come?"

"If they don't come, they are the ones who broke the bargain. You would be free." Father's voice held a heavy weariness as his breath puffed silvery in front of his face.

But Gijs would die.

Harm paced along the squishy mud yet again, trying to stifle his yawn. He'd spent most of his day reading all the books on the *feeënvolk* he could find in the palace and the city libraries. When all the knowledge to be gleaned there had been exhausted, he'd haunted the merchants' quarter, asking the far-ranging traders for stories from other kingdoms.

Until a few generations back, Tulpenland had very few dealings with the *feeënvolk*, except for the occasional merfolk getting tangled in fishing nets. The theory was that the land—so waterlogged and barely kept above the reaches of the sea by dikes, canals, and windmills—didn't provide the firm anchoring points for *feeën* circles like other nations.

After tulips were introduced, Tulpenland experienced more interactions with the *feeënvolk* during the spring when the tulips were blooming. Even then, such occurrences were rare and usually staved off by the farmers cutting the blooms off the flowers.

But that left Harm unprepared for what he was about to face. He didn't have generations of lore of the *feeënvolk*. Just a head full of hastily crammed book knowledge and secondhand stories told by the seafaring merchants.

As Harm turned to pace back along the row between the tulips once again, a shiver spread through the night, tingling against his skin and raising the hair at the back of his neck. He and his father both turned toward the *feeën* circle.

The white tulips glowed, the moonlight collecting in a pool of silver.

A figure appeared in the silver a moment before a woman stepped from the circle into the tulip field, followed by a well-muscled dog.

In the haze of moonlight and shadows, Harm couldn't make out much of her features, though he guessed she was only a handful of years older than him. She had brown skin and straight black hair that she wore unbound down her back. Her clothes were leather and more form-fitting than anything he'd ever seen a woman wear before. The dagger belted at her waist was all business.

The brown dog at her side only came up to the woman's knees. But its square head was set on a thick neck over such a muscled chest that it looked like it could plow over a cow.

The *feeën* woman halted before them and rested a hand on her dagger's hilt. "Duke Johannes?"

"Yes." Father took a step forward before halting again, as if he wasn't sure how to address this strange, warrior-like woman. She must not be the same *fee* who Father had bargained with before as he didn't seem to recognize her. "Who are you?"

"I'm the mercenary tasked with delivering this and retrieving the package." She held out a stoppered glass vial. The contents glowed with a milky blue light at odds with the silvery moon overhead. "Have your son drink this as soon as you return tonight. He will be well by morning."

Father took the vial, closing his fingers over it almost hesitantly as he glanced at Harm, the moonlight glinting in the pained depths of his eyes. With that action, he sealed his choice of one son's life for the other's.

Harm gave his father a slight nod, and Father hugged the vial to his chest. His father might have promised his life away, but that didn't mean this wasn't Harm's choice.

"Then you must be the other son." The woman turned to Harm, her eyes appearing like black pools in the shadows of the night. "You'll be coming with me now."

Harm caught his breath, shifting back a step. He'd expected it, and yet...

"No." Father still gripped the vial to his chest, even as

he glared at the *feeën* woman. "The bargain was a life for a life. I will not hand over my eldest son until my younger son is healed."

"That vial holds your younger son's life already." The woman's fingers flexed on her dagger's hilt. "What is in that vial will cure him and restore him to health, returning his life to him fully, as you bargained."

Harm rolled those words over in his head, but he could hear no fault with them. The *feeënvolk* were wily. If his father had merely asked for a cure, then he might have received something that would kill Gijs quicker, as death could be considered a cure. But as far as Harm could tell, his father had bargained well and left no wiggle room in the wording.

But the woman's explanation also held the hope of Harm's salvation. If handing over that vial counted as a life, then Harm handing himself over to the *fee* would also count as his life. The bargain would be complete in that moment, and he would be free to escape without jeopardizing Gijs.

"For the bargain to be complete, your son must come with me now." The *feeën* warrior woman's posture grew more belligerent. Her dog gave a faint growl.

"It's all right, Father." Harm didn't want to go right now. If only he could see for himself that Gijs was cured.

But if this was the price, then so be it. He'd said his farewells already, knowing this would be the likely outcome.

Father nodded and took a step back.

The woman's posture relaxed, but she didn't take her

hand from her dagger as she turned to Harm. "Stand still while I search you and your pack for weapons."

Harm eased his pack to the ground, then held his arms away from his sides to indicate that he wouldn't resist. He didn't have any weapons for her to find.

She strode up to him, carrying with her the scent of leather, oil, and a sweet fragrance he couldn't identify. She was as close as if they were about to dance, her hands reaching for him.

Yet her movements were brisk as she patted him down, starting at his shoulders, checking each of his arms and down his chest and back. He tried not to react as she ran her hands over the waistband of his trousers, then down each of his legs. She paid special attention to his boots before she went through each of the pockets of his jacket.

As she straightened, she must have gotten a glimpse of the look on his face because she gave a huff as she opened his pack. "Your dignity is fine. Another mercenary might have made you strip naked to ensure you didn't have any hidden weapons."

Father made a choking noise, and Harm coughed, his neck heating as he tugged at his collar. He'd known the *feeënvolk* didn't have the same sense of modesty that Tulpenland held in high regard, but he hadn't expected it to be stated so baldly. Nor to have the indignities he might face start so soon. "And you deemed such a search unnecessary?"

She glanced up from rifling through his pack to sweep a glance over him from head to toe. "I could take you."

Harm's pride wanted to protest but…she probably could. She seemed far too comfortable with the weapon she carried while he was a Tulpenland prince who had only cursory training with weapons. "Good to know."

"Yes. Keep it in mind." The woman went back to poking through his pack. She inspected the wedges of cheese, unstoppered the flask to sniff at the cassis juice inside, and frowned at the salted pork. But at least she returned all the food to his pack without confiscating it. According to the stories, it was dangerous to eat *feeën* food.

After a moment, she held up a blue-and-white pottery plate and raised an eyebrow.

"Trade goods for bargains. Not a weapon, and thus something I'm allowed to take." Harm held her gaze without backing down. He wasn't going to budge on this.

He needed something in his favor, and this was the only thing he could think of. He'd gotten his hands on a variety of pottery plates, teacups, and even a teapot, and he'd used his spare set of clothes as padding to keep them from breaking or rattling. Hopefully the pottery would be unique enough to appeal to the *feeënvolk*.

"It's a lot of extra weight to carry." She lifted his pack with her free hand as if to test its weight.

"I know." Harm crossed his arms.

"I'm not carrying it for you." She stuffed the plate back into his pack.

"I don't expect you to."

"Fine. If that's what you want to take, it's no business of mine." She buckled his pack shut, then pushed to her feet. After reaching into a pocket, she drew out what looked like a slim rope, though it shimmered in the moonlight. "Now, let's—"

"Wait!" Father stumbled forward, holding out a hand, even as he stuffed the vial into his coat pocket with the other. "Please, let me have a moment to say goodbye to my son."

Harm met his father's gaze. They'd already said goodbye over an hour ago as midnight had been approaching. They hadn't wanted to say farewell with a *fee* watching.

There was something in Father's gaze. A glimmer that was more shrewdness than tears.

Whatever Father had in mind, Harm wasn't going to protest.

Harm strode the two steps to his father, even as his father stepped to him and, inexplicably, embraced him.

He stiffened, his arms at his sides. He couldn't remember the last time he'd been hugged. Grown men didn't hug. Women didn't even hug all that often. Tulpenlanders simply weren't the type.

As his father leaned close, as if to share a few parting, emotional words, he whispered, "There's an iron knife tucked into the back of my belt."

Harm hesitated only a heartbeat before he brought his arms around his father as if to return the embrace. Trying to keep his movements slight, he patted his father's back until his hand closed on the knife. As he pulled it free, he could feel straps for securing it to an arm or a leg, if he had the chance.

For now, he simply had to hide it as best he could.

She'd already searched him, so hopefully she wouldn't think to search him again.

Harm stuffed the knife up the sleeve of his coat, tucking the hilt into the seam at the end of his sleeve to hold it there as best he could. With a pat to his father's back, he stepped out of the hug. "Look after Gijs. I will come back as quickly as I can."

Father slid his hands free, as if reluctant to let Harm go to the fate that awaited him in the land of the *feeën-volk*. He didn't say *I'm sorry for trading you to the* feeën-volk. Nor *I love you*. Instead, it was a stiff, "Take care of yourself." But that meant the same thing.

Harm faced the *feeën* woman again and strode toward her, his heart hammering in his throat as he was all too aware of the iron knife up his sleeve. "All right. I'm ready to go."

"Hold out your arm." She gripped the shimmering, roughly ten-foot long cord in both of her hands.

She knew about the knife. Heart roaring, Harm held out his other arm, the one not hiding the knife.

Instead of ordering him to reveal the knife, she slipped the loop at the end of the cord over his hand and pulled the slip knot tight around his wrist. It didn't seem like a secure way to tie his hands—he could simply loosen the knot and slide his hand free—but he wasn't going to argue with her.

With a glance at him, she stuck her hand through the loop on the other end of the cord and pulled it tight.

In a flash, the cord became more transparent, though it still appeared as a string of sparkling moonlight running between them.

"What—" Harm stumbled back, staring at his wrist. When he moved his arm, the soft fibers of the cord rubbed against his skin, even though it didn't look so much like a rope anymore.

"Come." She spun on her heel and snapped her fingers.

Harm picked up his pack, swung it onto his back, and trotted to join her.

As he reached her side, she gave him a glare. "I wasn't talking to you." She patted the top of her dog's head before she held up her wrist with the tether. "I have *you* on a leash."

In other words, her dog had more freedom of will—and thus the need for a command—than he did right now.

So that was how it was going to be. Harm forced himself to merely grin back at her. The most annoying thing he could do was give her a dose of his Tulpenlander cheer. "I see. Your dog must be very well trained."

"Yes, she is." The *feeën* warrior shot Harm another sweeping glare. "I have yet to see how well trained you are."

Ouch. She left no doubt where he stood with her.

She strode straight toward the still glowing silver circle inside the white tulips, her dog trotting faithfully at her side.

Harm cast one last glance over his shoulder at his father, taking in his lined face, the agony in his eyes, the slump to his shoulders, before the cord tightened around Harm's wrist and he was yanked into the *feeën* circle.

Chapter Three

Valeria of the Wild Hunt had been saddled with a puppy.

Not her dog Daisy. No, Daisy was a mostly mannerly, somewhat trained, useful kind of dog.

No, the puppy trotting at her side was the far-too-pleasant, naïve kind of puppy that made one rather sorry when one had to kick him. Not that she ever kicked actual dogs. But people puppies? She was a fae mercenary; she kicked those all the time. It was just part of the job, and she did her best not to feel too guilty about it. But occasionally there came along a puppy that made her just the tiniest bit sorry for what she had to do.

Val rested a hand on Daisy's back as the two of them stepped into the faerie circle. The whirling disorientation of walking between the realms tore at Val, and she would have struggled far more to move, much less breathe, if she hadn't been touching the fae dog.

Animals had an easier time moving between the realms than people did.

Before she could drag in a breath, she and Daisy popped out onto the other side, the warmth and magic of the Fae Realm closing around her with a familiar weight after the strange, magicless feel of the Human Realm.

Here in the Fae Realm, the moon was only a sliver, and the night shrouded deep and dark around them. The stars overhead twinkled with a hint of blue she hadn't seen in the fainter, less brilliant stars of the Human Realm. On this side, a circle of red-and-white toadstools formed the faerie circle while tiny red flowers dotted the moss. As they were in the Court of Dreams, one of the Spring Courts, the thick air was choked with the overwhelming scent of flowers and moonlit dew.

Val gave a yank on the cord still attached to her wrist, and the human puppy stumbled out of the faerie circle to land on his hands and knees on the thick, brilliant green moss.

The human gave a cough, then sucked in a shuddering breath. "That was…a mind-shattering experience."

It was, but she wasn't going to give him any sympathy over it. If he couldn't even handle crossing between the realms, he wouldn't last long in the Fae Realm.

"Get up. We need to keep moving." Val spun away from the puppy. He would be forced to follow; the binding cord would ensure it.

"Where are we?" The puppy appeared in her peripheral vision, strolling at her side as he gaped at the sights around them. "Are these trees? No, they're gigantic ferns! Are they huge or are we small?"

Val marched forward beneath the spreading leaves of the ferns stretching high over their heads and tried to ignore him. He couldn't go away, but maybe he'd fall silent if she didn't respond.

He paused for just a few footsteps, gaping at the scenery like an utter loon, before he spoke again. "Where are we going?"

"Queen Mab. The bargain won't be complete until I hand you over to her." Val spat the words between gritted teeth. She shouldn't encourage his yammering, but she also didn't want him getting any ideas about trying to escape from her. He wouldn't succeed, but his resistance would be a hassle.

"I see." The puppy's expression turned contemplative for a moment before he looked at her again. "What should I call you?"

That did it. Val drew one of her knives, grabbed the cord to yank him forward, and shoved the point of her knife beneath the human's chin. "Look. I'm not your friend. I'm not your tour guide. I'm merely delivering a package, and that package happens to be you. We have a short walk, then I'll hand you over to your new mistress. We aren't going to be stuck together long enough for names or chitchat or whatever. Got it?"

"Yes." He started to nod, seemed to think better of it, and swallowed, his eyes flicking between her and the knife with all the wide-eyed innocence of someone who had never had a blade to his throat before. Such a hapless little pup. He was absolutely going to die here in the Fae Realm.

Oh, well. Not her problem.

Her problem was merely getting him from here to Queen Mab's court. That was it.

It had been strange that Queen Mab hired a mercenary for such a mission. The walk between her throne and this faerie circle was not that long, nor was this section of the Fae Realm particularly monster-infested. The Human Realm on the other side wasn't all that dangerous to the fae, not like trying to retrieve a human from the Greenwood where the foresters assiduously guarded the woods from fae incursions. She would have understood hiring a mercenary for that kind of mission.

But this? This was well below Val's caliber of skills.

Whatever. The sooner they hiked to the palace in the Court of Dreams, the sooner she could ditch this puppy and be on her way. Surely her Hunt Leader would have something more challenging for her by then. Even better if the mission needed multiple mercenaries, and she could set out with the close group of fellow mercenaries she'd formed within the larger Wild Hunt band.

Val sheathed her knife, stepped away from the human, and marched into the darkness beneath the foliage. Daisy ranged around them, sniffing the bushes and investigating all the animal trails.

After a few moments of blessed silence, the puppy felt the need to go back to yapping. "I'm not supposed to talk to you, but may I at least pet your dog?"

Perhaps he thought he'd survive longer if he made

friends with her dog. But if he wanted to pet Daisy, she wasn't going to stop him. That would count as entertainment rather than an annoyance.

"Sure." Val gave a whistle.

Daisy froze, her head lifting as her floppy ears pricked. Then her ears went back, her mouth opened in a toothy grin, and she took off at a full tilt run toward Val and the human. Daisy only barely slowed before she flopped into a sit even as she rammed into Val's leg. Only the fact that Val had braced herself kept her upright. Daisy peered up at her, tongue lolling, toothy grin on full display.

Val ran her fingers over Daisy's short, sleek fur and soft ears. "You're a good dog."

"Hello, puppy. May I pet you?" The human held out one of his hands, bending as he did so. "What's her name?"

Being the snuggly dog she was, Daisy didn't even take the time to sniff his hand before she got to her feet, tail wagging so hard her butt wiggled along with it. She pressed against the human's legs before sitting on his foot.

"Daisy." Val crossed her arms and resisted the urge to tap her foot. This would be worth the few seconds' delay.

"Daisy?" The human paused in petting the dog and glanced up at Val, eyebrows raised.

"Yes. What of it?" Val shifted her weight, her feet itching to get back to walking.

Daisy wiggled closer to the human, bumping his hand with her head as she insisted he go back to petting.

"Nothing. It's just very…normal." The human ran his hand over Daisy's head and down her back. He smiled, scratching Daisy behind the ears. "You're such a good dog. Yes, you are."

Daisy's grin grew, and she flopped onto her back, presenting her belly for a rub.

The human obliged, going down on one knee to better pet the dog.

Daisy wiggled and squirmed, her tongue lolling in happiness. Then, as Val had expected, two more heads, identical to the first, emerged out of her main head to join that one in grinning and tongue lolling.

"Aaah!" The human gave a cry as he fell back onto his rump, unbalanced thanks to that heavy pack he'd insisted on taking.

Daisy took that as a sign to tackle him, trying to wiggle onto his lap for some aggressive cuddling even as all three of her heads licked his face.

"Your dog—pft—three—blegh—heads." The human tried to cover his face and fend off the heads, even as he was trampled by the squirming, overexcited dog.

"She's a fae dog." Val wasn't going to coddle the human. A three-headed dog wasn't the scariest thing he'd see here in the Fae Realm.

Overstimulated, Daisy's eyes went wild as she leapt off the human and tore away into the forest, running in random circles before she raced back the other way. She spun a few more times before she flopped onto the ground, panting and teeth still flashing in her doggy grin. The two extra heads merged back into her main head, leaving her looking like a normal dog once again.

The human rolled into a sitting position, adjusting something up his left sleeve. A knife, probably. He likely thought she didn't realize he had a knife tucked up his sleeve, as if she hadn't noticed that highly suspicious exchange with his father and the way the fabric hung heavy.

But it wasn't her business. She'd searched him for weapons as instructed, and she could truthfully say she hadn't found any. She wasn't obliged to confiscate any weapons he gained after her search as long as she didn't see them.

"Daisy is way too normal of a name for that dog." He swiped his sleeve over his face before he climbed to his feet, hefting the pack. He glanced from Daisy to her. "You enjoyed that."

"Yes." Val turned and headed into the nighttime fern forest once again. They'd already delayed enough.

The human finally lapsed into a longer silence as they hiked over the moss and flowers, Daisy racing back and forth through the darkness.

After about an hour of walking, the fern forest brightened ahead of them, lit by thousands of faerie lights. Figures moved through the shadows headed in the same direction, from a tree nymph with her hair of leaves trailing down her back to the flitting pixies shedding glitters of dust behind them as they flew on their buzzing dragonfly wings.

The human had gone back to gawking. Fine by Val. If he was gawking, he wasn't talking.

Val led the way as the ferns opened into a field of moss with humongous flowers growing from it. Some of the flowers loomed high above them on tree-thick stems. But others were simply buds growing right up from the earth. Occasionally, one of the petals on the buds flopped aside, and a fae would step out of the flower-house.

As they headed for the center of the flower field, the buds grew closer together while ten-foot-tall stands of grass formed something almost like walls, hedging them in.

Music drifted on a sweetly scented breeze, coming from a building formed of various rose- and ivy-covered arbors. Elaborate gardens of hedges, fountains, and flowerbeds with non-ginormous blooms extended around the building in a chaotic, meandering manner.

Fae dressed in everything from swirling silk dresses in vibrant colors to outfits of leaves and flower petals drifted through the gardens and beneath the arbors.

As Val, her charge, and her dog approached, the fae halted their conversations, turning to stare at her. They whispered to their companions, sneering expressions twisting their lips and narrowing their eyes.

Whatever. Val didn't care how much they scorned her for being a courtless mercenary. She would much rather be a member of a Wild Hunt band than bound to a court and the whims of its often fickle ruler. She knew firsthand what those in power did to those who couldn't fight back.

Beneath an arbor festooned with trailing ivy, Queen Mab's throne of flowers and thorns perched, as sweet and spiky as the faerie queen. Her sycophants buzzed around her, attempting to win her favor, while the rest of her court swirled around the room-like space formed of the various flower-covered arbors.

To one side, a cluster of humans played various instruments, blood dripping from torn fingers. Their faces were blank-eyed and hazy, too dazed with faerie fruit to know their own names, much less what they were doing.

Her package's gaze lingered on the other captive humans, his blue eyes as wide as the plate she'd found tucked in his pack.

The crowd parted for her, and Val strode through them without meeting anyone's gaze. She halted in front of Queen Mab's throne, not bothering to bow. After all, Mab wasn't her queen.

Daisy sat behind Val's legs. Relaxed, but still guarding Val's back.

Queen Mab, an over-dressed pink-haired pixie, sprawled on her throne, her tiny heart-shaped face barely peeking above the layers of frothing lace piling around her neck. "Is this the human you were sent to fetch?"

"Yes. Here's the human for which your emissary to the Human Realm bargained." Val gestured to the human puppy. All Mab would have to do was claim the human as hers, and Val's job would be complete.

Her long lashes sparkling with pixie dust, Mab swept a greedy glance over the human. "He's a handsome specimen, isn't he?"

The human straightened his shoulders, his jaw working, as he faced the pixie queen. A good show of bravado, but all that bravery would be nothing but dandelion fluff once he was faced with the cruelties this realm enacted on captive humans.

"Whatever. Just claim him as yours, and I'll be on my way." Val resisted the urge to fiddle with the end of the cord looped around her wrist. The binding rope—and that loss of freedom that felt too much like moments from her past—was her most hated part of retrieval missions. Well, that and being stuck with whatever whining, pathetic puppy she'd been sent to retrieve.

"That fae had been quite correct when he said I would procure a delicious morsel for my collection if I did what he said." Queen Mab's gaze remained latched on the human, as if he were a piece of fudge she wished to devour. Or perhaps more like a dog with a bone she wished to chew to splinters.

The human blinked, then lunged forward so quickly that Val barely managed to snatch the cord and hold him back before he reached the faerie queen. "What fae? What did he tell you to do?"

"Hush, pup. Heel." Val yanked on the cord, forcing the human to stumble back to her side. The human didn't realize the perilous position they were in. Technically, Val was still under Mab's employ until the retrieval was complete. Still, Val stood on shaky ground when it came to operating in the Fae Realm, unbound to a court as she was.

"Mouthy thing, isn't he?" Queen Mab waved a delicate hand bedecked with rings formed of flowers.

"Please. I need to know what that fae said." Undeterred by Val's reprimand, the human brushed at his coat and faced the faerie queen again.

Queen Mab's gaze sharpened. "What will you give me, human? Information isn't free."

Val yanked on the cord again. "Wait to make bargains until after I hand you over."

If he made an unwise bargain now, he'd drag Val into it as well, unless she could extract herself from this situation first.

"Let him speak, mercenary. I'd like to hear what he has to say." Queen Mab's smile smeared too slick for her petite face.

Val sucked in a breath to protest, but the human was already stepping forward, his shoulders squared. "I would request that you tell me who this fae was and what precisely he told you when it came to me, my family, my duchy, and my father's bargain, and how that led to my present predicament."

"What would you give me in exchange?" Queen Mab's rosebud mouth pursed, as if she was looking forward to pouncing on whatever the human offered.

Val braced herself with an internal sigh. The binding magic of a bargain already hung heavy in the air. There was nothing for it now but to plot her way out of it when it went wrong. For it would go wrong. An innocent pup like this would no doubt stumble into something terrible.

He swung his pack off his back, knelt, opened it, and reached inside. He paused for a moment, his shoulders rising and falling as if he was preparing himself for something difficult.

Then he straightened, presenting one of the blue-and-white plates from his pack. This one had a depiction of a tulip field with a windmill in the background. "This pottery has been incredibly precious to me and my forebears. It was cherished by my grandmother, and I…" The human's voice grew rough, almost choked. "This is one of the last things I have to remind me of her."

Val worked to keep her face blank, even as she all but gawked at the human. He had a whole stack of that pottery in his pack—including everything from plates to teacups—and he hadn't acted at all sentimental about them when she'd come across them.

But he had mentioned using them as trade goods. She'd brushed it off as wishful thinking on the part of a naïve puppy, but was it possible she'd underestimated him?

With each word, Queen Mab leaned forward, the greed in her eyes so rampant she was nearly drooling. She'd drink up all the implications that taking that plate was robbing this human of something precious to him.

"And…" The human paused, as if he hesitated to go on. When he spoke, his voice was lowered, as if he were imparting a great secret. "It is a source of our wealth and power in the Human Realm. I will give it to you once I have heard the information I requested."

Queen Mab held out her hands and flexed her fingers, as if she wanted to snatch the plate from the human's hands. "Very well. I agree to your bargain."

Magic snapped into place, sealing the bargain.

The human held the plate away from Mab's grasping fingers. "The information?"

The faerie queen slouched on her throne, all but

disappearing in the mound of her swathing garments. "Fine. A fae came here. I don't know his name, so don't ask. He said that a prince in a human kingdom connected to my court was sick and that his father would soon attempt to bargain for a cure. I was to send one of my people to wait in the faerie circle to make the bargain when the king came. The bargain needed to be a life for a life, and the older prince's life was the one that must be demanded. I was to use a mercenary from the Wild Hunt to fetch my prize."

Val flexed her hand on the knife. A curious tale, indeed. One she would've brushed aside as not her business, except that whoever this fae was, he'd roped her into the deal by including that tidbit about using a mercenary from the Wild Hunt. That had made it Val's business.

Why would this fae go through all this trouble of meddling if he wasn't even going to stick around or get a prize of his own out of this bargain? It didn't make sense.

Had Diego, her Wild Hunt leader, known what was going on when he sent her to the Court of Dreams, telling her that her services would soon be needed? At the time, Val had assumed he meant that she would soon find work here in the troubled section of the Fae Realm, thanks to the skirmishes between the Court of Revels and Court of Knowledge. But had this mysterious fae contacted him too?

The human nodded, his eyes still slightly distant as if he were mulling over what he'd heard.

Queen Mab reached out her hands, making a grab-bing motion.

A trick. If the human handed the plate over now, Mab wouldn't be obligated to tell him anything else. As far as he would know, she had told him everything.

The human's gaze sharpened, holding the plate out of the queen's reach. "Is that all?"

Val eyed him, frowning. Good thing she was handing this human over soon. He might look as tooth-less as a newborn puppy, but he actually had something of a brain behind that grin.

The faerie queen huffed. "I was told to provide a cure for a particular fae poison. That's all I know."

The human puppy's eyes widened. "Then my brother was poisoned by a fae."

"Or someone who bargained with a fae for poison." Queen Mab flapped a careless hand, brushing that aside.

Even more curious. And dangerous. Just what was this human tangled up in? Val needed to hand him over before his problems became *her* problems.

A shower of pixie dust raining onto her skirts, Queen Mab wiggled her fingers again. "I have kept my end of the bargain."

With stilted movements, his face still pallid, the human stepped closer to the throne and held out the plate.

Queen Mab snatched it, clutching it in her tiny fingers. While the plate had appeared small in the human's grasp, it was as big as a platter in Mab's hands.

"Now that everyone is satisfied with that bargain,

can we complete the other bargain?" Val tapped her fingers along the hilt of her knife.

Queen Mab stopped stroking the plate long enough to scrutinize Val. "As much as I wish to add a human this delicious to my collection, I gave in to Titania's whining."

Something twisted in Val's stomach. Surely the queen didn't mean…

"I'm afraid I've already traded his bargain to Queen Titania to pay off a debt I owed her." Queen Mab clutched the plate in both of her hands. "He's not mine."

Of all the swamp-infested, dragon-eaten things! Val bit back her growl and forced herself to grit out in a reasonably personable tone, "In that case, I invoke the Law of Hospitality and humbly ask for a safe and secure room along with safe food for myself, my dog, and this human until the time that I should decide to continue my journey."

Queen Mab shrugged. "The Law of Hospitality doesn't apply to you. You don't have a court."

"No, but as long as I'm on a retrieval mission for one of the courts, I'm to be afforded the hospitality due a member of that court."

"Fine. The room and food are granted." Queen Mab gestured grandly in a rather overblown and bored magnanimity. "You're fortunate I'm still friends with Titania. The Court of Revels is on the outs at the moment. I wouldn't travel through the Court of Knowledge if I were you, nor would I depend on your tenuous link to the Court of Revels to grant you hospitality in many places of the Fae Realm."

Val wasn't going to thank Queen Mab for the advice or act like she was in the queen's debt in any way. "I can handle myself."

"Hmm. Perhaps. Though I'd keep an eye on the human. He's one worth snatching, I think." Queen Mab gave both of them a cruel smile before she returned her focus to her new plate. "Chicory, please see our guests to their room."

A wispy sprite woman with little blue flowers trailing from her hair stepped out of the crowd, nodded to Val, then pivoted to walk in a new direction in a clear indication to follow.

Val headed after the girl with Daisy sticking close to her legs. The human hurriedly shrugged on his pack, running to catch up before the cord dragged him.

As they left the structure of arbors and started down a meandering path between the giant blossoms, the human leaned closer to Val. "What does it mean that I've been traded to Queen Titania?"

At least he'd had enough sense to wait to ask until after they were well out of earshot of Queen Mab and her court.

"It means"—Val gritted out between her teeth—"that I'm stuck with you for a while longer."

Chapter Four

Harm stumbled after the *feeën* warrior woman and her dog, his mind reeling.

Someone had poisoned Gijs with a *feeën* poison. And that enemy was still out there, with his father and brother unaware and unprepared.

Had it been a *fee*? A human who bargained with the *feeënvolk*? And how had that mysterious *fee* known about all of this to set up the bargain with Queen Mab?

Harm's stomach churned. Hang the bargain. He needed to escape. Now.

The *feeën* girl leading them halted before what looked like a yellow tulip bloom, except that it was the size of a small cottage and rested directly on the ground instead of on a stem. The girl gestured to it. "Your room."

The warrior woman nodded. "Deliver food at midday."

With a bob of her head, the girl spun away, not giving Harm a glance. As if he didn't even exist.

Perhaps he didn't. Not here in the realm of the *feeënvolk*.

The warrior woman brushed aside one of the petals, then stepped into the flower, her dog trotting at her side.

Harm had little choice but to follow, tied to her by the cord as he was.

The inside enclosed them in yellow folds, the floral scent thankfully faint. A small round space held several spindly wooden chairs with moss cushions while what appeared to be two more petal doors filled the far side.

As soon as the flower petal door closed behind them, Harm tugged at the knotted cord at his wrist. The knot was a mere slip knot. He should have been able to loosen it and slip the cord off.

But no matter how much he tugged and pried, he couldn't seem to make the cord budge.

"Why won't it come off?" Harm tugged even more frantically. He needed to leave. To go home. His brother and father were in danger.

"It's a threefold cord crafted of moonlight, silver, and the fleece from a golden sheep." The *feeën* warrior faced him, crossing her arms. "Once it's put on, it won't come off until the bargain is complete. And before you get any ideas…"

She lashed out, a blur of black hair and brown leather, and gripped his wrist. Before he could even think about fighting back, her knife was out, swinging toward his arm.

Harm cried out, flinching away even as the knife came down.

But instead of slicing off his hand, the knife slammed into an invisible *something*, halting only a breath away from his arm.

"Why would you do that?" Harm yanked at his hand again, but he couldn't free himself from her grip.

"You can't cut off your hand or arm to free yourself. Nor can you cut off any of my limbs, so don't even think about it. But..." Her blade flashed as it whipped up from his arm to rest beneath his chin, the point digging into his skin. "You can still be killed, and I would be left dragging around your rotting corpse until you were delivered."

Then if he killed her...

She must have read the thoughts in his eyes for the knife dug harder against his skin. "Don't even contemplate killing me. First of all, you'd never manage it. Second, you'd end up hauling my corpse around with you for the rest of your miserable life, short as it would be. Third, you'd still have to keep the bargain your father made, otherwise you'd take the perils of a broken bargain back with you to your kingdom. Trust me, you don't want to do that. I'm your best chance of surviving long enough to fulfill the bargain, understood?"

Harm stilled, swallowing against the point of the knife. Even if he freed himself from the cord, he was still bound by the bargain. His first impulse had been to ignore it but...he couldn't.

From his research, a broken bargain would be more of a risk than whatever danger his father and brother were in. One of the merchants Harm talked to mentioned that a kingdom to the south had experienced a severe drought for nearly a decade thanks to a *feeën-volk* bargain.

Harm couldn't risk that, loath as he was to abandon his family to the peril they faced. "I understand."

Strangely, her words also implied that *she* couldn't get this cord off any more than he could. They were well and truly stuck together by this cord until he was delivered to Queen Titania.

"Good." She stepped back and sheathed her knife. "And don't even think about drawing that knife you might have up your sleeve."

Harm froze, a chill dousing him. He and his father had been so careful passing that knife. But if she knew about it…if she took it…then Harm would never escape.

"Look, I don't care if you have a knife. I did my job and searched you for weapons. If you acquired another weapon after my search, that's none of my business." She shrugged and turned away from him. "Just don't let me see it."

In other words, as long as she didn't see it, she officially didn't know about it. It was a strangely compassionate gesture from a *feeën* woman who hadn't shown him a lot of sympathy so far.

Or perhaps she just plain didn't care. About him or about whatever *fee* he might ambush with the knife down the road. Maybe she expected the same lack of caring from him when it came to prying into her business.

"Now I'm going to get some sleep. I don't care what you do, but we'll be heading out when I wake whether you are rested or not." She marched toward one of the tulip petal doors and pointed first at the other door, then at the one in front of her. "That's your room. This is mine. If you try to come in, I will kill you."

No chance of that. He wasn't the type to press those boundaries. Besides, sharing a flower-house like this was already beyond the pale when it came to Tulpenland standards of propriety between an unmarried man and woman.

With that, she stepped inside, the petal door falling shut with a soft shushing sound. Strangely, the cord connecting their wrists didn't go around the petal door. No, the strand of silver and sparkles went *through* the door.

Daisy, the sometimes-three-headed dog, curled up on what appeared to be a moss rug, though she eyed Harm with such big, liquid amber eyes that he couldn't help but stagger the few steps to kneel beside the dog and pet her. She rolled onto her side, presenting him with her belly.

As cute as she was, Harm just patted her side. He didn't want to risk bringing out those two spare heads again.

His pack and exhaustion pressed heavily on Harm's shoulders. He couldn't remember the last time he'd slept.

With the dog still watching him hopefully, Harm gathered his remaining strength and pushed to his feet. He glanced from the cord on his wrist to where it stretched through the *feeën* woman's door.

With a shrug, Harm shuffled across the strangely springy floor of the tulip house and gripped the petal door to the room she'd assigned to him. The petal was soft and smooth beneath his hand, exactly like a tulip petal back home. If a tulip were the size of a small windmill.

When he stepped inside, he found a bed formed of mounds of flower petals against the inner wall. A basin and pitcher of water set on a spindly wooden stand stood by the outer wall where it curved in the shape of the flower.

The yellow petal door slid shut behind him. When he glanced down at the cord, it ran through the wall that separated him from the *feeën* woman's room.

Such a strange magic. Where it passed though the wall, the cord appeared more light than fiber. And yet on his wrist, it was as firm as an iron manacle, though thankfully far softer.

When he slid his pack off his back, the strap went right through the cord. Same when he shrugged out of his black coat. But when he tried to pass his hand through the tether, it remained solid.

Mind-bendingly strange. All Harm could do was shake his head, too weary to puzzle over the oddness of this place, and collapse onto the flower petal bed.

Dogs who only had three heads occasionally, cords that were sometimes solid, sometimes not, and tulip bloom houses were the least of the bizarre things he would face in the realm of the *feeënvolk*.

———

Harm was dragged from hazy, outlandish dreams of pink frogs and talking tulips when something jerked his arm so hard that he was yanked from the petal bed. He fell to the springy floor with an *oomph* that was more a startled exclamation than pain.

"Get up, pup, or you'll be dragged." The *feeën* woman's voice came harsh and clipped from the other side of the door.

"At least give me a moment to wash up and change." Harm pushed himself off the floor. "If you drag me through the door now, I'll be in a state of undress."

Granted, he was only lacking his jacket and boots, but she didn't know that. The *fee* didn't seem as bothered by such things, but Harm was betting she'd still be reluctant to drag him from here if she thought he might be unclothed.

"Fine. Hurry up." Her tone rang even more brusque.

Harm rushed through splashing his face with water and changing into his set of more practical clothing, which included thick canvas trousers stuffed into his boots, a plain shirt, and a leather overcoat.

The last thing he did was strap the iron knife his father had given him to his lower leg, tucking it underneath his trousers, then inside his boot. It was a clunky weapon, with a rounded knob at the top and a hilt that lacked any sort of grip over the iron tang. The knob would surely give him a bruise.

Hiding it like that didn't make it very accessible, but he shouldn't draw it until it was time to escape. Until then, it would be safely out of the warrior woman's sight.

With that settled, Harm took out some of his salt pork, repacked his nicer clothes around the blue-and-white pottery items in his pack, shrugged on the heavy load, and strode from the room with his head high.

The *fee* wore the same leather outfit and weapons as she had that morning, though her hair was now tightly done in a single braid down her back. She stood in the center of the room, munching on what looked like an egg on toast—except that the egg was green and the toast was pink.

She jabbed a finger down at the tray of food sitting on what appeared to be a toadstool table. "Eat. These foods should be safe."

More of those green eggs and pink toast sat on the tray, along with an assortment of other strangely colored food. Her *should be* was not enough reassurance, given the odd colors.

Harm held up the unappetizing salt pork. "I have food."

"Suit yourself." She shrugged and kept eating, even as she headed toward the door. "We might as well eat and walk."

She didn't have a pack or seemingly anything to gather besides her dagger, which she already wore. She snapped her fingers for her dog, and that was that.

Harm trailed after her. Not that he had much choice, given the roughly ten feet of glimmering cord stretched between them.

She set a brisk pace as she wound through the towering blooms. Various *feeën* meandered around them, though the court seemed strangely quiet for the middle of the day. Then again, it had been bustling late at night. Perhaps these *feeën* were more nocturnal creatures.

Harm finished his meat, but he didn't say a word until they were back in the fern forest. Only once they were well away from all the other *feeën* did he ask, "How far of a walk is it to Queen Titania's court?"

"Too long." She all but growled the words as she stalked through the fern forest.

"We won't arrive tonight, will we?" Even with his long legs, Harm struggled to keep up with her quick pace.

"No." She rested a hand on her knife's hilt but didn't look at him.

Harm nodded. That confirmed something he'd been mulling over. He chose his words carefully. Saying the right thing now could be the difference between life and death. "I understand that you don't want to play tour guide or act as my friend. I'm not asking you to do so. However, given that we will be stuck together for a while and that dragging around my dead body would be a hassle, I think it's in your best interest to explain a few basics of this realm to me so that I don't die before we arrive."

He'd worded it so that it wasn't a bargain but an obligation of captor to her captive.

For long moments, she kept marching forward as if she hadn't even heard him. Her dog disappeared into the surrounding foliage, sniffing along a trail.

When she finally spoke, her voice had that aggravated tone that seemed to be her default. "Fine. But only because showing up with a dead body would be a hit to my reputation."

"Ah, yes. I can see how a mercenary's spotless reputation would be important for business." Harm worked hard to keep a straight face, his voice bland. No annoying the prickly *feeën* lady, no matter how tempting it was. "What should I call you? I'm not asking for your name or whatever is dangerous to share here in this realm. Just something to call you."

"Val." She crunched through a patch of smaller ferns that were an odd counterpoint to the otherwise enormous ferns stretching over their heads. "Call me Val."

Well, proper addresses would go the way of proper attire, it seemed. "And you can call me Harm. If you get tired of calling me *pup*."

The look she shot him said that she wasn't going to stop with that moniker anytime soon.

"Did you have strange dreams last night?" An impertinent question, perhaps. But his dreams had been… odd. Too odd to be normal.

"This is the Court of Dreams." One of her shoulders lifted in a semblance of a shrug. "Be glad we were guests last night. Our dreams tonight might not be as pleasant."

Good to know. Harm suppressed the urge to grimace. He didn't want to imagine what a nightmare induced by this place might be like. Better to move on to asking his next question.

"Where are we? Queen Mab has a court, but this Queen Titania also has a court?" No matter how much Harm had researched, he'd come up with very little information on the politics and kingdom-structure of the realm of the *feeënvolk*. If he were to escape—especially since he wouldn't be in the court attached to his human kingdom—he would need this knowledge.

Val glared at him, as if she knew this question had more to do with his eventual escape than keeping him alive now. Yet she sucked in a breath, her shoulders rising and falling. "There are many Courts throughout the Fae Realm. Each Court belongs to the broader Spring Court, Summer Court, Fall Court, or Winter Court, where the weather is perpetually that season. Right now, we are in the Court of Dreams, which is a Spring Court. We'll be walking to the Court of Revels, a Summer Court."

That sounded like a complicated system. "And we'll be walking the whole way? There isn't a public coach or river barge we can catch?"

Val huffed and rolled her eyes. "We don't have such things here in the Fae Realm. We do have the Anywhere Doors, which is how most fae travel between courts, but those are inaccessible to us."

"Anywhere Doors?"

She gave another huff, as if she was frustrated she had to explain something this basic. "They are doors that are magically linked to each other. By stepping through a Door, you can step from one place to another no matter how far apart those two places are."

"Huh." Harm tried—and failed—to wrap his mind around such a thing. He probably shouldn't find it so mindboggling. He was currently walking through a forest of ferns that stretched taller than the tallest trees in Tulpenland. "And we can't use them because…I'm human?"

"No. Humans are allowed to use them if they are a part of a court, just like any fae attached to that court." Val shoved aside a six-foot-tall stalk of grass with violent force. "But I'm not a part of any court."

"Queen Mab mentioned that last night." Harm swept a glance around the sunlit fern forest, the sky bright overhead, the moss beneath their feet dappled with shadows and light. "What does that mean?"

"All the fae here in the Fae Realm are pledged to one of the Courts. Well, nearly all of them. There are a few independent islands." Val shrugged, her jaw working. "But I'm not pledged to any court. When I'm not on a mission, my home is in the realm beyond this one. The Realm of Monsters."

Something called the Realm of Monsters didn't sound very habitable. No wonder she walked with violence wrapped around her like a cloak.

"The Realm of Monsters doesn't seem like a pleasant place to live." Harm spoke carefully, not sure if prying into this part of her life was a question too far.

"It isn't." She kept marching forward, not looking at him, her tone quelling. But at least she answered his question. That was more than she had been willing to do the evening before.

Perhaps it had something to do with the look that had bordered on respect that she'd given him after he'd bargained with Queen Mab. Or a good night's—well, morning's—sleep had vastly improved her mood.

"Then why live there?" Harm tromped around one

of the trunks of the ferns and adjusted the straps of his pack where they were cutting into his shoulder muscles.

"Most of us don't have a choice." That growl was back in her voice, her shoulders stiffening. "We're banished from the Fae Realm or cast out for various reasons. Some of us chose to live there rather than swear allegiance to a manipulative ruler. To survive, we join the scattered bands of the Wild Hunt. As a part of the Wild Hunt, sometimes we ride in force to raid the Fae Realm or Human Realm. Sometimes we hire ourselves out as mercenaries. But we're free, and that's enough."

He had the sense that was all she would say on the matter. It had already been more than he expected, though he hadn't missed the fact that she'd never clarified her particular reason for living in the Realm of Monsters.

As she was so fond of saying, it wasn't his business. Time to switch the subject back to something less personal.

"Last night you claimed the Law of Hospitality because you're on a mission for the Court of Revels. Wouldn't working for a court and gaining the rights of that court also transfer to the Anywhere Doors?" Harm needed to understand how the complicated laws of this realm worked. It could be the key to his eventual escape.

"No. The Anywhere Doors are pickier than the Law of Hospitality." Val grimaced, flexing her fingers on her knife. "Nor would claiming the rights of the Court of Revels help in this case. The Court of Knowledge, which controls the Anywhere Doors, has banned members of the Court of Revels from using the Anywhere Doors. They've also banned any use of the Doors that involves the transport of humans into captivity."

That would explain why they were walking instead of just using the magic of these Anywhere Doors.

The Court of Knowledge sounded intriguing. He would have to learn more as that sounded like the place to go for help, should he manage to escape.

"I have a question for you." She gave him a sidelong glance. "Where did you learn to bargain like that?"

"Like I did with Queen Mab?" Harm just shrugged, the motion reminding him of the weight of the pottery on his back. Heavy as it was, he didn't regret bringing the items along. "Every Tulpenlander learns to haggle from the cradle. Getting a good bargain is a way of life. The bargains are more monetary and less binding, but the concept is still the same."

"Hmm." Her hum held something that almost bordered on grudging approval. As if for the first time, she had some hope that he wouldn't get himself killed off through sheer foolishness. After a moment, her face hardened again. "Don't get used to such success. Mab is a pixie. She can be bought with any pretty bauble. Other fae aren't so easily bribed."

Harm sighed through his teeth, hoisting his pack high to try to relieve the strain on his shoulders. So much for bonding with the prickly *fee* who was attached to the other end of his rope.

A shrill, animalistic scream pierced the air, coming from a stand of brush ahead.

Harm reached for his boot before he stopped himself, his heart hammering in his throat. "What's that?"

"Our supper." Val strode forward without so much as a hitch in her stride, even as the animal shrieked again.

The animal's cries ended a moment before Daisy crashed through the brush, all three heads making an appearance. The dog gripped something brown and furry in the mouth of her middle head. She halted, then whipped her head back and forth, the muscles all along her sturdy frame standing out, as she made very sure the creature was dead.

Harm swallowed and forced himself to straighten.

Val strode to the dog. "Drop it, Daisy."

Daisy whipped the dead creature back and forth yet again, as if it was her new favorite toy.

Val slipped her hand into a pocket, pulled out what looked like a dried piece of meat, and held it out. "Sit."

Daisy sat, the eyes of all three of her heads focused on the meat Val held. After a moment, the dog dropped the animal carcass and tipped her noses up, her ears going back in a seal-pup appearance that would have been cute...if she hadn't had three heads.

Val tossed the treat, and Daisy raced after it. As soon as the dog's back was turned, Val snatched up the animal carcass. Even as Daisy's two spare heads merged back into the middle one and she snarfed down the treat, Val stuffed the animal carcass into a pocket without so much as a flinch. Strangely, her clothes didn't bulge with the size of the animal. It just…disappeared.

Harm adjusted the fit of the straps on his shoulders and gave himself a good shake. This strange *feeën* woman and her dog weren't on his side, exactly. But right now, that was as good of allies as he was going to get.

Chapter Five

As evening settled deeper around the seemingly endless fern forest, Val turned a spit over a crackling fire, roasting the carcass of the rodent Daisy had killed earlier that day. The pleasant spring warmth abated into a mild chill while a crisp breeze whispered through the ferns overhead.

The human—Harm—sat on a toadstool seat across the fire from her, the flames doing nothing to the cord that lay between them. His eyes were still slightly wide after watching her produce a tent, bedrolls, firewood, and miscellaneous camping supplies from her pocket.

Not the same pocket that held the dead rodent. One should never use the same pocket for dead things as one's other supplies.

She had then started the fire with her bottled dragon fire in its small stone jar, which had earned her further wide-eyed astonishment.

As she turned the spit, Val kept a wary eye on the darkness surrounding their little camp. She'd picked a spot among a tight cluster of ferns, the moss beneath them dotted with yellow flowers. The ferns weren't a circle, which would have been a cause for concern, yet they were close enough that they would provide some shelter for their camp.

Mischievous sprites roamed these wilds between the Court of Dreams and the Court of Revels, venturing out of their toadstool homes once the sun retreated below the horizon. They weren't dangerous, exactly. But they weren't *not* dangerous either.

Besides the sprites, there were also the faerie circles and the rifts where monsters could slip between the realms. Sure, Val lived in the Realm of Monsters and dealt with monsters all the time. But in the Realm of Monsters, she had the rest of her Wild Hunt backing her up. Grutte, with his massive muscles and even more massive great sword. Ignatius and Abelardo with their tricks. Chela and Jesenia, who always had Val's back. The rest of the Wild Hunt who, though they were not part of her gang of acquaintances, would still ride at her side into battle.

Here, she was alone with just Daisy to help her guard the hapless human.

Well, he wasn't as hapless as she had assumed. He'd bargained like a fae with Queen Mab.

But his soft hands and the bewildered look he got around weapons told her that he couldn't handle that knife he had tucked in his boot. If it came to fighting monsters, he would be about as much help as a log chained to her arm.

Once the meat was done cooking, Val hacked off a

hunk, stabbed it on a skewer, and held it out to Harm. "Eat."

He took the skewer, staring at the hunk as if he wasn't sure how to go about eating it. "No proper plate and utensils?"

"Are you volunteering to wash a whole stack of dishes once we're done?" Val chopped off another chunk for herself, stabbing it on a stick as well.

"No, I guess not." He shrugged but still eyed the meat warily.

"It's safe for you to eat." Val waved her spit at him, the swishing motion through the air helping to cool the meat.

Harm frowned at the meat, as if weighing his options. "I suppose it would be best to save my human food for my escape. Now that the journey is going to be longer than expected." He finally took a tentative bite.

If that logic was what got him to stop being picky, then she wasn't going to correct his assumption that escape was possible.

Daisy bounded into the firelight and skidded to a halt in front of Val. The dog plunked her butt down, her tail wagging, as she tilted her face up in a huge-eyed, begging posture.

Val bit into the meat and ripped off a chunk with her teeth. Then she juggled her own skewer while she sliced another chunk of meat from the carcass. She chopped it into smaller bites, making sure there weren't any bones, so that Daisy wouldn't choke. Then she set the pile of meat on a flat rock.

Daisy dove onto the meat, all three of her heads making an appearance as she snarfed the food down.

Val barely had time to take another bite before Daisy was back, begging for more.

She spent her meal alternating between eating and cutting up more meat for Daisy. Harm managed to finish his meat well before she finished hers, even with his persnickety, small bites. Such a mannerly human prince. Too bad for him that good table manners wouldn't keep him alive here in the Fae Realm.

Not unless he used them to seduce Queen Titania. But he didn't seem the type.

Harm glanced around before scrubbing his greasy fingers on the moss by his feet. "Will we arrive at the Court of Revels tomorrow?"

"No. The day after tomorrow. It will be a long walk." Val held out her greasy hands to Daisy, who licked them clean. Once the grease was gone, Val wiped the dog slobber onto her trousers before she pushed to her feet. "We should head for bed. We have an early morning tomorrow."

She didn't want him asking too many questions about the Court of Revels. Not that she was feeling guilty about handing him over to Queen Titania or anything like that. He was a package, and this was her job. No reason to get a conscience over it just because this particular package had the wide-eyed innocence of a friendly puppy.

"There's...only one tent." Harm eased to his feet, eyeing her, then the tent. "Will I be sleeping outside?"

"Don't be ridiculous." Val rolled her eyes as she used

a stick to scatter the remaining logs and coals so that the fire would burn itself out during the night. "I'm not letting you that far out of my sight even with the tether. A monster would get you in your sleep before you'd wake up to so much as scream."

Not that the flimsy canvas of the tent would do much to stop monsters. But Val would need to keep the human close enough that she and Daisy could defend him if they were attacked by monsters or sprites or whatever might stumble across them here in the Fae Realm.

Harm swallowed and glanced at the tent again. "But...last night...you said..." He trailed off, as if he couldn't think of a delicate way to phrase his question, as a red flush rose up his neck. "It's hardly proper."

Val huffed and ducked to crawl into the tent. "Just get in here."

She crawled inside, sitting on the end of the bedroll she'd laid out on the right side of the tent. She started unlacing her boots.

After a moment, Harm pushed aside the flap at the end and tentatively peeked his head inside. His shoulders relaxed beneath his stiff coat. "You could have mentioned there's a divider down the center."

It wasn't much of a nod to privacy. The divider was more a curtain, and it wasn't attached to the floor. With the tent so small, their bedrolls were only inches apart regardless.

"If you roll onto my side of the tent, I will stab you." Val didn't even bother to glare at him but continued taking off her boots and setting them at the end of her bedroll.

"Understood." The word scratched out, as if his throat were tight.

Good. She made him nervous. She preferred it when her packages feared her. It made things simple. The ones who wanted to be her friend were far worse.

"Stop dawdling in the door. You're letting in a draft." She unbuckled her knife and set it next to her pillow where she could easily reach it in the night.

Harm hurriedly tumbled the rest of the way inside, and the flap swung shut, plunging the inside of the tent into darkness.

For several minutes, she could hear Harm shuffling around as he tried to set up his bedroll in the dark. She hadn't set it up for him, of course. Why would she?

Once Harm had finally settled, Val gave a whistle.

With a leggy bound, Daisy burst into the tent. She trampled over first Harm's, then Val's legs, nearly getting herself tangled in the dividing curtain.

"No." Val kept her voice stern, even as she shoved Daisy back. "Stay at the end of the bed."

Finally, Daisy settled down and curled up at the end of Val's bedroll. Val wouldn't be able to stretch out all the way, but she was willing to give up space for Daisy. After all, the dog was their best defense if a monster came sniffing around during the night.

⎯⎯

HARM TRIED to keep his mouth shut as he all but gawked at the forest surrounding them. His coat hung over his arm, leaving him in just his shirtsleeves.

Partway through the day before, they had crossed a stone bridge over a gurgling creek—after Val had bargained with the troll who guarded the bridge. The fern forest had given way to towering deciduous trees, though the mossy ground remained the same. Across the distinct line, the forest was noticeably warmer, as if they'd stepped from a balmy spring day to a glorious summer one.

He'd kept his coat on for a while, but when sweat had slicked down his back and beaded at his hairline, he'd finally given in and taken it off.

There was no one here to care if he dispensed with the proper layers of clothing. He would still have more clothing on than many of the *feeën* he had seen two nights ago.

The only way he was going to survive was if he adapted rather than clung to things that would hinder him. No, he wouldn't discard his virtues. But ditching his coat to go around in his shirtsleeves was hardly the start of a slippery slope into immorality.

Now dusk settled around them, but even then the air remained so warm that he wasn't even tempted to put his coat back on. Lights danced in the distance among the trees while the ever-present floral scent on the air grew even heavier.

A music so lilting and chaotic that it was almost savage sawed on the breeze, ringing louder with each step they took.

A pair of *feeën*—a male and a female dressed in so little that Harm quickly averted his eyes—stumbled through the forest, holding goblets that sloshed something red. The two *feeën* clung to each other, so wrapped up in their drunken tryst that they didn't even glance at Val and Harm.

The breeze drifted past the two, carrying with it a scent so strong and sweet that Harm stumbled, his mouth instantly watering, his eyes going blurry for a moment.

Val gave a tug on the rope, as if to hurry him away. "Wine made from faerie fruit. It's the only thing that makes fae intoxicated. For humans, it makes you lose control of yourself and become fully susceptible to commands."

Harm swallowed, not sure how to brace himself against the shudder coursing through him. Just a whiff of the faerie fruit wine had been enough to mess with his senses. What would happen if he ate or drank some of it? "I appreciate the warning."

"That wasn't a warning." Val faced the lights in the forest ahead of them, the gleam reflecting in her dark eyes. "I was stating your reality. A warning won't do you any good. If Queen Titania wishes to make a plaything of you, you'll be forced to consume faerie fruit whether or not you wish to do so."

That knot in the pit of his stomach tightened. This Queen Titania sounded far worse than Mab.

Harm forced himself to take a deep breath and straighten his shoulders. He didn't regret the fact that he was here. After all, this was the price of his brother's life.

A price some *fee* had set for an unknown reason. Once Harm was turned over to Queen Titania, he could finally escape and warn his father and brother about the danger they were still in.

Val strode forward with the same iron-edged determination she'd shown before when trying to hand him over to Queen Mab. Apparently she was just as eager to hand him over and complete her mission as he was to finally escape this place.

They stepped into a broad space formed of trees arching overhead like the beams of a castle's hall. At the far end, a jagged cliff rose toward the starry sky, its ledges dripping with vines and moss.

As Val and Harm strode down the promenade, Daisy trotting at Val's side, they passed figures sprawled among the foliage, emitting giggles and whispers and other sounds Harm didn't want to dwell on. The *feeën* he could see wore everything from draping folds of silk to dresses formed of flowers to some outfits that could barely be termed clothing as they were nothing but a strategically placed leaf or two.

He'd thought Queen Mab's court was underdressed, but this court made them appear downright modest. The back of his neck burned with the utter embarrassment of standing in such a debauched place. He'd never so much as wandered the dock district of Tulpenwerf after dark.

At the far end near the cliff, a *feeën* woman with a glittering, gem-studded crown resting in her golden hair lounged on what appeared to be some kind of moss-covered rock doubling as a bed or a couch. Her pink lips pursed almost too full while her cheekbones were too sharply defined.

Her clothes—a generous word for what she was wearing—were a bizarre seductive armor. Her well-endowed bosom was barely contained in a scanty covering of what seemed to be chain mail while another little bit of chain mail draped over her white loincloth. Two golden pauldrons rested artfully on her shoulders, but other than that her arms were bare. Perhaps she wanted to appear the warrior queen, but she paled compared to the true warrior woman marching at Harm's side.

Now Harm's whole face flushed with embarrassment, and he kept his eyes firmly locked well above the queen's head. He was going to die of mortification before he managed to escape this tawdry court.

Val halted, a hand on her knife as she faced the *feeën* queen. "Queen Titania, I have brought the human that Queen Mab gave you to pay her debt."

Queen Titania slunk to her feet, her overly plump lips twisting into something that might have been a salacious smirk, if her cheeks could have moved that much. She stalked toward Harm, and he barely managed to stand his ground when everything in his mind was blaring with the instinct to run.

"Queen Mab knows exactly what I like." Queen Titania purred the words in a husky voice as she slinked closer. "I don't know how she let a handsome delicacy like this go."

Harm stumbled back as a chill swept through him. He understood all too much. About what it meant to be Queen Titania's plaything. About what his father's bargain would cost. About his chances of escape.

Then Val was there, tugging him behind her. A wall of prickly, reluctant safety between him and the *feeën* queen.

At least until she opened her mouth, her hand on her knife. "Until he's yours, no touching the merchandise."

This was no rescue but a mere reprieve. As soon as Queen Titania said the proper words and the cord around their wrists released, Val would happily turn him over to this queen and walk away without so much as a backward glance.

Harm gripped his coat in front of him, barely stopping himself from reaching for the iron knife. Not yet. As soon as Val was gone, he'd have to draw the knife and attempt his escape. He didn't have a plan. He had no idea how to get back to the Human Realm. But he couldn't risk staying here a moment once he was free of the cord and the bargain. If he waited, Queen Titania would have him drugged on faerie wine and doing whatever she wished, and then he'd never escape.

"Can't I at least have a little fun?" Queen Titania's wheedling whine grated along Harm's spine.

Daisy eased between them, all three of her heads out and her hackles raised. She even appeared bigger than she'd been a few moments ago.

Val's scowl deepened. "No. Claim him first. Unless he isn't yours?"

Queen Titania's blue eyes shifted away from Val, her

whole stance changing in a way that fluttered the first bit of hope in Harm's chest.

With an elaborate sigh, Queen Titania draped herself on her moss-covered rock once again. "Most tragically, he is not. There was this gem I just had to have, so I traded him sight unseen to Golbet of Flight Talonstorm."

Her fingers dropped—involuntarily drawing Harm's gaze—to an obnoxiously large white diamond nestled in her bosom. He hadn't noticed it before, given that he had been decidedly not looking in that direction. He quickly snapped his gaze back up to the crown in her golden hair.

He didn't belong to Queen Titania. The relief of that pounded through his skull.

Sure, this Golbet of Flight Talonstorm might be even worse—hard as that was to imagine—but that reckoning would wait for another day. Today, it was the reprieve he needed.

Val backed up a step, one hand gripping all the slack in the cord between them so that Harm was on a mere foot of tether. "If he isn't yours, then—"

"Titania!" The enraged baritone voice boomed off the cliffs with such force that Harm ducked behind Val again before he'd even realized what he'd done.

Queen Titania bolted partially upright, her eyes going as wide as they could in her strangely stiff face, before she seemed to gather herself to return to her languid sprawl. "Oberon, darling."

Harm turned to get a look over his shoulder while not fully putting his back to Queen Titania.

A *feeën* man stalked down the promenade between the trees, his face twisted in such a state of fury that his eyes were nearly invisible. His brown curls were so waxy that they didn't even move with the force of his march, and even his golden crown seemed to be glued to his head with whatever he used on his hair. Beneath the thin, decorative chest plate he wore, his pectorals puffed out almost grotesquely above his jiggling paunch. Besides the chest plate, the only other bit of clothing he wore was a leather belt with a little bit of chain mail hanging down in the front and back. A short sword hung from his belt, and it banged against his bare leg with each step he took.

"Who is that?" Harm leaned closer as he whispered to Val. At their feet, Daisy had turned to face the *feeën* man, her growl growing louder.

Val's hand was now gripping her knife's hilt, though she didn't draw it. She, too, spoke at a whisper. "King Oberon. Queen Titania's husband."

"She has a *husband*?" Harm glanced back at the approaching wrathful *feeën* king. This was not good. "Their marriage isn't…happy, is it?"

"Not at all." Val's mouth barely moved as she tugged on the cord, easing the two of them toward the edge of the outdoor hall. "It's the unhappiest relationship in the entire Fae Realm."

Really not good. Was this the moment Harm should pull out that iron knife to defend himself?

"Titania! What is the meaning of this?" King Oberon halted and jabbed his hand at Val and Harm.

A green-skinned *fee*—boy? Man? Harm couldn't tell

—halted just behind King Oberon, dressed in a similar chain mail loincloth, though he didn't have the chest plate.

"We need to get out of here." Val hurried them faster toward the trees. Daisy planted herself between them and the *feeën* royal couple, her snarl flashing lots of white teeth.

"Right behind you." Harm plunged into the trees at Val's heels, not needing the tugging on the cord around his wrist to hurry him along. The rising shouts of the fighting *feeën* couple chased him as he and Val disappeared into the surrounding forest.

Chapter Six

Val stirred the pot of stew bubbling over the fire, trying to ignore the pinching feeling in her chest. At her feet, Daisy gobbled down the shredded dried meat and veggies Val had prepared for her.

Across the way, Harm sat on a raised root that was as tall as a fallen log, his elbows braced on his knees as he stared listlessly into the fire. The picture of a puppy who had endured his first kick and wasn't sure how to handle it.

She shouldn't feel this squiggling sourness in her chest. She'd escorted many a package over the years as a mercenary, and she'd always managed to squash the niggling thoughts before.

But there was just something about this particular puppy that brought out...regrets. He should have treated her as his enemy. Lashed out at her at least once or twice.

Instead, he looked at her with trusting blue eyes and

acted like they were allies. No one other than her fellow Wild Hunt mercenaries had ever treated her that way.

She couldn't afford to entertain such inconvenient emotions. Emotions got a mercenary killed.

Worse, she was stuck with this puppy yet again. Her freedom was still restricted. And the walk from the Court of Revels to the Court of Stone wasn't short. If she was already feeling this uncomfortable, how much worse would it get before the trip was over?

Val wasn't familiar with the dragon shifter Golbet in particular, but Flight Talonstorm was fairly indifferent to humans. They didn't defend humans the way Flight Clawstone did, but they also didn't treat humans as badly as Flight Icewing. Turning Harm over to Golbet should, at least, be better than handing him over to Queen Titania.

Yet he'd still be a captive. And escaping from a dragon was nigh impossible. She should explain that to him with all the ruthlessness of the cold truth. It might even be the kindest thing to do.

But she couldn't bring herself to do it. At least, not yet. It would be like kicking a puppy a second time in one day.

Perhaps it was that foolish beginning of a conscience that had her opening her mouth and asking, "Are you all right?"

Harm sighed, lifting one hand long enough to drag it through his hair. "I'm fine. I just..." He glanced off into the dark forest surrounding them before he returned his gaze to the fire. "I'm a man. A prince. I've never been in...*that* kind of danger before. I knew what I'd face here. I knew it could come to that. But knowing it and actually facing it are two different things."

They were. Just like turning a package over to a new master and actually seeing what he would face once she was gone were also two different things. With the one, she could wrap herself in the pretense of ignorance and claim innocence in whatever happened next. But with the other…she wasn't ignorant and thus wasn't innocent. And that was…far too uncomfortable to contemplate.

Harm released a long breath and finally lifted his head to look at her, his face smoothing back into that cheerful puppy look. "But I'm fine. Where are we headed next?"

Val shook herself. Yes, right. Far better to get this conversation on a familiar and safer topic. Even if she had to work to keep her emotions buried at the mention of a particular court. "Flight Talonstorm is a clan of dragon shifters in the Court of Stone. The shortest way to get there would be to cut through the Court of Sand, but that court is the most dangerous in the whole Fae Realm. The heat and the shifting sands make the barrier between the Fae Realm and the Realm of Monsters especially thin there. Monsters and rogue fae run rampant."

The Court of Sand was the easiest way into and out of the Realm of Monsters. As such, she'd been through the Court plenty of times since joining the Wild Hunt.

But that didn't mean she particularly liked that Court, given her history there.

"That sounds…daunting." Harm started to reach for

his ankle before he seemed to remember himself and halted. It was a good thing he wasn't stuck with one of the other mercenaries or the knife that he had hidden there would have been confiscated long ago.

"It is." Especially if Val had to cross the court with a human puppy on a leash. "Or we can go through the Tanglewood, across the top of the Court of Knowledge, and through the Harvest Court until we reach the pass into the Court of Stone. It will take longer, but there will be fewer monsters."

"Not that I get a vote, but the longer route sounds safer to me." Harm shrugged, resting his elbows on his knees again. "I want to get to our destination as quickly as possible, but I also want to arrive alive."

"I said fewer monsters, not no monsters. The Harvest Court is rife with nuckelavee and particularly nasty grain sprites." Val still had the scars from the last time the little biters had gnawed on her ankles. "But it would be somewhat less arduous than crossing the deserts of the Court of Sand."

Why was she leaning toward the longer option? Sure, she preferred to avoid the Court of Sand, especially anything that would entail coming in contact with one of the warlords. But she faced the Court of Sand nearly every mission, and she'd face it again. She wasn't a coward who let her past rule her.

Then why did a part of her *want* the longer option? As if she wanted to delay handing Harm over as long as possible?

It was the regret, that was all. Pesky emotions.

With more time, she could prepare him for survival. After all, why shouldn't she teach him how to fight?

It wasn't as if she actually liked whoever she would hand him over to at the end of this. She couldn't care less about anyone here in the Fae Realm. They'd never done anything but cast her out. So what if they got stabbed? It wouldn't be her problem, even if she trained the one who did the stabbing. It might not be the best for her mercenary reputation, but who was to know?

"Look. You wanted me to tell you what you needed to know to survive. So here it is." Val took two bowls and spoons from her pocket, then ladled the stew into them. After setting the pot aside so that it could cool, she held out one of the bowls to Harm. "You need to know about the Laws of Bindings and Bargains that rule the Fae Realm."

He took the bowl of stew, stirring it with a spoon. "Is that like the Law of Hospitality?"

"Yes, though the Law of Hospitality is a lesser law, not a binding law." Val held her bowl of stew in her hands, waiting for it to cool. "Right now, you're under the power of a bargain. It compels you to fulfill it and will enact destruction on you and your home if you don't. But it also gives you the ability to eat some fae food and to communicate. Even though you're speaking your language, and I'm speaking mine, we both understand each other."

Harm nodded, his gaze going distant. After a moment, his forehead puckered. "Then how could my father understand the fae when he made the bargain?

And I could understand you even before you put the threefold cord on my wrist."

"Queen Mab likely sent a fae who could speak your language. It was probably why the fae who told her about your brother's illness didn't go himself." Val tried to ignore the way Harm's jaw tightened at the mention of the mystery fae who had set this into motion. She didn't like not seeing the whole picture either, but there was nothing either of them could do about it. "Once the bargain was in place, the magic of the bargain gave all involved the ability to communicate."

Harm rested his elbows on his knees, his bowl cradled in his hands, but his posture was more relaxed and less hunched than before. "So once I'm delivered and the bargain is complete, what happens then?"

"You'll then be under a captive binding. You'll still be able to communicate and eat most fae food, except for faerie fruit. It'll make you susceptible to commands, though you can resist, and you'll struggle to go far from your captor." Val held up her wrist with the sparkling cord attached. "Kind of like this, but a fully magical version wrapped around your very being. In theory, a captive binding is supposed to grant you some protections—your captor can't kill you and you can't kill them —but the fae can torture you a great deal without killing you."

"So I've seen." His tone held a coldly dry note. Perhaps he was remembering the tortured musicians of Queen Mab's court. His gaze dropped to the bowl in his hands, his grip tightening on his spoon. "If I can't kill them and can't go far, then is escape impossible?"

"You can't kill them with faerie steel." Val placed emphasis on the words, flicking a glance at his ankle where she suspected he had an iron knife hidden. But she wouldn't say anything more pointedly than that. If he couldn't figure out what she meant, then he wouldn't have the brains for escaping.

"I see." Harm drew out the syllables, giving a nod. "What about the captive binding? How do I escape that?"

Val probably shouldn't tell him. Her fellow fae wouldn't like that she was educating her package.

But that tight knot was easing in her stomach, and not just because she was satiating her hunger with the stew.

"There are three main ways. You can be rescued by someone else, who returns you to your home and sets you free. That's the main way humans are freed." Val hesitated, then decided not to mention the Primrose League, a shadowy organization that existed to rescue humans. That would have been too helpful, especially when they were headed into the Court of Knowledge, the court that allegedly harbored the League's leader. Besides, if he sought out the League now, he might just get her killed. "You might be able to free yourself, though you would be left in the Fae Realm without the ability to communicate or eat any food whatsoever. The third way is to override the captive binding with an even stronger binding."

"Such as?" Harm leaned forward, his stew seemingly all but forgotten in his hands.

"Any binding involving love. Most often that is the

marriage binding." Val couldn't help the curl to her mouth. All such sappy stuff. Anyone in the Realm of Monsters could tell one just how rare such things were.

"Marriage." Harm raised his eyebrows. "After what we saw today?"

"Hard to believe, I know. But the truly strong marriage bindings involve love, and those are the powerful ones. Supposedly. I've never seen it." Val scraped the last of the stew from the bottom of her bowl. "You'll need to be wary. Some fae might try to trick you into a marriage binding, hoping you'll fall in love with them. A marriage with a human—when there is love—makes a fae immune to iron and gives them the ability to lie in the Human Realm. Both things that fae who prey on humans long to achieve."

"A marriage binding could save or doom me." He took a bite of the stew, chewing before he swallowed. "Anything else I should know?"

So much, but they'd be up all night if Val tried to explain every nuance of the Fae Realm. Instead, there was only one last thing she'd warn him about now. "Just be careful that your captor doesn't shed your blood and his or her blood. That would place you under a blood binding. Blood magic is banned here in the Fae Realm, but even then, some fae will still do it. Blood bindings put you fully under the control of your captor. You won't be able to refuse any command, and escape is nigh impossible."

Harm set aside what remained of his stew. "Avoid a blood binding. Understood."

Daisy's ears perked up at the sound of the bowl

clunking against the tree root. She stopped licking her already clean bowl and placed her nose in Val's lap, giving her the begging eyes.

"All right, I'm done." Val set her bowl on the ground for Daisy to lick out.

Harm eyed Daisy. "We are washing the dishes, right?"

"*You* are washing the dishes." Val touched the side of the pot. It had cooled enough so she set it next to her bowl for Daisy to lick out next. "Daisy is just helping you out by pre-cleaning everything."

Harm made a noise in the back of his throat. So ungrateful. She'd only made stew—and its excess of dishes—as a comfort food because he'd looked so disconsolate after their run-in with Queen Titania.

Daisy's head shot up, her whole body stiffening, as she stared into the forest behind Val. A low growl emanated from the dog's chest.

Val rose to her feet as she cocked her head to better listen to the forest sounds.

Harm braced himself, as if preparing to stand. "What is—"

Val held up a hand, and he fell silent.

Daisy's other two heads appeared, her fur rising along her back. She gave one last, low growl before she bolted into the night.

"Monsters." Val drew her knife, spinning in that direction.

"Should I..." Harm fumbled with his trouser cuff where it was stuffed into his tall boots.

"No, use mine." Val drew a second knife and tossed it at him.

Instead of catching it, he stumbled backwards, eyes wide, as he let the knife fall to the ground.

Val huffed and turned toward the forest. Yes, she would definitely have to teach him to use a knife. He'd never survive if she didn't.

Chapter Seven

Harm tentatively picked up the knife, gripping it in his hand and facing the forest as if he actually knew what he was doing. If it had been a sword, he would at least have had some clue. But a knife? Nope.

He'd had some perfunctory training with swords and blunderbusses. But most of his training had been focused on overall war strategy as he was expected to remain behind while the generals took care of actual tactics and the men did the fighting. Not that the Duchy of Tulpenland got in many battles.

Sure, a few of the neighboring kingdoms and duchies were jealous of their booming economy. King Hendrik to the south especially had been making threats lately. But he'd never invade. Tulpenland remained safe behind their network of canals, which could be used to flood the land and impede any attempts to march an army across the lowlands.

But Harm didn't think monsters cared if he could

negotiate a trade treaty or list the seven principles of warfare as laid down by the ancient general Sirit Tou.

Something squealed deep in the underbrush. Then with a roar and a crackle of breaking branches, a huge and hideous beast with far too many gnashing fangs leapt into the pool of light cast by the fire.

Her jaw set in a grim line and her black hair limned with firelight, Val stepped forward and stabbed her knife with a brutal force that belied her otherwise graceful movements.

The monster roared and lashed out at her, but she evaded the teeth, dancing away. As she did so, she reached into a pocket and withdrew a long spear tipped with a barbed head. The weapon was far too long to have fit in a normal pocket, but Harm had concluded the pockets must be magical, given the number of impossibly large things he'd seen her pull from them.

Val stabbed the monster again, fending off its head with her spear. She didn't even look hampered by the fact that she couldn't go more than ten feet away from Harm because of the cord.

Daisy appeared in the circle of firelight. One of her jaws was clamped at the back of the neck of a rat that appeared to be nearly as big as she was. Another of the obscenely large rodents burst out of the forest, and one of Daisy's other heads chomped down on it with such force something snapped. Daisy's muscles bulged along her shoulders and sides as she viciously shook the rodents, further snapping bones.

Then a slavering wolf even bigger than Daisy leapt toward Harm. Its black fur blurred slightly sludgy, and its eyes gleamed red around the edges. Its fangs glinted, even though they were brown and rotting.

Harm yelped and tried to scramble back, but he was pinned between the wolf and the crackling fire. He held out the knife in both hands, but the wolf just dodged instead of nicely impaling itself.

Harm avoided the snapping teeth and swung down at the wolf, trying to stab it. The wolf danced away from the blade. Without meeting the resistance of the wolf's body, Harm's wild swing continued, and he sliced the side of his thigh just above his knee with his own knife.

Harm yelled in pain, then yelled again as the wolf clamped its fangs around his arm, bowling into Harm with such force that he fell backward. Unlike when he'd been pinned by a too enthusiastic Daisy, this wolf was all fangs and claws, biting and tearing.

Where was the knife? A weapon? Something? Harm wordlessly shouted as the wolf ravaged his arm and tried to get to his throat.

Then the wolf yelped, and Val appeared beyond the wolf's head. She stabbed the wolf again, then gripped it by the scruff and yanked it off Harm.

The wounded wolf tumbled a few feet, rolling onto its side. Before it could scramble to its feet, Daisy attacked with a savage growl, all three heads snapping down.

Harm slumped more fully on the ground, trying to catch his breath past the drumming of his heart and the pain spreading through his body.

Val glanced around before she pulled a cloth out of her pocket and cleaned her dagger. As she scrubbed the blade, she stared down at Harm. "You were supposed to use the knife."

"I tried." Harm gripped his injured arm with the other, blood welling between his fingers. Blooming tulips, that hurt. Between the searing pain in his arm, burning lines of agony across his chest, and the pulsing throb of the cut on his leg, he might just pass out.

"Where's my knife?" She sheathed the one she'd finished cleaning and propped a fist on her hip.

"Don't know." Harm gritted his teeth. He wasn't sure he could even sit up right now. "I was trying not to die."

"Trying not to die usually involves holding on to the knife, not losing it." Val cast about for a moment before she took a step, bent, and retrieved the knife from where it had somehow gotten half-buried in the moss. Instead of sheathing it right away, she set to work cleaning it with her cloth.

"I'm bleeding." Harm didn't think cleaning her knife should be the priority right now. Not that he wanted to be a bother, but he didn't want to bleed out.

"Fine." She sighed and sheathed the knife. "Sit up and take your shirt off."

"I...er..." The back of Harm's neck was heating again. Perhaps he'd just lie here and die instead. It would be the proper thing to do rather than disrobe.

"If you don't take your shirt off, I'll cut it off. And I promise, I won't be gentle about it. So up and off." Val wasn't even looking at him as she stowed her cloth in one pocket, then began taking various items out of the other pocket.

As that sounded even more improper than somehow

getting his shirt off himself, Harm gritted his teeth, gathered his strength, and rolled into a sitting position, leaning his back against the root he'd been sitting on before this whole mess started.

His fingers were trembling so much with the pain that he fumbled to unbutton his shirt. He shrugged his shoulders out of the shirt and got it off one arm. But the fabric was stuck to his wounded arm. Bracing himself, he slowly peeled the fabric off, gritting his teeth and only groaning once or twice, blackness crowding the edges of his vision, as the fabric came away.

Long scratches ran down his chest and across his abdomen. Most were superficial, but some of the deeper ones dribbled blood. Bites ravaged his left arm while his breeches were soaked with blood from the slice on his leg.

While he'd been gritting his way out of his shirt, Val had set up a second pot over the fire. At least she wasn't going to boil water for wound cleaning in the one Daisy had been licking out.

With that done, she turned to Harm and sent a scouring glance over him, making him all too aware of how much of a bloody mess he was. And how unimpressive his chest was compared to some of the *feeën* he'd seen the previous few days. He wasn't flabby, exactly. But his muscles weren't defined.

Val knelt before him, grabbed his injured arm, and turned it this way and that as she inspected it. She wasn't rough, but she wasn't gentle either.

Harm hissed at the rush of pain jolting up his arm. "That hurts."

Val ignored him as she poked at a few of the gashes on his chest. "Are you wounded anywhere else?"

Besides his pride? Harm pointed. "My leg."

She tugged aside the fabric of his breeches and inspected the wound. Her frown deepened as she lifted her gaze to his. "This was done by a knife."

"Yes." Might as well grind what was left of his pride under his heel while he was at it.

Val huffed a breath as she sat back on her heels. She drew one of her knives from its sheath, held it up, and gestured at the blade. "This is the pointy end. It goes in your enemy, not in yourself."

Harm pressed his hand over the bites again, cradling his wounded arm to his chest. "I don't think my lack of knife skills is our highest priority right now. I'm bleeding out."

"I left you alone with one of my knives for less than five minutes, and you managed to cut yourself. Yes, your lack of knife-handling skills is the priority." Val sheathed her knife again, then removed the now boiling water from over the fire, setting the pot next to her. The steam wafted a stringent, herbal scent. "And you are not bleeding out. You'll be fine."

He was seriously questioning her definition of the word *fine*.

She reached into her pocket and withdrew a vial filled with some kind of green and glowing sludge. She shoved it at him. "Drink this."

Harm took the vial, eyeing it. "This won't kill me, will it?"

"Of course not. It's an expensive healing potion, so

don't complain." Val touched the tip of her pinky to the water, then started arranging various supplies on a patch of moss next to her.

"Then I'm honored you're using it on me." Harm winced as he moved his injured arm to uncap the vial. With one bracing breath, he tipped the vial back and downed the whole thing as quickly as he could.

Despite the green color and sludgy consistency, it wasn't as bad as he'd expected. Rather than tasting like mud or seaweed or something nasty, it tasted like a strong perfume smelled: cloying and overly floral.

"Don't be. It's just practical. I can't have you dying on me." Val continued fiddling with the supplies, though everything seemed arranged. "We'll start your training in the morning. This mission will be more expensive than it's worth if I have to keep using potions on you."

Harm choked on the last swallow of the potion, and he coughed to clear his lungs. "Training?"

"Yes. Training. With a knife." Val took the empty vial from him, jammed it in her pocket, and picked up one of the clean cloths she'd set next to her. "Now hold still."

She grabbed the wrist of his injured arm, yanking his arm toward her as she dipped the cloth into the pot of steaming water. As she sloshed the dripping cloth onto his arm, the hot water and whatever she'd put into it stung like embers being ground into the wounds.

"Ow! Ow! Hey, stop that! Ow!" Harm tried to yank his arm back, but her grip might as well have been iron.

With head low, tail wagging slightly, Daisy crept closer before she pressed herself to his right side. For a moment, Harm held his arm out, not really wanting to touch her. She had gore smeared underneath her chin and down the front of her chest, but all the mess was from the rodents and wolf. Daisy didn't have a scratch on her.

"Stop squirming." Val kept ruthlessly cleaning the wounds in his arm, dipping the cloth into the water again and again. "You don't want to risk infection."

"Shouldn't that healing potion take care of it?" Harm forced himself to hold still, gritting his teeth at the rush of pain. This hurt worse than getting chomped on. At least during the attack, he'd been so busy trying not to die that he hadn't even registered the full extent of the pain.

He gave in and rested his free hand on Daisy's back, digging his fingers into the coarse fur at the scruff of her neck.

"Yes, but you are a human and therefore more fragile." Val turned his arm back and forth. As if satisfied with her work, she dropped her rag into the now pink-tinted water, popped the lid off a small pot, and revealed what looked like some kind of herbal paste. She dipped her fingers into it and spread it over his wounds. "It doesn't hurt to help the potion along."

"Doesn't hurt *you*," Harm grumbled between his clenched teeth. "Your bedside manner leaves a lot to be desired."

"I'm keeping you alive. That's about all you can ask for in your position." She tipped her head toward the cord that coiled between them, the one end gripped tightly beneath her hand on his wrist and the other sparkling around her wrist.

He supposed that was the best he would get, captive that he was. At least Daisy seemed sympathetic, pressing into him as if offering comfort.

Once she was finished with the paste, Val wrapped his arm with bandages from his elbow down to his wrist. After tying it off, she reached for the rag in the water again. Without so much as a warning or hesitation, she brought the rag to one of the scratches high on his chest.

"Hey, ow!" Harm squirmed away from her as much as he could with his back to the root and Daisy pressed to his side. "Now that you've taken care of my arm, I can do the rest myself."

"Have you ever tended wounds before?" Val's eyebrows rose as she speared him with a look.

"No." He dragged the word out. Tempting as it was to lie, she'd see right through it.

"Then I don't trust you to do it properly." Val dipped the rag into the water again and scrubbed at his wounds.

Harm lowered his hand to rest on Daisy's back again. She had a point, little as he liked subjecting himself to more of her rough ministrations.

Once she finished cleaning the wounds, she set to work spreading the same herbal paste over the scratches and gashes.

She leaned closer to him, her hair only inches from his face. When he inhaled, he caught the faint scent of leather and oil and some kind of spice he couldn't name. He was all too aware of her hand on the bare skin of his chest and abdomen. Not that her touch was at all romantic or even gentle.

He gave himself a mental shake. She was a *fee*. And if his guess was correct, she was several years older than him. More than that, she held the other end of the cord that kept him here. She was only helping him and keeping him safe from the other *feeën* and monsters in this realm because it was her job.

As if oblivious to his thoughts, Val briskly wrapped his chest with bandages, then cut the slit in his breeches wider so that she could give the cut on his leg the same scrubbing, herbal paste spreading, and bandage wrapping treatment.

Once she tied the knot on the last bandage, she sat back on her heels. "That's done. We had better get moving. All the death and bloodshed here will attract more monsters."

"Does this mean I get out of doing the dishes tonight?" Harm grimaced, leaning his head against the root behind him. His wounds throbbed, and a bone-deep exhaustion settled into his body. The last thing he wanted to do was walk more that night.

But she had a point. If predators were attracted by the scent of blood in the Human Realm, then how much more would monsters be attracted to such things in the realm of the *feeënvolk*?

"Yes." Val began stuffing the medical supplies back into her pocket.

Harm glanced to the side where Daisy had left the two rodents and the wolf she'd killed. For a long moment, he couldn't spot the bodies, though they should have been obvious on the forest floor.

A few gray tufts of fur poked between a layer of roots and moss that seemed to be growing up and over while the gray plume of a wolf's tail stuck from the moss. Even as he watched, a chill spreading through him, the ground gave something almost like a gulp and slurped the tail down into the earth.

"The forest ate the monsters!" Harm hugged his injured arm closer again, holding tightly to Daisy.

"Well, yes. What else are the trees supposed to eat?" Val didn't even look up as she packed away her supplies. She stood, grabbed the pot, and dumped the bloody water out to one side of their camp. With a grimace, she tossed the bloody rag into the forest as well. When it fell, the moss gave a ripple and little tendrils wrapped around the fabric, beginning the process of consuming it.

Harm shuddered, all too aware of the moss and roots surrounding him. "The forest won't eat us, will it?"

"It only eats dead things." Val shot him another one of her stern looks. "So don't die."

Don't die or the forest would eat him. If the monsters didn't give him nightmares, that surely would.

Chapter Eight

Within moments, Val had packed up their camp, scattered the coals of the fire, and turned to Harm.

He'd eased into the remains of his shirt and shrugged on his coat. An odd juxtaposition of bloody tatters and stuffy propriety. Such a strange human.

Using the root, Harm pushed to his feet, swaying for a moment before he steadied. After those injuries, he needed sleep, not a long nighttime hike. The healing potion she'd given him would work best while he was resting.

But she didn't dare stay here. She'd just have to push the human a little farther and hope they could get far enough before he collapsed entirely.

He took a step, then braced himself with one hand on the root as he stared at his pack at his feet. Amazingly, it hadn't been smashed in the struggle.

Val sighed. The human was too weak to carry his pack himself. Not to mention, the straps would dig into those gashes across his chest. If she wanted to make any progress tonight, she'd have to carry his pack for him.

She reached for the pack before he could, though she looked up at him, meeting his gaze, rather than picking it up. "If you trust me to carry it for you, I'll put it in my pocket."

Harm's jaw worked for a moment before he nodded, something in his eyes both hopeful and wary. Once this pack was in her pocket, he would have no way to guarantee he would get it back. She had the power to withhold it from him.

Val picked up the pack, her muscles tight at the heavy weight of it. Harm might not have the warrior's physique of her fellow mercenaries in the Wild Hunt, but he was tall and sturdy to have carried this around with so little complaint. He had the build to become a formidable warrior with the right training.

She stuffed the corner of his pack into her pocket. The opening to her pocket didn't seem to get larger, and his pack didn't seem to get smaller, yet somehow she was able to stuff it inside.

Harm was still looking at her, his mouth opening as if he was preparing to thank her. As if he thought this was a kindness.

Val turned her back and stalked into the darkness before he could get the words out. She didn't want to hear them and experience more of that uncomfortable itchiness filling her chest. "Come. We've already lingered here too long. More rifts are bound to open and let loose more monsters."

"Rifts?" Harm trudged after her, not trotting to catch up like he had before.

Daisy leapt to her feet, bounding into the forest ahead of them as if she wasn't the least bit tired.

"Rips in the barrier between the Fae Realm and the Realm of Monsters." Val shoved a branch aside. "They form when evil deeds are committed. Such as hatred in a marriage."

"Like whatever is going on between King Oberon and Queen Titania." Harm was already breathing hard. The human couldn't take much more tonight.

"Yes. They are infamous for causing rifts. I suspect the whole Court of Revels will be crawling with monsters tonight." Val searched the darkness around them, making sure they weren't about to be attacked. "If you can make it, I'd like to get across the border into the Court of Knowledge before we stop for the rest of the night. We'll be safer there."

"Isn't the Court of Knowledge the one Queen Mab said you should avoid?" Harm stumbled over a root, though he caught himself on a nearby tree.

"Yes." Val swallowed down the rising irritation. She wasn't sure if it was with Harm, with the king and queen of the Court of Knowledge, or with this mission as a whole. "King Theseus and Queen Hippolyta of the Court of Knowledge are the rare fae monarchs who are actually good. And I don't just mean good as in competent rulers, though they are certainly that. But genuinely *good*. Because of that, their court has taken a stand against the trade in humans."

"I see." There was a note to Harm's voice that she didn't like, his quiet afterwards far too contemplative.

Val halted and half-turned toward him. He walked for two more steps, nearly running into her before he seemed to realize she had stopped. He halted only a step away from her.

She waited until he met her gaze before she spoke. "Yes, the Court of Knowledge would be the place to go if you ever get free of your new master. But until then, even a fae monarch can't loosen this cord or break the bargain your father made. They might still do all they can for you, but they could make *my* life difficult, which would eventually make *yours* more difficult. So don't think you're going to find help there anytime soon."

Harm nodded, his gaze dropping from hers. His shoulders slumped still further as he hunched over his injured arm.

"Still, it will be a safer court to give you time to recuperate." And train him as much as she dared.

As tonight had shown, he needed some skills. She would never get him safely through the Harvest Court and into the Court of Stone if he wasn't somewhat competent enough to save his own skin once in a while. If that also gave him the skills to rescue himself once her part in this was all over, then so be it. That wasn't her problem. Getting him alive and mostly well to his destination was.

Val spun and set out into the forest once again, Harm stumbling after her.

They hiked for several hours, the forest growing darker around them. They were deep in the Tanglewood now. That enchanted forest separating the Court of Knowledge from the Court of Revels held secrets even King Theseus of the Court of Knowledge didn't fully understand.

At least the Tanglewood seemed somewhat benevolent tonight. Their path had been fairly smooth, not riddled with roots and dropped branches. Nor had they encountered any more monsters.

Then again, the Tanglewood tended to favor the innocent, and Harm was nothing if not innocent.

A tug on the cord halted her steady march, and Val turned to Harm.

He had fallen to his knees, his face even paler than before, his blue eyes glassy. Blood soaked the bandages and the shreds of his shirt. The man was well and truly done in.

Val strode back to him, bent, and pulled his good arm over her shoulder. He gave a moan as she hauled him back to his feet. "Just a little farther."

His head hung, but he gave something that might have been a nod. He had a core of stubbornness to him, she would give him that.

She wasn't sure if they'd crossed into the Court of Knowledge or not. Since both courts were Summer Courts, there wasn't a change in temperature, and within the depths of the Tanglewood, there was no distinct border. They might be in the Court of Knowledge. Or they might not. It was even possible that they had been walking in circles all night if the Tanglewood had decided to be particularly mischievous.

Val halted and rested a hand on the trunk of a huge

tree. She didn't normally attempt this since she was a courtless mercenary. But with Harm's weight sagging against her, she had to try. "I know I'm not a part of your court. Nor do I have a claim here in this realm. But for his sake, please show us a safe place to camp."

"Who you talking to?" Harm's voice slurred as his head tipped into hers as if he was too weak to hold it up.

"Not you. Shh." Val kept her hand on the tree. For a long moment, nothing seemed to happen.

Then a particularly clear section of forest opened before her, though the forest didn't seem to move or anything like that. It even seemed brighter ahead.

Daisy's mouth flopped open with a grin as she bounded down the trail before them.

Always trust a companion animal. They had better instincts than she did.

Val followed Daisy, hauling Harm along with her. Little red flowers lined the mossy path while bigger yellow flowers grew in waving stalks on either side.

After only a few minutes of walking, the path ended at a large boulder, which rested alongside a massive tree. Other trees clustered in a dense grove, creating what seemed to be a safe haven in the forest. A few yards away, a creek meandered between the trees, clear and clean.

It was about the most painting perfect campsite she'd ever seen. Suspiciously so. Was this the forest's benevolence or a malicious trap?

Daisy sniffed around the boulder, her tail still

wagging vigorously. She, at least, didn't seem alarmed by the place.

Harm all but hung from his arm over her shoulders. He wasn't making it much farther.

This would have to do. If it was a trap, she'd deal with it.

She lowered Harm to sit with his back to one of the trees. He slouched there, somewhat tilted to one side, as if he didn't have the energy to move even to make himself more comfortable.

Val set up the tent and both bedrolls as quickly as she could. Once done, she hauled Harm into the tent and onto his bedroll. He was only half-conscious, and he likely wouldn't even remember any of this in the morning. Sighing, she removed his boots and tucked him into the bedroll as best she could.

Trusting Daisy to wake her if there was trouble, Val crawled into her own bedroll, though it took a while before she managed to fall asleep.

***

HARM PEELED HIS EYES OPEN, his eyelids scratchy. His mouth felt strangely gummy, his tongue so dry it stuck to the roof of his mouth.

Blinking to clear his vision, he found he was staring at the underside of the brown canvas tent. He was bundled in the bedroll, his boots at the end of the bed, though he still wore his coat and bloody shirt.

How long had he been asleep? He had no memories

of crawling into the tent and only vague recollections of stumbling through the forest after the monster attack.

He pressed a hand to his chest, then held up his arm. His wounds mildly ached, but not nearly as much as they should.

Sitting up, Harm peeled the bloody shirt and bandages away from his chest, the fabric stiff with dried blood, and peered at his wounds. Strangely, the gashes had closed, new pink skin already showing.

How long had he been asleep? That healing potion must have been strong stuff to have healed him this much in a single night. If it was a single night.

Without so much as a knock or a warning, the front flap of the tent flipped aside, revealing Val crouched there, peering at him.

Harm gave something of a yelp, reaching for the blanket though he managed to stop himself before he pulled it to his chin. "Knock before you enter! What if I'd been dressing?"

"Oh, stop squealing like a blushing maiden." She rolled her eyes. "I didn't even know if you were awake."

"You'd squawk if I burst in on you." Harm flapped his good hand at her.

"You wouldn't dare. I'd stab you." She patted the knife at her belt.

"So just because you have the power to enforce your boundaries makes them the only ones worth considering?" Harm started to cross his arms, but the movement tugged at his still healing wounds. He dropped his arms to his sides instead.

Val opened her mouth, then hesitated, her eyes going

distant for a moment. Perhaps she was thinking of Queen Titania and her grabby hands for her jaw hardened.

Then her gaze sharpened, and she gestured at him again. "And how much of all your proper layers and protestations have to do with your actual morality and how much is merely a performance?"

Like her, Harm opened his mouth, but the words caught in his throat. A performance. Just like Queen Titania's and King Oberon's performance of being warriors. How many of his own actions were done for the appearance of virtue rather than actual virtue?

Instead of continuing this discussion, Harm eased his feet out of his bedroll. "How long was I asleep?"

"The rest of the night and all morning." Val gestured toward the brightness outside of the tent. "It's early afternoon now."

At least he hadn't slept a week or something like that.

Val's expression returned to that impassive, no-nonsense one, her tone brisk. "Now, let's have a look at your wounds."

And…there it was again. Harm sighed, but he didn't protest as he peeled off the bloody remnants of his shirt.

As soon as he dropped the fabric to the side, Val grabbed his injured arm and set to work unwrapping the bandages.

Harm tugged the bandages off his chest as best he could with one hand. No way was he going to let Val do that.

She let the last of the bandages drop, then inspected

his arm. The bites were now pink patches of new skin, healing but not yet fully healed. The gashes across his chest and the slice across his leg looked the same. Still sore, but he wasn't in danger of bleeding more.

She dropped his arm and gave a sharp nod. "Get dressed. We'll start your training after you eat."

"Training?" Harm rested his injured arm on a knee, his whole body still feeling strangely weak and weighed down. Likely the blood loss and the exhaustion of completing several weeks of healing overnight.

"Yes, training." Val gestured from his arm to his chest. "You clearly need it."

"I have some training with a sword." Harm couldn't help the defensive note in his voice. "Last night was an off night for me. I've never fought a monster with a knife before."

"If you have a good foundation of training, that will make my job easier." Val eyed him, as if she seriously doubted it.

Not that he could blame her. He'd made a poor showing the night before.

But he couldn't keep delaying. His family was in danger.

"How long will training take?" Harm ran a thumb over one of the new patches of skin on his arm. "I need to get home as soon as possible."

"You'll never get to the Court of Stone, much less escape, without training." Val speared him with a far-too-frank look in her dark brown eyes. "If you want to see your family again, you will take the time now to train."

Harm clenched and unclenched his fingers, hating how right she was. He hadn't even managed to fend off one monster wolf. How could he possibly survive long enough to find his way home, even if he managed to escape? He'd only made it this far because of Val.

"Fine. I'll train." Harm reached toward his ankle, where the knife was still hidden underneath his stocking, even though Val must have removed his boots. "Should I…"

"No!" Val shook her head. "If you have an iron knife, I don't want to see it, remember? I'll lend you a knife for training, when we get up to it. But that will be a while. You aren't ready to be trusted with pointy objects."

He would have protested, but even shifting his injured leg reminded him of how hopeless he was.

"Now hurry and dress." Val leaned back on her heels and let the flap fall closed again, her voice coming through the canvas. "Daylight is wasting."

Harm cast about, then sighed. "My pack is in your pocket."

He couldn't see her, but he could almost imagine he heard her huff a sigh of her own. A few moments later, her hand appeared, shoving his pack past the tent flap. At least she had enough patience that she hadn't tossed the pack and broken the precious pottery.

Harm took the pack, waited for the flap to fall closed and stay closed, and dug through it for his only other set of clothes. He quickly changed into his white shirt and gray breeches, though he left the black coat where it was. Once done, he stuffed his bloody clothes into the pack. As much as he wanted to simply discard the rags, he had so few things that he couldn't afford to lose anything. Nor did it seem safe to leave things with his blood simply lying around, even if the forest would probably eat it.

Once that was done, he crawled out of the tent, leaving his pack beside his bedroll.

As he straightened, Val took in his loose shirt and breeches, then gave a nod as if she approved. She faced the length of the clearing in the forest just outside of their sheltered nook among the trees. "Today, we're going to take it easy and work on your reflexes. You'll be throwing a rope for Daisy."

At the sound of her name, Daisy raised her head from where she sprawled in a patch of sunlight.

Harm had been braced to do something more physical. But throwing a rope for a dog didn't sound so bad. He played fetch with Gijs's puppy Vlek back home.

Val reached into her pocket and pulled out a thick rope of about an inch and a half in diameter. The rope was three feet long and had four large knots tied in it at regular intervals.

At the sight of the rope, Daisy sprang to her feet and bolted into a sprint, heading straight for Val, her mouth open as she reached for the rope with her gleaming teeth.

At the very last moment before being bowled over, Val sidestepped the dog, almost casually lifting the rope out of the dog's reach as Daisy sprang. Daisy's teeth snapped on air only inches away from the rope before she landed, immediately spinning back toward Val, her eyes fixed on the rope.

Before Daisy could spring again, Val pointed at the ground with her free hand. "Sit."

Eyes still pinned on the rope, Daisy plunked her butt onto the ground, though her whole body remained tense.

Val whipped the rope forward, throwing it all the way across the clearing.

Even before the rope left Val's hand, Daisy had already sprung to her feet. She raced after the rope, running low to the ground, her ears pinned to her skull. She sprinted so fast that she skidded past the rope as she tried to stop. Once she snagged the rope, Daisy whipped it back and forth like she had the rodent she'd killed. The knots of the rope thumped into the dog's sides, but she didn't seem to feel any pain at the whacks.

"Here, take this." Val held out a second rope.

Harm took the rope, gripping it just before the knot on the end and bracing himself.

Daisy raced back toward them, the first rope in her mouth. As her eyes latched on the rope in Harm's hand, she dropped her rope and leapt for Harm, her jump so high that her flashing teeth were nearly level with his face.

Harm stumbled backward, trying to lift his arm fast enough, aware of the teeth far too close to his face.

Daisy's jaw snapped onto the rope, the claws on her front paws scratching the front of Harm's legs, and she landed on the ground. She ripped the rope right out of his grip and swung it viciously, as if she felt the need to kill it.

The knotted end slammed into Harm's shin, and he

hopped backward yet again, grimacing. That was sure to bruise. As if Harm's body wasn't battered enough as it was.

"Grab the other rope." Val pointed to where it lay a few feet away.

Harm hobbled to it, but even as he reached for it, Daisy abruptly went from killing the other rope to diving for the one Harm was reaching for. He tried to snatch it from the ground, but Daisy was already there, her teeth knocking into his hand as she snagged the rope. Her teeth didn't draw blood, of course. She'd been going for the rope and only got him by accident. But he was probably going to get yet another bruise out of the deal.

"You need to be faster than that." Val waved at the rope Daisy had abandoned.

Hand and leg throbbing, Harm rushed back the way he'd come and snatched the rope off the ground. Even as he turned, Daisy was already rushing toward him, her mouth open, her eyes almost crazed as she focused solely on the rope.

Out of sheer panic, Harm threw the rope. It wasn't a good throw, only going a few yards, but Daisy skidded before she could run into him and tore off after it.

Val sighed. "You need to make her sit before you throw the next rope. She'll lose all her training if you indulge her and just throw it."

Gritting his teeth, Harm rushed to grab the rope Daisy had left. She was already sprinting back. He had only seconds.

He snagged the rope and straightened even as Daisy

leapt for him. He jumped backward, and this time he managed to lift the rope out of Daisy's reach.

When she landed, she immediately jumped again, and Harm had to whip the rope high out of her reach yet again.

"Sit." Harm tried to make his voice sound calm and commanding instead of panicked and out of breath. And he'd thought an afternoon playing with a dog sounded easy. "Sit, Daisy."

She stared at the rope, her tail wagging, her mouth open.

"Sit." Harm didn't dare look away from the dog.

Finally, Daisy seemed to get the idea, and she more or less lowered her butt to the ground, though her haunches where still tensed to spring.

Good enough. Harm threw the rope, this time flinging it nearly all the way across the clearing, buying himself a moment to snag the second rope from where Daisy had left it and sprint back to Val's side by the time Daisy returned.

If this was what Val considered taking it easy with training, Harm could only imagine how hard the actual training would be.

Chapter Nine

Val strolled alongside Harm as he marched around the clearing, holding a large rock over his head. Harm seemed to have regained his strength well enough. She wasn't sure how long healing took in the Human Realm, but the Fae Realm had a way of accelerating things, from healing to training to romance.

She shouldn't invest this much time into ensuring a package's survival. She could tell herself it would make her job easier. Safer. Cheaper than bargaining for more healing potions.

No, the truth was that Harm was too frustratingly *good*. He was here in the Fae Realm to save his brother. Nor did he resent his father for trading him to the fae. He treated Val with respect despite the fact that she was his enemy.

She couldn't bring herself to just dump him at his destination in the Fae Realm. Not anymore. Not after she'd gotten to know him.

By the time they arrived at the Court of Stone, how attached would she be?

She couldn't let herself think of it. Right now, she had to focus on training Harm so that she could—hopefully—banish that squiggly discomfort in her stomach.

As Harm finished his circuit of the clearing, she halted. "That's enough of that."

Harm released a breath, likely in relief, and dropped the stone to the ground.

One of the nearby trees reached out and whacked his shoulder with a whippy branch.

"Ouch!" Harm gripped his arm and flinched away from the tree. "What was that for?"

"Don't drop the rock. The Tanglewood doesn't like it." Val pointed. "You need to put the rock back where we found it."

Harm grimaced, picked up the rock, and lugged it toward the boulder next to their tent. This time, he tucked the rock into its hole. The moss began growing over the rock again, subsuming the rock back into the forest floor.

Harm trotted back to her, halting with a look of focus that almost mirrored Daisy's.

When Daisy wasn't snoozing in the sun, as she was doing now. The dog was more than happy to spend a day here in the Tanglewood, sleeping in the sun, catching the occasional critter to keep them fed, and playing fetch with the rope.

"What tortuous exercise do you have for me now?" Harm spread his arms, though his grin took any of the bite out of the words.

He really was far too trusting. Too cheerful. She probably should break him of that. But she just couldn't bring herself to do that any more than she could just hand him over to his fate. He was just too…endearing.

Annoying puppies that got under one's skin.

Giving herself a shake, Val crossed her arms and eyed him. "You said you have some training with a sword."

"Yes." Harm crossed his arms as well, facing her. "You don't have to sound so doubtful."

Her eyebrows rose. Did he have to bristle at that after his dubious performance in fighting that monster wolf? "Yes, I do. Now go ask the Tanglewood to provide us two staves for sparring."

"You don't have swords stashed in your magical pocket?" Harm scratched his chin as his gaze dropped to her side, though he snatched his gaze back up to her face, his neck flushing, after only a moment.

"Yes, of course I do." She might prefer knives, but she also had a good collection of long swords, short swords, sabers, several war axes, two spears, and even a halberd. It was just easier to carry her weapons in her pocket than openly on her person. "But I'm not ready to trust you with anything sharp just yet."

Harm's grin took on a lopsided tilt as he turned away and strode back to their small camp, nearly reaching the end of his ten-foot tether before he halted. He rested a hand on one of the trees. "Tanglewood, could you please provide two staves suitable for sparring? I would appreciate it."

Val resisted the urge to shake her head. Harm had adjusted rather well to talking to the forest to request things.

The tree shivered for a moment before two lengths of wood dropped from the upper branches to land at Harm's feet.

"Bedankt." Harm gathered the staves and returned to Val.

He held out one of the pieces of wood, and she took it. The weight wasn't balanced quite like a sword, but it would do.

Across from her, Harm gripped the end of his staff, already dropping into a fighting stance.

Not a bad stance. Perhaps he had some training after all. Now if that training was adequate remained to be seen.

Val moved from casually holding the stave to whipping it forward in a blink, aiming to take Harm off guard.

His eyes widened, but he brought his stave up to block without so much as a stumble backward.

Val threw herself into her next strike. She couldn't maneuver as freely as she normally would, given the cord between them that would tangle around them if she tried too much fancy footwork. But she could still hit hard and strike fast.

Harm parried her blow, putting his shoulder and back muscles into it. With his longer reach, taller height, and greater mass, he could strike a decent blow of his own.

Val felt something like a grin tug her face. This sword practice might actually be a decent match after all.

———

VAL DREW HER SPARE KNIFE. She flipped her knife around to pinch it by the flat of the blade as she held out the hilt to Harm. "It's time you tried again with a knife. Just remember…"

"Don't cut myself with the pointy end." Harm took the knife, flexing his fingers on the hilt as if testing the grip. "And I shouldn't cut you with the pointy end either."

"No, you should absolutely try to stab or slice me with the pointy end. You won't succeed, but you need to try." Val unsheathed a second knife. That lack of ruthlessness was Harm's biggest weakness when it came to fighting. "While we're sparring, I'm the enemy. You won't learn if you hold yourself back."

She wasn't sure why she'd added the qualifier *while we're sparring*. She was his captor, his enemy, and she was taking him to an unknown, likely cruel fate here in the Fae Realm.

"I…see…" Harm's gaze dropped to the knife she held. "So you're going to be attempting to stab or slice me?"

"No, because I'd actually succeed, and I've wasted one healing potion on you as it is." Val eased into her fighting stance.

Harm just shrugged and dropped into a stance of his own. He had more of an uncertain edge to him with the knife in his hand rather than the stave. It seemed knives weren't a Tulpenland prince's usual weapon.

Well, she could fix that.

Chapter Ten

As Harm shouldered his pack once again, his muscles ached. After several days spent doing nothing but strength, sword, and knife training, his whole body *hurt*.

And he'd thought being mauled by a monster wolf was bad. Turned out training with Val was worse. Far worse. He looked forward to walking once again today. At least they'd only be training in the evening.

"Don't dawdle." Val marched forward, the cord yanking on Harm's wrist as she reached the end of the tether.

And there was the prickly *feeën* mercenary he'd come to know rather well. She'd been almost pleasant during the past few days. It had been unnerving.

Harm hurried to catch up, falling into step with her as they strode between the massive, vine- and moss-draped trees of the Tanglewood. The moss beneath their feet was soft and springy, the air warm and faintly floral-scented along with all the green smells of the forest.

They hiked through the Tanglewood for several hours, Daisy bounding ahead of them. Although they caught the occasional glimpse of *feeën*, neither *feeën* nor monsters bothered them.

At last, the forest grew brighter ahead, the trees becoming smaller as Val and Harm neared the treeline. At the edge of the forest, a meadow dotted with flowers in all colors and shapes spread out before them.

In the middle of the meadow, a city of tents, caravan wagons, and booths formed of everything from branches to stalks of grass to what might have been bones sprawled among the wildflowers. A lilting music filled the meadow while tantalizing smells wafted on the breeze.

Val halted, half ducking into deeper undergrowth.

Harm dropped into hiding beside her. "What's that?" And, more importantly, why were they hiding?

"A faerie market." Val's eyes flicked back and forth as she scanned it and the bustling meadow.

"And…that's dangerous?" Markets weren't particularly dangerous back home, but this was the realm of the *feeënvolk*.

"Right now during the day? No, not particularly, if you keep your wits about you." Val gave a hint of a shrug. "But at night? Absolutely."

"Then…why are we hiding?" Harm glanced from her to the bustling faerie market once again.

"It's never wise just to charge into places like a faerie market. Especially as a courtless mercenary. But I don't see a large presence of guards or librarians from the Court of Knowledge, so it should be safe enough for us." Val turned to him, gesturing at his pack. "I'd bypass it altogether, but it wouldn't hurt to acquire some supplies, especially a sword and clothing with a magical pocket for you. If you're willing to part with more of your trade goods. Faerie markets don't take coin. Just bargains."

Harm flexed his fingers on the strap of his pack. He didn't want to use more of the blue-and-white pottery he'd taken along. Who knew how much he'd need for bargains to return home once he made his escape?

But on the other hand, he'd need a sword, especially once Val left and he made his escape on his own. The clothing with a magical pocket would be handy as well. He wouldn't always have Val with him to carry his items in a pocket, and carrying everything in a pack advertised to everyone who saw him that he had items with him. A magical pocket would keep that a secret, and secrets like that were as valuable as currency here in the Fae Realm.

"All right." Harm gave a sharp nod. "Let's bargain for whatever you think is best. You'll know better than I do what I'll need."

Val straightened and pushed away from the tree. "Then stick close. We can't hide the cord tethering us together, but I don't want to advertise it either. I'm a courtless mercenary with few protections here. I don't want to draw the attention of the sovereigns of this court."

"Understood." Harm stepped even closer. Then,

following an impulse that even he didn't want to examine, he clasped her hand, the cord tucked close between them.

Val jumped, yanking her hand free of his. "What are you doing?"

"Hiding the cord as much as possible." He lifted his eyebrows. "If the method is all right?"

She eyed him like he'd just suggested swimming through a sewage-choked canal. But after a long moment, she reached out and took his hand. "Fine. Yes, this would be the best way to hide the cord."

Harm grinned at her sour expression and pushed through the undergrowth with Daisy leading the way. He didn't want to examine why holding Val's hand sent such a thrill through him. After all, once this was over, he'd escape back to the Human Realm, and she'd return to the Realm of Monsters. They'd never see each other again.

Yet he couldn't help but enjoy the feel of her fingers clasped in his, despite the slight awkwardness. Nor the way her shoulder occasionally brushed his as they strolled across the open meadow.

When he'd left home, all he'd wanted to do was return as quickly as possible. And he still did. His father and brother were in danger from whatever strange *feeën* conspiracy he was caught up in.

But would it hurt anything if he enjoyed the journey? With each day here in the Fae Realm, something in him was stretching, growing, *changing* in a way he never would have if he'd lived his whole life as a prince in

Tulpenland. By the time he returned to the Human Realm, who would he have become?

Harm and Val joined the crush of *feeën* entering the faerie market through one of the gaps between the caravan wagons.

Feeën of all shapes, sizes, and colors strode around them, from three-feet-tall sprites with skin in shades of green, pink, purple, and more to the tall, leafy people with bark-like skin and leaves shedding from their hair. Some of the *feeën* had animal features, like a mouse tail or fox ears while others were almost human in appearance, except for tapered ears and a sharp beauty.

Even stranger than the people were the wares displayed in the booths. One booth held jars of various substances with labels like *giant snail slime* and *belching toad spit*. At another booth, shrunken heads hung along the canopy, twisting and turning, their mouths moving as they spoke to passers-by.

The rows of caravans, tents, and booths meandered in a chaotic fashion with other rows branching off at sporadic intervals. Sometimes cleared sections held bonfires and dancing greens.

Val tugged Harm down a smaller, darker side row. The goods down here seemed to be more of the practical nature compared to the odd assortment of the main row they'd left behind. One booth displayed boots and shoes of all shapes and sizes. Another tent had only rugs while yet another had racks of clothing.

"Your boots seem serviceable enough." Val swept a glance over him. "But new breeches, shirt, and perhaps a leather jerkin or something similar are in order."

She switched her gaze to assessing the booths. Instead of going to the merchant directly in front of them, she continued down the alley until they reached another booth, which only had a few pieces of clothing of the sturdy and leather variety on display. The diminutive woman running the booth had large round mouse ears and a pointed nose complete with whiskers. Her pink tail swished her gray skirt back and forth.

Her nose wiggled as she glanced between Harm and Val before her gaze focused solely on Harm. "I see you are in need of new vestments." She held up a leather vest. "Can I interest you in a vest that will protect you from heartache?"

That sounded too helpful. Harm glanced at Val, questioning if this was something he should bargain for.

Val snorted and shook her head. "You'd probably lose your ability to love or feel emotions. I might be tempted, but I don't think you would be."

"No." Harm gave a shudder. Yes, losing loved ones hurt. He still hurt from the loss of his mother. But he wouldn't want to have never loved her at all.

"No shenanigans. I'm wise to your goblin tricks." Val wagged her finger in front of the mouse woman's nose. "We are just in need of breeches, a shirt, and a leather jerkin. The only magic needed in the clothing is a magical pocket and overall durability. Nothing else, understand?"

"Even that much magic has a price." The mouse woman's whiskers twitched as her tiny black eyes sharpened. "What will you bargain? A year of this human's life? The hair from his head?"

"He isn't mine to bargain with." Val crossed her arms. "But he has some items he is willing to bargain."

Harm swallowed as he swung his pack to the ground. No pressure. He now better understood the dangers of bargains than he had when he'd bargained with Queen Mab.

"What've you got, human?" The mouse woman's nose twitched even faster.

Harm dug into the pack and pulled out one of the pottery plates. "I have—"

She held up a hand, the back of the fingers covered with bits of soft gray fur. "No. What need have I of useless baubles?"

Right. He'd misjudged his audience. The pottery would do for a *feeën* queen who had an appetite for such trinkets. But for a practical working woman like this mouse *fee*? Not so much.

What did he have that would appeal to this woman? He wedged the plate back into the pack, shifting his good coat aside as he did so.

His coat. Would that work? She made clothing, and it was a fine jacket. He hated to part with his one piece of nice clothing so soon, but it did him little good here where *feeën*-made clothing was more practical.

Harm held up the coat, giving it a shake to smooth some of the wrinkles. Even with the wrinkles, the silver threads of the embroidery around the cuffs and collar stood out nicely against the rich black fabric. "I have a jacket fit for a prince and sewn by skilled human tailors."

The mouse woman leaned closer, her eyes almost as

greedy as Mab's had been. "This was made entirely by human hands? No magic went into its creation?"

"None whatsoever." Harm brushed a hand over the coat, making the embroidery catch the light.

"There is value in something that is untouched by the magic of this realm." The mouse woman eyed the jacket before she swung her gaze back to him. "But this one item of clothing isn't enough for what I've been asked to create."

Harm hesitated. Would he be caving too quickly if he immediately searched for something else to add? Or would he anger the woman if he insisted that the coat was enough?

Val tipped her head in a suggestion of a nod.

Hanging the jacket over his arm, Harm dug through his pack once again. What else did he have? He had the rest of his good set of clothing, though he was currently wearing them. Or there was his ripped and bloody clothing, but he was uncomfortable trading something with his blood on it. That seemed like a bad idea, especially after Val's mention of blood bindings.

Or...his hand closed on the inner pack that held his stash of human food. He hadn't used much of it yet since the rodents Daisy caught seemed to be safe enough to eat once Val roasted them.

He had several wedges of cheese. And this goblin woman was part mouse. Would it be offensive to offer her cheese?

He dug out a wheel of the cheese Tulpenland was known for. There was only one way to find out.

Even as he straightened and started unwrapping the

cloth, the mouse woman's nose twitched even more vigorously as she sniffed, the light in her eyes turning downright ravenous. "What's that?"

"This is a wedge of some of the finest cheese produced in my kingdom." Harm unwrapped the last of the cloth.

The mouse woman leaned closer, and Harm held it out of her reach before she snatched it or took a bite of it right out of his hand. "Not a bite until we have completed our bargain."

The mouse woman's gaze never left the cheese. "I will create breeches, a shirt, and a jerkin with a magical pocket as requested for the jacket and two wedges of that cheese."

"The jacket and one wedge." Harm used his foot to shift his pack farther away from her before she got any ideas.

The woman's eyes narrowed, still entirely focused on the cheese.

"We are headed for a Winter Court." Val's arms remained crossed, her tone disinterested. She was prompting him without taking over the bargaining.

Good thought. Harm would have met the mouse woman's gaze, but she had eyes only for the cheese. "The jacket and two wedges of cheese if you include a coat or a cloak suitable for winter, along with thick stockings, mittens, a hat, and a scarf, in addition to the items already discussed."

"Done. It's a bargain." The mouse woman lifted her hands, making grabbing motions with her fingers.

Harm lowered the cheese, not about to torture the woman further.

She snatched it, took a bite, and moaned as if it was the best thing she had ever tasted.

Harm reached into his pack and fished out another wedge of cheese, making sure to grab one that he liked less than the others he had left. He held out both it and the jacket.

The mouse woman snatched the second wedge of cheese first, then took the coat almost as an afterthought. "Come, come. Step inside my booth, and I'll get your measurements."

Having his measurements taken was something he was used to back home, but was it safe to step into this strange mouse woman's booth? Harm glanced at Val.

Val waved to him, Daisy sitting on her feet. "Go on. Now that the bargain is struck, it's safe enough. Besides…" She wiggled the cord. "You can't go far."

Very true. It wasn't like the mouse woman could bundle him into her wagon and kidnap him. He was already well and truly held captive as it was, and no one was taking him from Val.

Harm followed the mouse woman into the booth, resisting the urge to reach for the iron knife tucked in his boot as the flap fell closed behind him, plunging him into semi-darkness.

A single candle flared to life, providing a small pool of illumination. The mouse woman bustled forward, setting the candle on a tiny table next to him.

Something skittered in the darkness, and Harm jumped. "What was that?"

"Just my mice." The mouse woman gestured as a tiny gray-furred mouse ran along the floor by Harm's feet.

It took all his self-control not to shriek and leap back. "Your…mice…" Was it strange for a woman who was mostly mouse herself to keep mice as pets or was that a perfectly normal thing for this realm?

"Of course. Mice make the best seamstresses." She whipped a measuring tape out of a pocket, grabbed a three-legged stool, and set it next to him. "Hold still. This will only take a moment."

The process of taking his measurements wasn't all that different than it was back home, except that he had to lean back several times to avoid being whacked in the face by a large mouse ear. The woman's mouse tail occasionally brushed against his legs while mice squeaked and skittered all around the tiny space.

As soon as she finished the measurements, the mouse woman ushered Harm out of the booth and into the alley once again. She nodded to Val. "I'll get started right away. Please come back an hour before sunset to claim the items."

Val's mouth pressed into a tight line—she likely wasn't happy that they would have to stay in the area until then—but she nodded. "Very well."

The mouse woman went back to nibbling on her cheese as she bustled around her booth. Did that mean the mice were making Harm's new clothes?

He shook that thought away. He'd never bring himself to wear them if he dwelled on that thought too long. And after bargaining so much for them, he wasn't about to not wear them.

Val set out along the alley once again, snapping her fingers in a command that Harm hoped was for Daisy rather than for him.

Shrugging on his pack, he fell into step with Val once again. "Off to find me a sword?"

"Yes." She marched onward for a few more strides before she cast him a glance. "It would be best if I did the bargaining at this next booth. I've gotten weapons here before. Many of the mercenaries in my Wild Hunt band have. Besides that, we'll draw too much attention to ourselves if you—a captive human—were to procure a sword."

"That would probably go against your *he's not armed as far as I know* deniability." Harm didn't mind ceding this bargaining to her. She would know better what to look for when it came to bargaining for a good sword.

"That too." Val kept her gaze forward. "Technically, it'll be my sword that I'll loan to you."

He didn't dare ask if she'd take the loan back before he was handed over to his new master. He wanted to trust her and believe that she'd let him keep it.

But she was still a mercenary, and in the end, he was just a package. He couldn't let himself forget that, no matter how much of a thrill he got holding her hand or how hard his heart started beating around her.

Especially then.

Harm shoved the doubts away, keeping a smile plastered on his face. "Do you need some of my pottery for the bargaining? Or are swordsmiths not into that?"

"No and no." Val still wouldn't look at him as she scanned the booths around them, taking them down an even darker, narrower aisle between the tents and market stalls. "As I'm doing the bargaining, I'll provide what's required."

That was cryptic, but Harm wouldn't argue if he could hold on to his pottery a little longer. He adjusted the strap where it was cutting into his shoulder. He looked forward to that evening when he could stuff his heavy pack into a magical pocket and stop having to tote it around.

As they strode down the tiny alley, the *feeën* who crept around them appeared even more disreputable, sporting even more weapons than Val did. Daisy stuck close, her hackles raised even though she had more manners than to growl at everyone. Just at the ones who stepped a little too close.

Val finally halted about nine feet away from a darkened booth with a variety of weapons piled almost haphazardly on a rickety table. The grizzled figure behind the table had huge arms and a tiny body, and Harm couldn't have said what kind of *feeënvolk* he might be.

"Stay here." Val pointed to a somewhat sheltered spot next to the post of the booth adjacent to the weapons booth. "Right here."

Harm nodded and placed his back to the post. With the variety of large and menacing figures tromping through this alley, he wasn't too comfortable being left alone, even if Val would only be ten feet away.

"Daisy, stay." Val gestured to the dog, and Daisy obligingly sat on Harm's feet, staring out at the crowds.

Some of Harm's tension eased. He would be far safer with the sometimes-three-headed dog protecting him.

A hand on the hilt of her knife, Val strode nearly to the end of the tether and was soon locked in what seemed to be tense bargaining with the proprietor.

Harm watched for a few moments, but then he swung his gaze to the crowd, taking in the strange sights. A booth a few yards away was made of bones while another market stall held harps that were singing. Not just playing but keening at an eerie pitch. The people in the crowd ranged from the grotesque to the macabre, yet the ones who were the most beautiful set Harm's teeth on edge.

"It's a strange sight, isn't it?" A low tenor spoke from behind him.

Harm jumped and whirled as much as he could with Daisy sitting on his feet.

A young man of about Harm's age leaned against the wall in the shadows between the two booths. He was dressed in a bland green shirt, brown trousers, brown boots, and a leather jerkin. A quiver of arrows and an unstrung bow were strapped to his back.

He held a piece of fruit in his hand. It would have resembled an apple, except that it was turquoise. Several bites were already missing from it. Even as Harm watched, the man crunched another bite, munching on it as if he didn't have a care in the world.

"Who are you?" Harm clenched his fists at his sides. Should he call for Val?

"Not going to tell you that." The young man turned

his head to the side, revealing reassuringly normal, rounded ears. "But I'm as human as you are."

"That could be a glamour." Harm had learned about such things in the past few days. He couldn't trust his eyes.

Daisy stood and approached the man, her tail wagging even if her head was low and wary.

The man held out a hand. Daisy sniffed it, and her tail wagged faster. She pressed her head into the man's knees, wiggling as he ran his fingers over her ears. Even as he scratched Daisy behind the ears, the young man glanced at Harm. "Your dog likes me."

"She isn't my dog." Harm wasn't sure why he felt the need to make that point.

"Belongs to your mercenary guard, does she?" The man gestured with the turquoise apple at the rope around Harm's wrist. "Is that a threefold cord?"

"Yes." Harm didn't see any reason to lie. He peeked at Val, but she was so locked in her bargaining that she didn't seem to be paying any attention to Harm or who he might be speaking to.

The man gave a nod, something of a grimace flashing across his face before he smoothed it into a smile once more. He took another bite of the fruit. "Where is she taking you?"

Perhaps it was foolish, but Harm was inclined to trust him. He seemed to be human, and Daisy liked him.

Harm settled a shoulder more comfortably against the post again. "To Golbet of Flight Talonstorm in the Court of Stone. I was originally bargained to Queen Mab of the Court of Dreams, but she bargained me away to Queen Titania, who in turn bargained me to Golbet."

"You dodged a quiver of trouble with Titania." The man didn't even try to hide his scowl this time. He reached into a pocket. When he withdrew his hand, he held out a small red flower. "This is a wild fae primrose. They often grow around faerie circles, and it's said that they lead travelers home. If someone hands you a wild fae primrose, you can trust them. You'll just need to get free of that cord first."

When the young man continued to hold out the flower, Harm took the delicate thing. It had five petals in a deep red color. Growing up as he did in Tulpenland where flowers were so highly prized, he'd easily recognize this flower again now that he'd taken the time to study it. "Thank you."

"Don't thank me. I've done nothing to help you yet." The man tilted his head in Val's direction. "Last piece of advice. I wouldn't mention any of this to her."

Harm couldn't help but look at Val, his gaze catching there. It felt like a betrayal to keep something like this from her.

But then again, this was survival. He didn't owe her any allegiance, no matter how many times she saved his life here in the Fae Realm. She was only protecting him because he was a package she needed to deliver in one piece.

As he debated, a tall *feeën* man with weathered brown skin and black hair streaked gray at the temples strode up to the weapons booth and halted next to Val. She whirled toward him, her eyes lighting with something Harm couldn't identify. Loyalty. Respect. Deference.

The sight speared painfully inside Harm's chest.

"Thanks..." Harm turned back to the stranger, only to find that he had vanished. The only sign that he'd ever been there was the core of the apple-fruit left in the dirt.

That was odd. Should Harm trust the man? Had he truly been human or had he been a *fee* in disguise? But why would he attempt to trick Harm? Harm was already a captive and bound to a *fee*.

With one last glance at Val and the strange *fee* she spoke with, Harm quickly stuffed the wild fae primrose into a pocket. It seemed he had made his decision after all.

Chapter Eleven

The swordsmith was proving particularly stubborn and uncooperative.

Val gritted her teeth. "One vial of basilisk venom and the tooth of a hydra. That's my final offer."

A movement at the corner of her eye was her only warning before the shadow of a figure stepped far too close into her space.

She whirled, hand already dropping to her knife. Then she stilled. "Diego?"

Her Wild Hunt Leader halted at the swordsmith's booth next to her. Hints of gray threaded through the hair at his temples while his black beard and mustache were trimmed thin. Multiple daggers filled the bandoleers crossing his chest.

"I see the ease of this mission hasn't dulled your edge." Diego's smile glistened in the depths of his dark brown eyes. "Though I became concerned when you didn't return as quickly as expected."

"There were complications." Val tried to put a note

of frustration into her tone. She placed her back more firmly to Harm. As if he was nothing but her package. Just a puppy she planned to kick. "His bargain was traded away. It's currently held by Golbet of Flight Talonstorm."

"Unfortunate." Diego clapped her on the shoulder. "At least one of my best is on this task. I know you'll keep the package alive. Deliver it and return when you can."

"I will." Val hesitated. But she should warn him since she had the chance. "There's something strange about this mission. The package was set up. Someone sickened his brother with a faerie poison. There's a fae involved in this, and that fae specifically asked for a mercenary to transport the package."

"I know. It's a situation that I'm handling, never fear." Diego shrugged with all the grace of a prowling jaguar.

Listening to rumors and handling the politics of working with fae monarchs on behalf of his mercenaries was, in part, Diego's job as the leader of their Wild Hunt band. So why did her chest tighten, her instincts prickle? As if he wasn't telling her the whole truth?

What was he even doing here? How had he managed to find her in the faerie market when he couldn't have known she would even be here?

"But I see I'm impeding your bargaining. Acquiring a new sword?" Diego gestured from her to the sword lying on the table in front of them.

"Yes." Val wasn't about to explain further. Hopefully

Diego wouldn't notice that the length and heft were more suited to Harm's longer reach and taller height. To keep him from studying the sword too closely, she gestured at the swordsmith. He had his burly arms crossed over his otherwise tiny frame, a scowl thrusting his lower jowl farther forward. "Except he's being stubborn."

Diego made a noise in the back of his throat as he shook his head. "After all the business my Wild Hunt has given you over the years? I insist you take whatever bargain my mercenary has offered you. No, better yet, consider it a part of our other deal."

What other deal? Val hurriedly shook her head. "No, I'll stick with my original offered bargain."

The swordsmith eyed Val for another moment, grunted, and held out a meaty palm. "Fine. The bargain is accepted."

Val dug the promised vial and tooth out of her pocket, handing them over before she claimed the sword. She immediately stowed the sword in the pocket, getting it out of Diego's sight. She tried to appear casual as she turned back to her Wild Hunt leader. "What other deal? What are you doing here? I didn't think you had any upcoming missions in the Fae Realm."

Would he think her questions too prying?

Why was she even worried? This was Diego. Her Wild Hunt leader. She had nothing to fear from him.

"I was just fetching a weapons order of my own." Diego waved at the swordsmith in a silent order.

The swordsmith scowled, but he ducked through the

curtains that divided the front booth from the back where he must have kept his tools and additional inventory.

As soon as the swordsmith was gone, Diego lowered his voice. "I'm planning a raid for the full Wild Hunt, and I'm calling in everyone who isn't on a mission. As soon as you and the others return, we'll ride."

A Wild Hunt ride. A pounding thrill of monstrous steeds, swinging blades, and rampant destruction to any in their path. The Wild Hunt bands existed for such ravaging.

Once Val might have longed for such a thing, calling it freedom. Maybe even vengeance.

Now she could only imagine what Harm would think of her, if he saw her participating in such scourging.

Not that he'd ever see it. He'd be left far behind with his new master when it came time to ride.

Val worked up a blank expression and a precise nod. "I will be ready to ride once I return."

"I knew I could count on you." Diego flashed his glittering smile again before turning as the swordsmith stepped past the curtain, lugging a bundle of swords, spears, halberds, and other weapons.

The swordsmith handed them over without any hesitation or bargaining, so whatever price Diego was paying must have been arranged in advance.

Diego stuffed the whole bundle of weapons into his magical pocket. With one last parting nod to Val, he spun on his heel and slunk down the alley, disappearing from sight among the disreputable market stalls and even more disreputable fae browsing through them.

Still fighting her itching instincts, Val stalked to Harm's side. "Let's go."

Harm peeled away from the post, something in his stance stiff and wary. "Who was that?"

"Diego. My Wild Hunt leader." Val spun on her heel, marching down the alley in the opposite direction from Diego. The companionable warmth had fled, replaced with the reminder that she was supposed to be a cold mercenary. Not befriending Harm. Or helping him to survive the Fae Realm.

Then why did that uncomfortable twisting return to her stomach at the thought of going back to kicking human puppies and merely delivering packages?

She kept up her furious pace until they left the darker part of the faerie market behind. By the time she located several booths containing basic food items, some of her dark mood had dissipated. She didn't see Diego again, and he was likely already on his way back to the Realm of Monsters, taking advantage of the chaos in the Court of Revels to hop through a rift.

Harm, too, eased from whatever stiff wariness had gripped him, and gawked once again.

In a cleared space in the market, a wooden platform had been set up with logs for benches placed before it. Currently, a troupe of actors pranced about the stage. Though, *actor* was a loose term. Val was no experienced critic, but they didn't seem to be very good.

Harm cocked his head. "Is this…normal for performances in the Fae Realm?"

"No." Val scowled as the donkey-eared man on the stage seemed to forget his line. Half the other actors hissed words at him, speaking over each other in a way that seemed to just confuse the man all the more.

"They're awful." Harm took a step closer. "But it's strangely fascinating to watch."

The audience was hooting: some with laughter and some with jeers. But the actors doggedly kept on with their performance, even as one of them—dressed as a tree with a plethora of branches strapped to his body— tripped over his fake trunk and fell in front of one of the actresses, and she took a tumble, her wide skirt flying up and over her head.

Val sighed and indicated a bench in the back row. "Then have a seat. We might as well watch in comfort."

They had plenty of time to waste while the mouse goblin woman made Harm's new clothes.

Harm slid onto the bench, and Val sat beside him, close enough to keep the cord tucked out of sight. Daisy wiggled her way between their legs, and Harm scratched her ears.

After the theatrical performance—*farce* would be the more accurate word—two librarians from the Great Library—a man and a woman wearing the green coats designating them as assistant librarians—took the stage. Both of them had golden hair and pale skin, and while Val couldn't get a good look, she suspected the female librarian might have been a human.

The two librarians did a dramatic reading of a passage from a book, made all the more dramatic because the two librarians seemed to hold some kind of animosity for each other. Or perhaps romantic tension. It was hard to tell which it was.

After them, a smirking male fae led a string of cringing humans carrying musical instruments onto the stage.

Harm paled, clutching the edge of the bench with a white-knuckled grip.

Val stood. "We should go."

Harm just nodded, rose to his feet, and followed her as they eased through the crowd that had gathered.

Once they popped out on the other side into the relative quiet near the booths that faced the performance stage, Harm glanced over his shoulder, a pucker between his brows. "I thought you said the Court of Knowledge is against the captivity of humans?"

"They are. But faerie markets are considered neutral. The Court of Knowledge doesn't have jurisdiction here, even though the faerie market is on the court's land." Val looked back the way they'd come, though she could barely see the cluster of humans over the heads of the crowd. The raucous jeers nearly drowned out the almost painful dirge the humans had struck up. "It still was bold of that fae to bring his captives here. He's bound to lose a few by the time he returns to his own court."

"Good." Harm spoke the word under his breath, his fists clenched at his sides.

Val swallowed, turning away and forcing herself into a brisk pace. She agreed with Harm. She shouldn't, but she did.

And yet here she was with a captive human at her

side with every intention of delivering him and no plans to aid him more than she already had.

———

IN THE DARKNESS OF EVENING, the last light of the fading sunset lingering behind the trees, Val tossed the rope for Daisy. After the day spent in the market, Daisy had an excess of overstimulated energy, and she raced after the rope. As she reached it, she tried to stop and ended up tumbling for a moment before she rolled back to her feet and scooped up the rope. As she whipped the rope back and forth to kill it, she gave a low growl.

With Daisy occupied, Val risked a glance over her shoulder at the tent only a few feet behind her. The crackling fire cast a pool of light onto the side of the tent and the surrounding grass.

Not that Val was anxious to see Harm emerge in his new clothes. It was just that they'd lost a whole day in that faerie market trying to obtain the items, and Val needed to make sure it was worth it.

If that goblin woman had tried to trick them by creating less than optimal clothing, Val would march back there and wring a better bargain out of her. Nevermind the lateness of the hour or how wild the faerie market would be by then. She was in the mood to crack a few heads.

Once they'd retrieved the clothing from the mouse woman, Val hadn't wanted to linger any longer. She'd hurried Harm out of the faerie market, and the two of them—three of them counting Daisy—had hiked as far away from the faerie market as they could before darkness fell.

Daisy finished killing the rope and raced back toward Val. With only a few feet of room to maneuver, Val held her ground until the last moment, sidestepping Daisy.

Daisy nearly barreled right into the tent before she caught herself, pivoted, and jumped at Val.

Val lifted the second rope out of the way. "Sit."

Daisy landed, then plopped her butt on the ground.

Val tossed the second rope and searched the gloom for where Daisy had dropped the first one.

There. The darker length of the rope lay against the grass several yards away. Well out of Val's reach, unless she dragged Harm out of the tent by the cord.

Daisy, at least, seemed happy enough whipping the other rope back and forth.

At a whisper of canvas, Val turned. Harm stood there, wearing a light blue shirt that brought out the blue of his eyes even in the evening shadows. Given the warmth of the weather, he'd rolled the sleeves to his elbows. The leather jerkin over top was well-fitted, and he'd left the ties loose at his neck. His new breeches were sturdy tan fabric while the sword belted at his waist completed the look.

His blond hair was long around his ears while the scruff of a beard covered his chin and cheeks. Dressed in fae clothes, tall, and broad shouldered as he was, he could have been a mercenary in the Wild Hunt.

At least, until he smiled. Then he didn't look at all

like a fellow mercenary. Instead, he was the cheerful puppy she was coming to appreciate.

Not appreciate. Seeing her Wild Hunt leader had reminded her of all the reasons why she should never harbor appreciation for one of her packages.

Val shook herself, shoving thoughts of Diego and the Wild Hunt away.

Harm spread his hands wide. "What do you think?"

"Either that goblin seamstress has a soft spot for you or that cheese was exceptional." Val gestured from Harm's head to his feet. "Because that is among her best work."

"Tulpenland is known for its cheese." Harm shrugged and smoothed a hand almost self-consciously over the front of the jerkin.

"That could be it. Goblins aren't animals, despite the discrimination against them here in the Fae Realm." Val checked on Daisy again. The dog had dropped the rope and was now sniffing around their clearing, uninterested in more play. "But they do sometimes have characteristics of those animals. It's part of their magic."

"Huh." Harm rocked back on his heels for a moment. Then he dug into his pocket, where he must have stashed everything from his pack, and pulled out a wedge of cheese wrapped in a cloth. "Would you like to try some Tulpenland cheese? I still have several wedges."

"I thought you were saving the food from the Human Realm for your escape?" Val took a seat on a log next to the fire.

Harm slid onto a seat on a log across from her. The cord between them partially fell into the fire, but it didn't burn. He dug into his pocket again. "I can spare some to share. Besides, I'm tired of carrying around so much."

"You have a magical pocket now. It won't be heavy." Val poked at the fire with a stick to give her hands something to do. She wasn't sure why this conversation felt strangely charged. They were merely discussing food.

"Yes, but I can still afford to share." Harm withdrew one of the blue-and-white pottery plates, a fork, and a small knife.

Val waved the stick at him, its end smoldering. "It isn't a good sign when you start to become attached to your captor and do friendly things like share your food."

Harm paused in cutting the wedge into chunks and raised his head to eye her. "And it isn't a good sign when you start to become attached to your captive and do friendly things like get him new clothes and arm him with a sword."

Val snapped her mouth shut. He had a good point.

"Besides, you aren't precisely my captor. That's whoever is waiting at the end of this journey because of the bargain." Harm lifted his right arm. "You're just as bound by this cord as I am."

"Don't mistake my own binding for innocence." Val wasn't sure why her voice held such a snap. As if this topic made her uncomfortable. She'd delivered many packages and had always successfully pushed off the discomfort before.

"Delivering a captive to his captor isn't what I'd call virtuous." Harm dropped his gaze back to the cheese, concentrating almost too hard on his task. "Just pointing out that you aren't my captor."

She shouldn't encourage his line of thinking. She might not be his captor by a strict definition of the word here in the Fae Realm, but that didn't make her *good*.

That had never bothered her before. Like the other mercenaries in her Wild Hunt, she'd scorned those from the Court of Knowledge and others who were taking a stand against the practice of keeping humans as captives. There just didn't seem to be any point in fighting something that had been the norm in the Fae Realm for generations. It wasn't like the fae treated each other much better than they treated humans.

No, she hadn't kept human captives herself, but she'd aided in the practice no matter how much she might want to think her conscience was clear.

Prior to this trip, she would have said she hadn't had a conscience.

After stowing the rest of the wedge in his pocket again, Harm stood, walked closer, and held out the blue-and-white pottery plate. "Anyway, here's the cheese."

Val took the plate, glad to let the momentary discomfort slip away again. "Sharing your cheese and getting one of your precious plates dirty? You must be feeling pleased with the new clothes."

Harm shrugged as he retook his seat. "I can always wash the plate." He'd kept a handful of the cheese for himself, and he popped a bite in his mouth.

Still, he was trusting her with one of the plates. She

could so easily sabotage him by breaking it rather than returning it.

Perhaps he was right to trust her, at least in this case. She wasn't about to destroy it.

As she picked up one of the pieces of cheese, Daisy appeared at her side, placing her front paws on the log next to Val and wiggling her head beneath Val's arm as she tried to reach the plate.

Val held the plate out of Daisy's reach and gave the dog a firm but gentle shove to force her back to the ground. "No, down."

Daisy dropped her paws back to the ground before she sat, regarding Val with such big, amber eyes.

"Maybe I'll share the last bite." If she shared before then, Daisy's three heads would all appear, and there would be no keeping the plate away from her.

Val picked up one of the pieces of cheese, trying not to look at Daisy, and popped it into her mouth.

A tangy and yet savory taste filled her mouth with a rich depth she couldn't quite describe. It wasn't at all like the cheese found here in the Fae Realm.

She couldn't help her hum of appreciation at the taste. "This is really good."

No wonder the goblin woman had felt the need to go above and beyond when fulfilling the bargain. She would have to give her best work to match the worth of the cheese she'd gained.

Harm grinned, then fished in his pocket again, pulling out a flask. He stood and crossed the space around the fire again. "Here. Wash it down with this."

Juggling her plate while still fending off Daisy, Val

took the flask and popped the cap off with her thumb. She tipped the flask back and took a swig.

A taste that was both sweet and tart coated her tongue from the juice, a refreshing sensation that paired well with the cheese.

Val lowered the flask. "What is that? It's really good as well."

"Cassis. A drink made from black currants." Harm's grin now sparkled in his blue eyes as he stuck another bite of cheese in his mouth, as if he was enjoying sharing these bits of his home with her.

"I like it." Val resisted the urge to down another swig and instead nibbled a bite of cheese, trying to savor it.

Food in the Fae Realm didn't usually have such complexity of flavor. It was all sweet or all tart or all sour, and usually to the extreme, like everything here in the Fae Realm.

Try as she might to make the cheese last, Val was soon down to her last two bites. She ate one piece, then held out the last piece to the now drooling Daisy. Daisy nearly took Val's fingers off as she snapped it up, gulping down the cheese so fast the dog probably hadn't even tasted it.

With one more sip of cassis, Val capped the flask. Enough companionable sharing around the fire. They should turn in for the evening and remember that once morning came, they would be back to being a package and delivery mercenary, nothing more.

Chapter Twelve

After the time he'd spent in the Fae Realm, Harm shouldn't be shocked as he and Val stepped from the lush green moss shaded by towering trees into crisp air and fields with waving cornstalks ready for harvest, a stark contrast marking the boundary of the courts.

"Do you ever get used to that?" Harm halted, gaping at the fields bursting with ripe vegetables in a variety of strange colors and shapes. "The abrupt changes between the Courts?"

Val's mouth pressed into a tight line, her face especially hard. "No."

After the moment around the fire sharing cheese and cassis, Val had woken in a foul mood, going all prickly once again.

It was getting rather frustrating.

Perhaps she was right. He shouldn't be trying so hard and should just see her as his captor and enemy as much as the one who held his bargain.

Daisy bounded off to sniff around the fields and each of the ripe vegetables.

Harm reached for one of the vegetables that was cerulean and shaped like an eggplant. "These are really strange."

"Don't pick anything." Val halted and glared. "Don't even touch them. We're not a part of the Harvest Court, so we don't have permission to pick anything. We'll bring down the wrath of the nuckelavee if we do."

"What are the nuckelavee? You've mentioned them before." Harm fell into step with Val as they followed what seemed to be a meandering path between the plants. Unlike the farm fields back home, which were planted in straight lines, these fields were all higgledy-piggledy with no set rows and plants growing in various clumps. Haphazard seemed to be the organizational style of choice here in the Fae Realm.

"Monstrous creatures that are part nightmare horse that eats meat and part a headless rider perched on its back. Except that horse and rider are one, and both bodies are formed of rotting flesh." Val didn't even break her stride as she described the horrible thing. "They're monsters, technically, but monsters of this court rather than monsters belonging to the Realm of Monsters. The nuckelavee guard these fields, especially at night."

"Charming." Harm gave a vegetable growing into the path a wide berth. He didn't want to accidentally call the nuckelavee down on them. "Are you sure cutting through the Harvest Court is safer than the Court of Sand?"

"Yes." Val's jaw worked. "That court has sand dragons—those are animal dragons that spit venom—thunderbirds, and giant snakes. That's not even counting the shifting sands where the barrier between the realms is so thin you could stumble into the Realm of Monsters without even meaning to do so. Monsters stumble out just as easily. Oh, and it's abominably hot."

"Right. Yes, the Harvest Court is better." Harm rested his hand on the hilt of his new sword.

Val just sent him another sour look and kept walking.

Apparently she wasn't in a talkative mood.

They walked in silence for several miles, the fields around them never seeming to change all that much. Occasionally Harm caught a glimpse of small *feeën* with gray-brown skin. They trundled between the fields, pushing wheelbarrows laden with vegetables. Brownies, Val called them.

The path took them into a field of dry and rustling stalks of corn, stretching for as far as Harm could see. The tassels of the cornstalks were level with his head, even with his height, while every stalk held several plump ears of orange-colored corn.

Val halted so abruptly that Harm nearly ran into her. She reached behind her and gripped his arm painfully tight.

"What is it?" Harm kept his voice low, even as he scanned the area. All he could see was corn and a single scarecrow on a pole. It wasn't dressed in clothes but was formed of bundles of straw tied together with twine, a round orange vegetable for a head.

Val crouched so that the corn fully hid her, dragging Harm down next to her. When she spoke, her lips barely moved with her whisper. "Scarecrow."

"Scarecrow?" Harm dropped his voice to a whisper as well and reached for his sword. "I'm assuming you mean something different here in the Fae Realm than what we have in the Human Realm."

"Here, scarecrows are very, very protective of their fields. They move about under their own power and are relentless in their attack. The only way to kill them is to burn them." Val eased her knife from her sheath. "If that one spots us, it will be very angry to see strangers in its field."

Harm would have drawn his sword, but it was an awkward movement to do while crouching, and he didn't want to accidentally set the corn to rustling. Instead, he followed Val, both of them bent over. He tried to set his boots down carefully so his footfalls wouldn't crunch on the fallen leaves scattered on the ground.

With a crashing bound, Daisy burst through the nearby cornstalks, growling and barking in the direction of the scarecrow.

"Daisy!" Val hissed, reaching for the dog.

All three heads in appearance, Daisy danced out of Val's reach, still barking, her fur raised all along her back. Her hunting instincts had taken over, and there was no calling her back now.

Harm tensed, his hand tightening on his sword's hilt.

Val straightened and peeked between the stalks. Then she grabbed Harm's arm again. "Run!"

Harm caught a glimpse of the bundle of straw detaching first one arm, then the other from the pole before he was yanked forward. He broke into a sprint before he could be pulled off his feet. While he couldn't draw his sword while running, his fingers itched for a weapon. Anything that made Val run instead of fight must be dangerous.

There was an even more uproarious rustling sound behind them, and Daisy's barking intensified until it was shrill.

Harm glanced over his shoulder, then nearly tripped over his own feet.

The scarecrow ran after them with a lumbering but surprisingly swift gait for something made entirely of straw. Its straight legs covered yards with each lurching step while its vegetable head swayed back and forth on its body. Even though it lacked a throat or a mouth, it made a horrible screeching noise, like a wind shredding through a field of dead stalks.

Daisy leapt, sank her teeth into one of the scarecrow's arms, and ripped the whole arm right off the body. The dog landed and shook the arm, tearing and shredding the straw.

The scarecrow gave its roar again and lifted its other arm to take aim at Daisy.

Val glanced over her shoulder, then muttered something under her breath. She halted, spun on a heel out of Harm's way as he struggled to slow, and dug into her pocket. She withdrew a spear, cocked her arm back, and threw.

The spear took the scarecrow through the vegetable

head, the shaft sticking out of the creature's forehead like a horn.

The scarecrow halted its swing at Daisy, and instead turned its head toward them. It didn't have expressions, yet Harm felt a wave of pure malice wash over him. He drew his sword and braced himself.

The scarecrow charged them, raising its remaining arm, the spear still impaling its head.

Val drew a sword as well before she gave a yell and leapt for the creature. She sliced off its head. The vegetable made a hollow *thunk* when it hit the ground. But the scarecrow kept coming.

Harm chopped his sword at the creature's arm. The sword bit partway through, and he hacked until the arm came off.

Val sliced sideways, chopping at the creature's legs. She got one leg off just as Daisy pounced on the creature again, knocking it to the ground and tearing it apart.

Harm relaxed, lowering his sword as he caught his breath.

Yet even as he watched, some of the straw began moving along the ground toward the body. The head rolled back into place while the arms and legs reformed.

With a whistle for Daisy, Val spun and broke into a run again. Harm adjusted his grip on his sword and ran to catch up before he could be yanked forward by the tether.

"So…" Harm gasped between breaths. "Burn it?"

"That's a last resort." Val didn't sound nearly as out

of breath as he was. She glanced over her shoulder, her jaw tightening, before she faced forward and kept sprinting. "We might set this whole field on fire if we did, and that would bring the nuckelavee down on us for sure. The scarecrow won't chase us past the boundary of its assigned field."

"And how far is that?" Harm's glance showed that the scarecrow was trundling after them again.

"Don't know." Val sprinted as easily as walking, hefting her sword as she ran as if she wasn't afraid of impaling herself if she tripped.

Or maybe that was just Harm's worry. He had, after all, sliced himself once on this journey already.

With a louder growl, Daisy streaked along the path and leapt on the scarecrow again, the force of her blow knocking the scarecrow all the way to the ground. Two of her heads grabbed arms and ripped them off while the middle head and her paws attacked the vegetable head.

Val slowed and spun once again. "That dog is going to be the death of me."

As she raced toward Daisy and the scarecrow, Harm followed in her footsteps, and not just because the tether wouldn't let him get farther than ten feet away from her. He was rather fond of the dog too.

Val hacked at the scarecrow, chopping the straw into tiny bits. Harm joined her, the two of them—three of them, counting Daisy—reducing the scarecrow to chaff. Val even went so far as to slice the vegetable head into pieces. As she retrieved her spear and slid it back into her pocket, she patted her side.

"Come on, Daisy. Let's go. That should buy us some time."

This time Harm sheathed his sword, the better to run. He set off at Val's side, and all three of them sprinted through the cornfield, following the meandering paths. Harm could only hope they were headed for a border of the field and not just running in circles, lost in the giant field.

They'd put the scarecrow well out of sight when the scratching roar echoed through the field once again.

Val's jaw worked, and she put on a burst of speed. Harm had no choice but to match her pace. Next to them, Daisy ran with her mouth shut and her ears pressed to her skull.

"There!" Val changed direction, swerving up a smaller path barely wide enough for Harm's shoulders.

He dove after her, his pounding heart lifting as he spotted the bright line where the corn gave way to another field.

A crash came behind him, and he risked a glance over his shoulder.

The scarecrow plunged after them down the narrow row. Its head remained only half put together while orange pieces bounced over the ground behind it.

Harm pushed himself even faster, stretching his long legs and pumping his arms. Even Val huffed gulping breaths as she raced just ahead of him.

As Val crossed the line into the next field, Daisy halted and started to turn, preparing to attack the creature once again.

Harm slowed and hefted the dog into his arms, a

squirming mass of solid muscle. The top of her head smashed into his chin as she scrambled to get free.

"Harm!" Val's shout snapped his head up.

The scarecrow was only feet away, a hole still gaping in its vegetable head like a gruesome mouth and that same dry shriek shaking the cornstalks around them.

Harm's feet were rooted to the spot, and it was all he could do to keep his grip on the dog flailing in his arms.

Just as the scarecrow swung at him, something jerked him by the wrist. Hard.

Harm tumbled out of the cornfield, landing on his back on a bed of vines and tilled earth. Daisy's weight fell on his stomach and chest, knocking the breath out of him.

Before Daisy could scramble free of his loosened grip, Val dropped her two-handed grip on the cord, darted forward, and grabbed Daisy by the scruff of the neck of her middle head. "It's all right, Daisy. You held it off."

The scarecrow tottered to a halt at the very edge of the field, screeching and waving its arms, but coming no farther.

Harm sucked in a shaky breath and didn't try to get up. He was never going near a scarecrow ever again.

Chapter Thirteen

After the exertion, even Val's legs ached as she and Harm hiked across the endless fields of the Harvest Court. By the time the sun eased low in the sky, Val was more than ready to find a safe place to camp for the night.

"Keep your eyes peeled for a cave, a tall tree, or an abandoned house." Val scanned the rolling hills around them. She and Harm needed a safe place before nightfall when the nuckelavee came out to patrol the fields.

Yet all she could see were more fields. This was why she hated traveling through the Harvest Court.

"We can't just pitch the tent?" Harm rested a hand on his sword's hilt.

"The tent wouldn't be enough. Not in the Harvest Court." Val squinted at a splotch of color in the distance. Was that a stand of trees? Would it be safe or infested with something dangerous? "I was hoping to find a nice cave to hole up in for the night. Or a tree tall enough to string hammocks out of the nuckelavee's reach. Their one weakness—if the nuckelavee have such a thing—is that they can't climb."

"I see." Harm's posture grew more tense as he strode at her side.

Val changed their direction slightly to head toward the distant copse of trees. It was the only shelter to be found, and daylight was fading fast into long shadows and an orange cast on the rustling cornstalks of the nearby field.

She and Harm skirted the cornfield, then crossed a small squash patch—after checking for any more scarecrows.

A gravel road lay on the other side of the pumpkin patch, each side lined with soggy ditches filled with tall weeds. Daisy dove into the weeds, disappearing except for the waving grasses and the occasional flick of her tail.

"Jump the ditch." Val backed up a step to get a running start. "There's no telling what's lurking in those weeds."

"Should we be worried about Daisy?" Harm leaned forward to peer into the ditch.

Something squealed, hitch-pitched and terrified.

"Nope. Daisy will be fine." Val shot a glance along the road. Nothing and no one in sight.

Harm nodded, shrugged, and tensed next to her. Together, the two of them ran forward and jumped. With his long legs, Harm landed on the road, easily clearing the ditch. Val landed next to him, her boots crunching on the gravel.

Across the road, the slim gray trees with yellow

leaves clustered around a small, tranquil pond. The trees were far smaller than she'd been hoping, but she might be able to shimmy up them high enough to string the hammocks. Getting Daisy into one would be a feat.

Not to mention, the scene was almost too perfectly peaceful. Val found herself reaching for her knife.

"You have good instincts, dearie. I wouldn't step into that glade if I were you." A creaky voice spoke from beside Val.

She whirled, placing Harm behind her, as she drew her knife.

An old woman with straggling gray hair and a face full of wrinkles peered up at Val. She wore a shapeless gray dress with a knitted shawl wrapped around her shoulders.

Val brandished her knife, gritting her teeth. How had this old woman sneaked up on her and Harm like this? Sure, Daisy was still distracted with decimating whatever was in the ditch, but that was no excuse. "Where did you come from?"

"My house." The woman gestured over her shoulder.

Val blinked as she focused on the small house no longer hidden by the rise of the road. The cottage sported a small front porch, two gables, white siding, and red gingham curtains. Red flowers grew in the window boxes. The cottage would have been picturesque...except for the fact that it stood on two yellow chicken legs.

How had Val missed seeing that? She'd been positive the road had been empty a moment ago.

"Now why don't you and your young man come in

for a spot of tea." The old woman patted Val's arm as if oblivious to the knife pointed at her.

"He isn't my young man." The words popped out before Val thought them through. Harm made a noise in the back of his throat.

"You have him on a short leash. Of course he's your young man." The old woman gestured at the cord running from Val's wrist to Harm's.

"No, that's not…" Val huffed a breath between her teeth. This wasn't the point she should be arguing at the moment.

Nor should the old woman's words make her as uncomfortable as they did. Apart from a tether for a small child to keep them safe, keeping a person on a leash wasn't exactly a good thing to do. Thus her crisis of conscience.

Val tightened the grip on her knife. "Neither of us is setting foot in your house. You'll drug us or glamour us or trick us somehow."

"It's good to be wary, dearie, when you have a man like that." The old woman nodded, then waved toward the trees again. "A nixie lives in that pond. She'll kill you and steal your man."

Val dared to take her eyes off the old woman long enough to glance at the pond. Was the woman telling the truth? Or was it a trick to get Val and Harm into her house?

Yet Val had gotten a bad feeling when she looked at the glade.

"Do you need a place to stay for the night, dearies? The monsters will be coming out to play soon." The old woman gave them a crooked- and yellow-toothed smile. "You're welcome to stay at my place."

Val opened her mouth to refuse, but Harm spoke first. "Can you give us a moment to discuss it?"

"Of course, dearies." The old woman remained smiling almost too benignly.

Harm draped an arm around Val's shoulders and steered her a few feet away from the old woman, his head leaning close to hers. "You said we need a safe place to stay tonight, right?"

"Yes, but don't be fooled. She definitely isn't safe." Val would have shrugged Harm's arm off, but the ruse of being a couple was probably just as well.

And the feel of his arm around her shoulders wasn't as odious as she would have expected. He was warm, and so tall that she could actually stand tucked against his side like this. Even better, he'd placed himself on her left side, leaving her right arm still free to wield her knife if needed.

"I'm not fooled. She's fae. Of course she isn't safe." Harm leaned even closer, his breath warm again the side of her face. "But I think she can be bargained with. Look at her house."

Val shot a glance at the neat little cottage perched on chicken legs. Right. This old woman was exactly the kind of fae who would bargain for one of Harm's fancy blue-and-white pottery pieces.

"But do you think it would be worth it? Or should we risk the glade?" Harm eyed the copse of trees, as if he got a bad feeling from it too.

That settled it. If both of them didn't like the look of the glade, then something was off.

The chicken cottage it was.

—————

Harm shouldn't relish the feel of having his arm around Val's shoulders as much as he did. It was simply the old woman putting thoughts into his head. That was all.

"All right. Go ahead and bargain with her." Val pulled away from Harm, turned back to the old woman, and sheathed her knife.

Harm let his arm drop. Right. Back to the business of survival.

He put on a smile and strolled toward the old woman. "We'd like to stay the night, but we want an official bargain. You understand, I'm sure."

"Of course, dearie. Never can be too careful." Something sharper glinted in the old woman's eyes. "What would you bargain?"

Harm gave himself a moment to think. If he said a word wrong, he would get himself and Val into all kinds of trouble.

With a deep breath, he held the old woman's gaze. "You will provide me and my companions with safe shelter for the duration of our stay. We will be allowed to sleep in peace and to go on our way unharmed, unchanged, and unhindered in the morning at a time of our choosing. In exchange, you will be given a wedge of the finest cheese of my homeland and…this."

Harm reached into his pocket and pulled out a pottery teacup. It showed a Tulpenlander woman with her cap and wooden shoes next to a windmill, all done in blue against the white background.

The woman's eyes focused on the teacup with the same greed the mouse woman had shown for the cheese. As Harm had guessed, given her prim cottage and invitation to tea.

"You will be given the cheese now and this teacup in the morning. Is it a bargain according to the terms I've laid out?" Harm could only hope he'd bargained well. Val hadn't interrupted, so hopefully that indicated he hadn't stepped too wrong.

"Yes!" The woman swayed forward, as if she wanted to snatch the teacup out of his hands.

Harm returned the teacup to his pocket and withdrew one of his wedges of cheese instead, holding it out to her.

She snatched it from him, closing her eyes as she smelled it. When she opened her eyes, she grinned, showing off her yellow teeth again. "You bargain well, dearie. I had thought to lure you inside to bake into a pie—young men are so tasty—but for this, I'll happily let you go your way unharmed." She tilted her head toward Val. "You do, indeed, have quite the young man. Thanks to him, you'll both survive the night. Come, come."

The old woman turned and minced toward where her chicken-legged cottage crouched on the road.

Harm swallowed, not sure if he should follow. He

was more reluctant to enter that house, now that the woman had admitted to wanting to eat him.

Val leaned closer. "It should be safe enough. Just… don't eat any of the food."

"Yes, I gathered as much." Harm shuddered. "I don't want to accidentally eat some previous unlucky man."

Val grinned, as if she found that funny. "Well, there's that. And, while you bargained for a safe place to sleep, you didn't bargain for safe food. So don't eat or drink anything."

Right. He had forgotten something. But as long as they didn't eat or drink, they'd be fine.

The old woman finally reached her cottage and stepped onto the porch. She opened the door and beckoned for them.

Two black cats oozed from inside and wound around her ankles, meowing.

Val ground to a halt. "There's something we didn't—"

Daisy burst from the ditch, barking uproariously, as she lunged for the two cats.

The cats hissed and dashed back inside. Daisy just about knocked the old woman over as she pursued the cats.

The old woman's face mottled. "What's *that*? Get it out!"

Val smiled in a manner that was somewhere between sharp and sweet. "That is Daisy. My dog."

"And one of my companions." Harm grinned as well. He had, at least, taken Daisy into account when he'd been making his bargain, even if he hadn't realized the crone had cats.

The old woman grimaced, smelled the cheese again, and turned for the door. "Very well, dearies. But the dog must stay in your room away from the cats."

Something crashed inside the house, followed by more hissing and barking.

The crone muttered under her breath as she picked up her pace and hurried inside as quickly as she could.

Val sighed, shook her head, and followed. She didn't draw her knife so she must believe it was safe enough. As she reached the porch, her eyes widened, and she lunged inside. "No, Daisy! Down!"

Harm took the stairs to the porch two at a time and stepped inside the house as Val all but tackled a barking, leaping Daisy, dragging her away from a curio cabinet. Two black cats perched on top, puffed up and hissing.

A small wooden-topped table with white legs dominated the center of the room while a fireplace sat on one end and the curio cabinet on the other. The back wall featured two doors with framed paintings of flowers hanging between them. Doilies decorated the curio cabinet's shelves beneath all the teacups while more doilies hung over the backs of the chairs.

It would have been a quaint sight, if one of the chairs hadn't been toppled, Val wasn't rolling about on the floor as she restrained her currently-three-headed dog, and too many black cats to count weren't dashing all over the place, knocking around teacups and scattering doilies. One cat tried to claw its way up the curtains, nearly tearing it off the rod.

"Close the door behind you!" the crone shrieked as another cat made a beeline for the outdoors.

Harm grabbed the door and yanked it closed. The cat skidded and dug its claws into the wooden floor before it could smack into the door.

"Which room is ours?" Val wrestled with Daisy, the dog still squirming and barking hoarsely at the cats.

"That one!" The crone pointed at the door on the left before she lunged and snatched one of the teacups before it could fall to the floor.

Harm dashed across the room as quickly as he could, given that he had to step over the fallen chair, inch past the crone, try not to trip on the cats, and dodge Val and Daisy. He opened the door to the room the crone had indicated.

On her knees, Val shuffled across the floor, hauling Daisy with her, until she shoved the dog into the room. Harm jerked the door closed.

For a moment they all remained frozen where they were, Harm with his hand on the door, Val hunched on the floor, and the cats tucked into whatever hidey-holes they'd found.

Then the old woman held up the teacup she'd saved from shattering on the floor. "Would anyone like some tea?"

Harm released a breath, something almost like a laugh filling his chest. "I don't need any tea, but I'll sit at the table while you have tea."

Val shot him a look, but he shrugged as he righted the chair and sat on it. Sure, they wouldn't dare eat or drink anything but spending a few minutes in polite conversation with their hostess wouldn't hurt now that the bargain was in place. They could afford to be gracious.

Her shoulders stiff, her eyes glaring daggers, Val dropped into one of the other chairs.

The whole house gave a lurch, and Harm gripped the table before he fell over backwards. Thankfully, the table must have been bolted to the floor because it didn't budge, even as the cottage swayed the other direction.

"The house is moving." An unnecessary statement, but Harm couldn't help but blurt it anyway as he braced himself.

"Of course, dearies. What else would the legs be for?" The old woman bustled about her kitchen as she shooed cats out of her way and put a kettle on for tea. "Where are the two of you headed?"

Harm shared a look with Val. Perhaps this wasn't such a good idea after all. Who knew where this old woman was taking them, and he didn't need Val's sharp look to know not to share their destination with her.

"Across the Harvest Court." Val casually rested her hand on her knife, her posture almost too relaxed. "Where is your house taking us?"

"Oh, I wouldn't know. It goes where it wants." The old woman waved vaguely as she assembled her tea leaves for steeping.

That didn't sound promising. What if the house took them back the way they'd come and they had to walk across the Harvest Court all over again?

Catching his eye, Val shrugged, then murmured

under her breath for only him to hear, "At least this is a safe place to stay tonight."

There was that. Harm hadn't even seen a nuckelavee, but if the scarecrows were an example of the monsters that guarded the fields during the day, he didn't want to run into the ones that patrolled at night.

The various black cats settled into places along the windowsills, on the curio cabinet between the teacups, and on the kitchen cupboards where the crone was working.

One of the black cats jumped onto Harm's lap, and he ran his hand down the cat's back. It purred, kneading its claws into his thighs.

The old woman poured hot water over her tea leaves, set her teacup on the table, and creakily sat in the chair across from Harm. She nattered between sipping her tea and taking bites of the cheese Harm had given to her, though she didn't seem to need more of a response than the occasional nod or noise of agreement from Harm.

Once she finished her tea, Harm pushed away from the table. "This was pleasant, but we should retire for the night."

Val hopped to her feet and headed to the door without another word to their hostess. At the door, she motioned for Harm to go first.

Right. They couldn't let Daisy out.

Harm opened the door only a crack. Daisy's nose immediately stuck into the space as she tried to shove her way through.

Harm squeezed through, only opening the door as

wide as necessary, nudging her out of the way with his leg.

Val followed so closely that she pushed him the last few inches into the room before she yanked the door closed behind them.

Daisy pranced around the two of them, jumping with her front paws scratching at them as if trying to give them hugs, frantic after being locked in the room away from them.

Harm scratched Daisy's heads until the dog flopped over with her heads to the floor and her butt in the air for scratching. "At least we don't have to worry about our hostess trying to sneak into our room during the night. She'd never risk opening that door and letting Daisy get to her cats."

"That's one way to ensure a good night of rest." Val tugged her bedroll from her pocket. "I'll still sleep in front of the door regardless. You can have the bed."

Harm took in the small, brass-framed bed beneath the window. It was barely big enough for a child. "I can't sleep on the bed while you sleep on the floor. It wouldn't be gentlemanly. Besides, that bed is too short for me. I wouldn't fit."

"I wouldn't fit either." Val huffed and spread her bedroll on the floor.

Satisfied with her scratches, Daisy hopped onto the bed, snuffling and pawing at the blankets as she arranged them to her satisfaction. Her spare heads disappeared as she flopped into a sprawl.

"Looks like Daisy claimed the bed." Harm reached into the magical pocket, his fingers grazing the various items stuffed in there, before the bedroll Val had loaned him came to hand. He was getting better at retrieving things from the pocket. It wasn't even feeling that strange anymore.

The room had slightly more space than the tent, but when Harm spread his bedroll on the floor next to the bed, his proximity to Val felt all too…intimate. There wasn't even a handy curtain dividing the room to give them privacy. He could see the way the moonlight beaming through the window fell on her face as she unbelted her dagger and laid it next to her pillow. The silver light glinted in her black hair in a way that made him want to run his fingers through the strands.

Harm shook his head, shoving away those thoughts. What had he been thinking? Why had he been thinking it?

Val flopped onto her bedroll, squinted, and waved at the window. "Could you close the curtain?"

Harm leaned over the bed, running a hand over Daisy's back, and gripped one of the curtains.

His fingers stilled on the fabric. Outside, a huge black silhouette moved in one of the fields, a shadow even with the light of the moon coating the fields in silver. The figure was somewhat horse-like, except far more spindly with red eyes and flecks of red foam around the mouth. The protrusion on its back was part skeleton, part blackened flesh trailing in rotting strips.

"Is that…" Harm swallowed as another of the shadowy forms joined the first.

Val didn't even bother looking out the window. "A

nuckelavee? Yes. That's why staying here was worth the risk."

Harm tugged the curtain closed, gave Daisy one last pat, then lay down on his own bedroll. As he closed his eyes, the lurching sway of the chicken cottage lulled him into sleep.

Chapter Fourteen

Val kept a good grip on Daisy as she hustled her dog through the main room of the chicken cottage. Daisy lunged and barked, trying to reach the cats.

"Don't you want to stay for breakfast?" The old woman held up her tea kettle.

"No, no, we're good. Don't want Daisy to turn one of your cats *into* breakfast." Val didn't even try to smile as she dragged the dog past the table and curio cabinet.

The crone made a noise in the back of her throat, her face whitening.

Harm paused to shove the blue-and-white teacup at the old woman.

After taking the teacup, she patted his cheek. "The two of you make such a cute couple, dearie. I don't mind missing out on a pie."

Harm coughed, glancing at Val as if he wasn't sure what to do.

"Yes, yes, now we really must be going." Val fumbled

for the door's latch, but as soon as she released Daisy with one hand, the dog nearly ripped out of her grip. Val quickly returned to clutching the dog with both hands.

Harm hurried past her and opened the door.

Val dragged Daisy out the door, across the porch, and down the steps to the ground. Harm all but threw himself out the door. He skipped the steps entirely and jumped straight to the ground.

The old crone stood in the doorway and waved to them, three of her black cats twining around her feet. "Listen to an old wise woman, dearie. Don't let a man like that slip through your fingers. Nice ones come around only once in a pink moon."

Now it was Val's turn to cough. "I'll keep that in mind."

One of the cats slinked a little too close to the edge of the porch. Daisy lunged with such force that she pulled Val right off her feet.

Harm dove and got a grip on Daisy as well before the dog made it up the steps to reach the cat.

The crone's mouth puckered as her cat clawed its way up the side of her dress to perch on her shoulder. "One last piece of advice, dearie. Perhaps consider getting a cat. They are far less trouble."

With that, the old woman retreated into her house, her cats following with their tails up in the air. As soon as the last one was inside, she slammed the door, and the chicken cottage lurched into motion. It trundled with the same gait as a chicken as it pounded down the gravel road.

Harm gave a shudder as he brushed black cat hair from his breeches. "I know it was my idea last night, but can we avoid staying with crones from now on?"

"Agreed." Suppressing a shudder of her own, Val released Daisy. The dog gave a few last parting barks at the rapidly disappearing house before she set to work sniffing at their surroundings.

Val stood to better assess their location. The fields around the road appeared virtually unchanged from the night before, except that one of the fields contained wheat instead of corn.

A distant smudge of white blurred in the distance to their right while, directly in front of them, a line of trees cut across the horizon from one end to the other.

Val pointed in that direction. "Looks like the house took us straight north during the night rather than veering at an angle across the Harvest Court as we'd planned."

"Is that good or bad?" Harm spun on his heel on the road, the gravel crunching, as he, too, took in the scenery.

"Good, mostly." Val set off down the road, as it went in the same direction they needed to go. "It saved us two days of walking in the Harvest Court, but we'll need to take a day cutting through the Goblin Court instead of going straight into the Court of Stone. The Goblin Court is safer than the Harvest Court, so it isn't a great loss to change our route."

Val hadn't planned to go this way since it would have added an extra day of walking. But since the chicken house had done the walking for them while they slept, she could tolerate this change of plans.

"I'll take safer." Harm strode at her side along the road, his arms swinging easily. He absently reached out and brushed his hand over the pink tops of the wheat growing alongside the road.

"No! Don't!" Val grabbed him and hauled him away from the wheat field, the force of her movement making her stumble closer to the field herself.

Something clutched her leg. Before she could shake it off, more things swarmed up her legs, and she was yanked off her feet.

Her back hit the ground, knocking the breath from her body, even as she was zipped into the wheat field by the many, many hands gripping her. Wheat lashed her face, the stalks scraping against the back of her neck.

The glittering cord tied to her wrist snapped tight, jerking her arm nearly out of its socket. Harm gave a yell from somewhere behind her before there came an *oomph*.

Something brown flashed by her, then there was a shriek and a growl from somewhere ahead. A few of the hands left her legs, but not enough to even slow the breakneck pace.

Val lifted her head and tried to squint into the wheat whipping her face. Little golden *things* had a hold of her legs as they raced through the wheat field. They seemed to be somewhat humanoid but also stalky with golden skin and rows upon rows of razor-sharp teeth that were too big for their mouths.

Grain sprites.

Val tried to sit up enough to bat at them, but she couldn't move between the force of their dragging and the cord just about yanking her left arm off.

"Val!" Harm shouted from somewhere behind her, but Val couldn't crane her head around enough to see him. "Lean left!"

Gritting her teeth, she tried to roll in that direction. She shoved with her elbow, which only succeeded in digging a furrow into the dirt. She tried to lift one of her legs, but there were too many grain sprites clinging to her.

Something tall and leafy rushed toward them.

"Brace yourself!" Harm yelled as the tree flashed past to Val's left.

Val jerked to a stop by her wrist with such force that something popped in her shoulder. She cried out at the flash of pain, even as she twisted around to catch a glimpse of Harm. He had flung himself around the tree, and he currently gripped the cord in both hands, his feet braced on the tree trunk.

The grain sprites chittered. Then their teeth flashed as they swarmed over her, biting at her legs and working their way up her body as they chomped. Val's leather clothes protected her for the moment, but if the sprites got to her exposed skin, they'd take the flesh right off her bones.

With her free hand, Val reached into her pocket and fumbled to draw a sword, a spear, a halberd. Anything long and pointy with enough reach to beat off the sprites.

"Grab your fire thingy!" Harm's words ended with a

yell of pain, followed by a shout that didn't seem to be directed at her. "Get back, you blighters!"

"The bottled dragon flame?" Val caught a glimpse of a few of the sprites swarming Harm.

"Yes!" Despite the sprites chomping at him, Harm didn't let go of the rope to beat them off.

Right. Val fumbled through her pocket, willing the item to come to her hand.

Something smooth pressed into her palm, and she yanked it out of her pocket. She held a small, stone jar with a hinged lid. Even with the lid closed, it felt cozily warm in her hand.

With her thumb, Val popped the lid open. A tongue of blue flame licked out the top. Val brandished the stone jar at the nearest grain sprite. "Back! Get back! Or I'll set this whole field on fire!"

The grain sprites skittered backward, though the ones by her feet didn't let her go.

"I mean it! This is dragon fire! If I set this field on fire, it will go up in seconds, and there will be nothing you can do about it!" Val held the stone jar only inches from the nearest unbroken stalk of wheat.

Chittering in their strange language, the grain sprites backed away even more.

Harm released the cord, rolled to his feet, and drew his sword. Batting a few of the sprites aside with his sword, he rounded the tree to stand over Val as he pointed the sword at the sprites.

Val rolled upright. Her left arm hung uselessly at her side while she still gripped the bottled dragon flame in the other. She gathered her legs beneath her, then rose to her feet without using either hand. She nodded her head at the line of trees along the nearest edge of the wheat field. "Head for the border."

Before either of them could take a step, Daisy crashed through the wheat and bowled into the nearest grain sprite. All three of her heads were out as she barked and growled.

With shrieks, the grain sprites scattered into the field. Daisy raced after them, disappearing among the wheat, though the crashes, screeches, and barking rang over the whole field.

Harm glanced over his shoulder at Val, his sword still in his hand. "Do we make a run for it?"

"Yes." Val flicked the lid closed on the jar, then stuffed it into her pocket. Holding her dislocated left arm, she broke into an awkward run.

Harm kept pace with her as the two of them crashed across the field, heedless of the wheat stalks they broke and trampled. With one last leap over the creek dividing the two courts, Val stumbled from the wheat field into the fall forest of the Goblin Court.

Harm staggered to a halt next to her, gulping in a deep breath. He held up his sword. "Are we safe now?"

"Safe enough." Val stepped to the edge and whistled. She had to whistle several times before something crashed through the wheat and Daisy popped out. She plunged through the creek, heedless of whatever creature might lurk within the water, and clambered out on the other side, promptly shaking water all over the two of them.

Harm jumped out of the spray and sheathed his

sword. Then he gestured to Val. "Do you need…uh… your arm…"

"I'm fine." Val clenched her teeth, rotated her arm, and braced herself. With a firm motion, she snapped her joint back into place. "We should keep moving."

Harm gaped at her for a moment before he nodded and fell into step with her.

Val set out in the direction of the white-capped mountains in the distance. As she walked, she dug into her pocket, pulled out a vial of healing potion, and uncapped it. She tossed it back, swigging it down in a single gulp.

This trip sure was getting expensive.

Worse, Val couldn't get the image of Harm standing over her, his sword drawn, his stance protective, out of her head. When it had counted, he'd had her back.

Though it wasn't like he'd had much of a choice, given the magic rope tying them together. And he had been the one to bring the grain sprites down on them by touching the wheat.

Val cleared her throat and flicked a glance at Harm, trying to force the words out. He had a few scratches on his face and hands, adding to the rugged look he'd gained thanks to his growing beard and leather jerkin.

Harm caught her gaze, his thick blond eyebrows raising. "What?"

She cleared her throat again. The words were somewhat strangled, but at least she got them out. "Thanks. For back there. With the grain sprites."

Harm shrugged, his broad shoulders pulling the blue shirt tight across his muscles. "I did get us in trouble in the first place. The least I could do was try to get us out of it for once."

"Still, I appreciate it." She couldn't quite describe the shift. Perhaps it was the crone's parting words still ringing in Val's ears. Maybe all the time she'd spent with Harm was going to her head. Or it could be seeing him with that more competent, confident air just did stuff to her heart.

"What would have happened if we hadn't gotten away?" Harm shot a glance over his shoulder at the wheat field behind them.

"The grain sprites would have chewed the flesh right off our bones until we were picked clean." Val grimaced and swiped at the drop of blood trickling from one of the scrapes on the back of her hand. Grain sprites were particularly nasty creatures.

Harm swallowed, going even more pale as he held up his arm with the cord. Bruises showed around his wrist. "Even with this?"

"Yes. They could have eaten us. Our skeletons just would have been tied together for all time." Val didn't want to think about it too much.

"I'm really growing tired of this realm." Harm patted his sword's hilt. "Far too many things want to eat me."

Val rubbed her aching shoulder. She was from the Realm of Monsters, and right now, even she agreed.

HARM GRIPPED the knife Val had lent him as he faced her in the light of their campfire. To one side, Daisy snoozed after her grain sprite fighting earlier that day, her stomach full of the leftovers of their supper.

Darkness had long ago fallen over the fall-decked branches of the trees of the Goblin Court. During their walk that day, they passed small clusters of homes tucked into the rocks and trees. Little stone houses with wafts of smoke drifting from the chimneys. Mushroom cottages with red and white tops. Dens formed of caves with little fox-faced people peeking out as they passed.

Despite all the time Harm had spent in the Fae Realm, he hadn't been able to help his gaping. Everything was just so quaint and not terrifying that he almost couldn't believe it. There was just something about the villages framed in autumn colors that reminded him of home.

A crisp breeze rustled the leaves overhead, and Harm had to resist a shiver. "Are you sure your arm is healed enough for this?"

Val rolled her eyes, her stance as easy and lithe as ever. "Yes. Now stop stalling."

"I'm not stalling. I just…" Harm trailed off, not sure how much concern he should express.

"I'm fine. Even with a healing arm, I can still take you." Val darted forward, slashing with her knife.

Harm stayed light on his feet, but he kept his ground. Val was faster than him. Far better than him. But he had a few inches of height and overall mass on her, and she'd taught him how to use that. He shoved her hand aside, then stabbed with his own knife.

She grabbed his wrist, yanking him to force him off-balance as she aimed her knife for his throat.

He leaned to the side to avoid the knife, bringing up his forearm to stop her arm. He turned his other hand, breaking her hold and getting a grip on her wrist instead. He tried to get a leg behind hers to send her to the ground.

Instead, he lost his own footing. Val didn't waste a moment. She shoved against him, and the next thing he knew, he was falling backward.

He tightened his grip on her arm, wrapping his other arm behind her back even as he fell. Her eyes widened as she lost her balance, and both of them tumbled to the ground just outside of the ring of firelight.

Harm landed first, his back cushioned by the layers of fallen leaves. But then Val landed on top of him, all solid bones and muscles and weapons, knocking the breath out of him and bruising far more than the ground.

Val pressed the flat of her blade against his throat. "You're dead."

Harm tightened his arm around her, the tip of his knife resting against her back over her heart. "But I took you down with me."

Val huffed, her breath warm against Harm's face. "Mutual death isn't going to get you back home to your family."

Harm tried to think of a comeback to that. But he couldn't concentrate with Val's face only inches from his, her dark brown eyes meeting his. Her hand—the one not holding her knife—rested on his chest with only the thin layer of his shirt between their skin. His grip on her wrist had loosened, and he had the strange urge to rub his thumb over the soft skin of the back of her hand.

Could she feel the way his heart thumped harder and his breath caught in the back of his throat?

With a tromping of paws on the ground, Daisy bowled into the two of them, clambering and wiggling and licking, as if utterly overjoyed that they were down at her level. Her spare heads made an appearance, all the better to lick both of them at the same time.

Harm sputtered and dropped the knife to better fend off the dog. He tried to extricate himself, but everything was a tangle of limbs, flailing dog, and the cord wrapped around them.

Val shoved off him, rising to her feet and out of Daisy's reach. She swiped one arm across her dog-slobbered cheek before she sheathed her dagger. Her gaze landed on the knife beside him. "You dropped my knife. Again."

"Sorry—trying—Daisy—" Harm sputtered as he tried to push all three heads away from his face.

"That's no excuse." For a moment, Val remained stern as she glared down at him. Then the smile broke through as she held out a hand to him.

He took it and leveraged himself to his feet and away from Daisy's wet tongues.

Still riled up, Daisy burst into zooming circles, running crazily around the hollow where they'd camped.

For a moment, he and Val stood there, his hand still gripping hers.

Then she tugged her hand free and turned away. "We should get some sleep. We have another long day of walking tomorrow."

Harm swallowed. He needed to get a hold of himself. This spark between him and Val needed to be squashed.

He cleared his throat. "Right. Good. Yes."

He was supposed to be hurrying back to his family as quickly as possible. So why did a part of him want to keep lingering here with her?

Chapter Fifteen

Val stood next to Harm at the very edge of the boundary line between the Goblin Court and the Court of Stone, a stark line where colorful leaves turned into bare trees and a blanket of snow. A stream wound beside them, gurgling merrily on the Goblin Court side while it was frozen solid in the Court of Stone.

Harm was gawking first at the Winter Court ahead of them, then at the Fall Court behind them. "This is just so strange. No matter how many times we do it, I'll still never get used to stepping over a border."

Far less strange than the edgy, wrong feeling still plaguing Val. Perhaps it had been Harm's courage facing the grain sprites. Maybe it was falling into his arms during their training session the evening before. But it was as if Val didn't fit in her own skin anymore, and she wasn't sure what to do about it.

She reached into her pocket and pulled out her thick, fur-lined coat. "Bundle up."

If her words came out a little short, well, it was Harm's own fault for being just so annoyingly nice and good that it did things to her insides.

Harm dug into his own magical pocket, pulling out a winter coat, gloves, scarf, and hat. He pulled the things on quickly, not fazed by her grumpiness.

Val busied herself pulling on her gloves, then adjusting her hat. "Ready?"

With a grin, Harm plunged into the Court of Stone ahead of her, his boots sinking into snow that was nearly knee-deep on him.

Daisy plowed into the snow, bounding through it before she plunged her face into a snowbank.

"She doesn't seem bothered by the cold." Harm waved to the frolicking dog.

"No." Val trundled into the Court of Stone. A wall of cold slapped her face, stealing her breath for a moment. Daisy might not be bothered by the cold, but Val couldn't wait until they could leave this court.

No, not *they*. She would be turning Harm over to his new dragon master and leaving this court alone. Except for Daisy, of course.

Why did that ache so much? As if she didn't want to do it? This was her job. Her mission. Between the cord and the bargain, neither of them had much of a choice.

She trudged through the snow, headed for the mountains. This was going to be one cold, long walk. Worse, she didn't even know which mountain in the Court of Stone belonged to Golbet. She'd have to find the nearest dragon and ask for directions.

Walking briskly at her side, Harm was digging into

his magical pocket again. When he pulled his hands out, a grin spread across his face. "Yes! Looks like that mouse woman must have really liked the Tulpenland cheese. She included ice skates in my pocket."

"Ice skates?" Val took in the two sets of what looked like silver blades attached to leather soles, just with straps instead of the boot part.

"Yes. We have these in Tulpenland. I grew up skating on the canals." Harm's grin was that wide, enthusiastic one that used to itch at her and now…

Now it was far too endearing.

"This will be so much faster and more fun than walking." Harm hurried a few feet away to the edge of the frozen stream and sat on a rock. Setting the skates aside, he held one ice skate to the bottom of his boot and buckled it in place.

"I don't know how to ice skate." She tromped through the snow and paused at his side, staring down at the second set of skates.

"Really?" Harm barely paused in buckling on his skate.

"I was born a summer fae, and I usually try to minimize the amount of time I spend in Winter Courts while on missions." Val wiggled her fingers in her gloves. The cold already nipped at her nose and worked through her clothing.

Harm pushed to his feet on the ice, moving like he had been born on skates. He spun to face her, sticking within their ten feet limit. "Come on. Surely you of all people aren't scared of ice skating."

"I'm not scared." Val stated the words, but she

nudged the second set of skates with the toe of her boot. She was in no hurry to try them on.

"You taught me to fight with a knife. I can teach you to ice skate." Harm held his arms out to her. "Besides, ice skating involves sharp, shiny blades strapped to your boots. Surely that's something that appeals to you."

When he put it that way…Val sighed and perched on the rock, reaching for one of the skates. "Fine. Just give me a moment."

She strapped the skates on as tightly as she could. She didn't want them coming off. Once done, she planted her feet on the ice and tried to stand. The blades slid on the ice, threatening to take her feet right out from under her.

Harm skated closer and took her hands. "I have you. Try to stand now."

Gripping his hands, Val levered herself upright. She bit down on a shriek as her feet slipped. Only Harm's firm grasp on her hands kept her from falling on her rear on the ice.

"It's all right. I have you." Harm somehow remained firm on his feet. "Gather your feet beneath you. I know you have good balance. Stand lightly, like you're about to start a fight."

Val scrambled for a few seconds, her weight hanging from her grip on Harm. She finally managed to get her feet under her, shifting her weight so that she balanced more solidly on the far-too-thin blades.

She could do this. She just had to get her balance right.

Tentatively, she straightened up from her crouch and eased one of her feet forward.

"That's it." Harm slowly skated backwards, his movements both graceful and powerful. "Just glide on the ice."

Val pushed her other foot forward, feeling the way the blade moved over the ice beneath. As she gained a better sense for the interaction of ice and skate, she found a better rhythm, her movements more sure.

Harm's grin widened as he continued to skate backward, gripping her hands. "I was right, wasn't I? This is more fun than trudging through snow, isn't it?"

"Yes, it is." Val probably should let go of his hands. But his mittened hands were warm over hers, his grip steady even as they skated.

And it made her think that she might be in more danger of falling than ever.

———

HARM SHOULDN'T LET the feel of her hands in his go to his head. Nor dwell too much on that trusting look she'd given him when she put her hands in his.

Still, his heart was soaring, and he tried to tell himself it was because he was on skates again. But if that was all it was, then he would've let go of her hands and skated to the full extent the ten-foot rope allowed.

Instead, he kept holding her hands and skating at that slow, easy pace while Val got a sense of the ice.

He shouldn't confuse this *thing* between them. She was only with him because of a magical cord and a mission to deliver him to his destination. Once they arrived at the dragon's mountain, she would leave, and he'd never see her again.

But maybe it was all right that this wouldn't last. He could still enjoy this moment, still let himself fall just a little, even knowing how it would end. She'd shown him how to be stronger, more genuine, and he'd leave the Fae Realm the better for it.

Could he leave her better for having known him? Right now, all he wanted to do was make her smile. A true, genuine smile of joy and happiness, not merely one of those tight, smirking smiles. Not that he disliked those smirks either. But he'd seen so very little joy from Val.

Harm picked up the pace of his skating, and Val easily matched him, her grip on his hands loosening as she didn't need to lean on him as much. Daisy happily loped alongside the river, bounding through snowbanks and sniffing along rabbit trails.

Val released one of his hands and picked up her pace even more. Her brown eyes held the hint of a sparkle, the curve of a smile on her mouth. Not quite the full smile he was hoping to see, but it was enough. "Is that as fast as you can go?"

"Not at all." Harm spun to face forward and put more power into his glide, shooting across the ice.

Val matched him, and soon the two of them were flying over the ice, the breeze of their passing whipping at their scarves. The cold scoured Harm's cheeks and nose. He didn't try to stifle his grin at the exhilaration of the speed. He might have even chuckled under his breath.

Val's black hair streamed behind her, her smile growing the faster they went.

Dark green spruce trees blurred past, their branches laden with sparkling snow. The craggy mountains grew on either side of the stream, and the shadows of their peaks spread colder patches across the ice.

A valley opened before them, surrounded by the looming peaks all around. The stream ended in a large lake, the ice perfectly smooth and crystalline, bordered by thick stands of evergreens.

Harm and Val raced onto the lake, their skates swishing over the ice. As they neared the far end, Harm tightened his grip on Val's hand, dug in his skates, and tugged Val toward him.

She spun into his arms and the two of them skidded to a halt, ice shaving in a sparkling wave from their skates.

Harm held her for a moment, her mittened hands on his chest, his on her waist. With all their layers of clothing, he couldn't feel her warmth. But he savored holding her anyway, especially with the way her eyes were dancing, just the hint of a grin playing along her mouth as if she might just give in to joy.

Harm couldn't help the way his gaze dropped to her lips. His hands tightened on her, tugging her closer. "Val, I…"

Her head tipped up, her gaze meeting his.

Then her eyes widened, and she shoved away from

him with such force that he nearly fell, his heart thunking into his toes. What was…

Val reached for the dagger at her waist. "Dragon!"

Harm whirled, reaching for his sword. As he caught sight of the massive creature landing at the edge of the lake behind him, he froze without drawing his weapon. A sword would do little good.

The yellow-green creature was massive with glinting scales covering its whole body from the tip of its fanged muzzle to the end of its tree-trunk-sized tail. Spikes ran down the center of its back while all four of its legs featured deadly-looking talons. Huge batlike wings beat with such force that trees bent and the wind pushed Harm backward several feet on his skates.

With a crunch of breaking trees and a *thump* that reverberated into the ice beneath Harm's skates, the dragon settled onto the ground.

Whining, Daisy shuffled from the bank onto the ice, her belly low to the ground and her tail tucked beneath her butt. She pressed into the back of Val's legs, still whining.

Harm swallowed and eased closer to Val, though he barely resisted the urge to hide behind her along with Daisy. "That's…"

"A dragon. Yes." Val lifted her hand away from her dagger. Her smile had disappeared into a hard, tight look once again.

A dragon. Harm swallowed, his stomach sinking even farther into his toes.

There was no way he was escaping a dragon.

Chapter Sixteen

Val forced her hand away from her dagger as she faced the dragon before them. If the dragon wanted to cause trouble, there was little she could do.

The dragon swung his head, and his slitted, green-gold eyes fastened on them. "Are you the human bargained to me and the mercenary escorting him?"

"Are you Golbet of Flight Talonstorm?" Val worked hard to keep her voice from shaking. She didn't fear much, but she didn't know anyone, no matter how brave, who could keep their knees from knocking when facing a dragon in this form.

"Yes, I am." The dragon's deep voice held a growl.

"Then, yes, we are." Val couldn't relax, even though they'd found the dragon they'd been looking for.

"Finally." Golbet shook out his neck, then raised his wings, as if preparing to take off once again. "Took you long enough. I've been flying these mountains for the past few days, waiting for your arrival. The

Dragon Moot will be nearly over by the time we arrive."

"If you could just—" Val lifted her wrist with the magical cord.

Golbet pumped his wings and heaved his huge body off the ground. This time, the blast of air pummeled her so hard that she stumbled backward. With Daisy pressed tightly to the back of her legs, Val fell, landing on her tailbone on the ice.

Harm, too, tottered, though he stayed on his skates by crouching and bracing himself with a hand on the ice.

As Golbet rose into the sky, Daisy all but crawled into Val's lap, whining and shaking.

"Val, what is—" Harm started to scramble toward her across the ice, all his gracefulness disappearing.

The dragon swooped out of the sky. His front talons opened and reached toward them.

Daisy flailed, and Val wrapped the dog in both arms to keep her from racing off. Harm shouted, covering his head with both arms as if that would save him from a dragon.

Then the dragon scooped all of them up in his front claws. Val tumbled, unable to brace herself with her grip on Daisy. The dog's head clunked painfully into her jaw, and Daisy's frantic clawing left bruises on her legs.

Val's stomach dropped as the dragon rapidly ascended into the sky. The cold deepened into a chill that the dragon's warm claws around them only some-what mitigated.

After a few minutes, the dragon leveled off, and Val

squirmed upright, her back resting against the dragon's palm—pad of his paw? Despite his size, the dragon was at least gentle with his grip, cupping Val and Daisy instead of squeezing them tight.

Peeking between the talons, Val assured herself that Harm rested just as unharmed in the dragon's other front claw, only a few feet away thanks to the limitation of the magical cord.

Harm caught her eye. His mouth moved as if he were shouting, but his words were lost to the wind and the beat of the dragon's wings.

Val shook her head and pointed to her ear.

Harm nodded, then waved first at the dragon, then forward. Perhaps he was asking where they were going?

Val shrugged. She had no idea where the dragon was taking them. The Dragon Moot met whenever the Elders of the various Flights called one, but it changed caverns each time so no one besides the dragons knew where it would be held.

As she didn't know how long the flight would be, she might as well be comfortable. She leaned over Daisy as much as she could, somewhat squishing the dog, and fumbled to unbuckle her ice skates.

In the other claw, Harm did the same, though he got his skates off much faster since he wasn't hampered by a panicking three-headed dog.

Once she had her ice skates off, Val stuffed them into her magical pocket. After a moment, she fished out a harness and leash. She didn't put the leash on Daisy often, but she couldn't risk Daisy running off in fear once they landed at the Dragon Moot.

It wasn't easy, wrestling the frenzied dog into the harness. But Val managed it eventually.

Then she settled in as best she could with a shivering three-headed dog curled up in her lap.

AFTER SEVERAL HOURS OF FLYING, Golbet abruptly dove downward. Val braced herself while she held on to Daisy.

A black mountain stood out against all the white of the surrounding court. Rivers of glowing lava flowed down the mountainsides.

Golbet swooped through a large opening in the side, gliding down a long black tunnel.

The scent of sulfur and an overwhelming heat smacked into Val. She immediately started sweating beneath her layers of clothing. Daisy's agitated panting grew even worse.

At the edge of a huge cavern, Golbet landed on his back talons with a jolt. He dumped Val, Daisy, and Harm onto the floor, and Val barely managed to keep a grip on the end of Daisy's lead as the dog tumbled, scrambled to her feet, and attempted to bolt. Val was dragged a few feet over the ground before Harm's weight at the end of the tether halted her.

Val struggled to her feet, keeping a tight grip on the leash as Daisy's claws scraped desperately on the stone floor.

In a blink, Golbet shrank, and a large man with straggling brown hair and wearing a yellow-green shirt beneath a black jerkin stood in his place. When he spoke, his voice held a similar timbre, though it lacked the growling depth. "Keep moving. We're late."

After sharing a glance with Harm, whose eyes had gone wide, Val staggered forward, leaning back against the pull of Daisy's leash.

A few yards ahead, the tunnel opened up into a large, well-lit cavern, and the sounds of voices thundered down the passageway toward them.

Daisy stopped pulling toward the opening and instead scrambled back to Val, cowering behind her legs again. Not that Val blamed her dog. Daisy was plenty brave. But anyone would cower in the face of a Dragon Moot.

Val took the last step into the cavern, blinking at the smoky haze burning her eyes and choking in her lungs.

Daisy dug in her paws, refusing to move another inch. Val hefted Daisy into her arms, toting the dog rather than dragging her.

Before them, pools of lava were scattered throughout the cavern, and dragons in their dragon form lounged in them as if in a soothing bath. More dragons in their fae form stood in clusters on the raised edges of the room while a large walkway led to a central space.

"Golbet!" One of the dragons in fae form standing in the center raised a hand. "Finally!"

"Are these the captives you promised for the bargaining?" Another dragon, this time in his scaled form, climbed out of one of the lava pools. He shook lava off his scales almost like a dog.

"I'm not—" Val tried to speak again, but Golbet shoved her and Harm forward before she could get the words out. She tried again. "I'm a mercenary. He's the one with the bargain. If you would just—"

Golbet strode to the center of the raised area, looking over the gathered dragons. He motioned to Harm, Val, and Daisy. "As I promised, this human stands ready to bind himself in service to a dragon. What will you bargain for his service?"

"Now hold on just a moment." Val strode forward, gripping Daisy tighter as the dog squirmed in her arms. "I'm not a part of this bargain. I'm the mercenary tasked with delivering him. You need to accept the delivery and let me go my way."

Harm was looking at her with something almost like betrayal in his eyes. But he didn't understand. Yes, she was trying to save her own skin. But it was more than that. If she was bargained to a dragon alongside him, then she couldn't…

Couldn't what? Rescue him? Even if she was free, she couldn't rescue him from a dragon.

"Too late. I put him up for the bargaining before you arrived. He isn't mine to accept." Golbet gave her something almost like a shrug before he turned back to the gathered dragons. "Well? What will you bargain for him?"

A pair of blue dragons pushed off one of the upper ledges and glided toward the raised center of the cavern.

Yet even as those two dragons swooped closer, a black dragon with red highlights along his scales climbed onto the edge of the raised section and transformed into a tall man with long black hair and even blacker eyes. "I'll bargain for him."

"We'll bargain for him." The pair of blue dragons landed next to the black dragon. They transformed into a young man and young woman, both wearing blue shirts and with brown hair. The young man wore tawny-colored trousers while the young woman had a swirling blue skirt that ended at her knees with leggings and tall boots beneath.

"Damig of Flight Thunderwing has first claim." Golbet nodded toward the man who had been the black dragon. "Taran and Tora of Flight Clawstone have second claim if the first offered bargain is unsatisfactory."

Damig and Golbet launched into a back and forth bargaining that Val didn't even try to follow.

Harm eased closer so that his arm brushed hers. "This is barbaric."

"It is." Val adjusted her grip on Daisy. The dog was getting heavier by the moment. "Technically, they're bargaining for your services, not your person. An indenture, if you will. But it still amounts to the same thing. Once you're bound to a dragon, it's difficult to free yourself."

Harm's jaw flexed beneath his beard, something almost like despair filling his blue eyes.

Val clenched her teeth, looking away. This whole time, Harm had clung tenaciously to his belief that he would escape. She couldn't watch him break, watch that optimistic cheeriness die, as the dragons bargained over his fate.

"It's—" Golbet started to nod toward Damig.

"Wait!" The young dragon man—Taran—lurched a step forward.

"We can offer more!" The young woman reached out, as if to drag Val and Harm away.

Damig glared down a nose that was long even in his fae form. "Better luck next time, dragonlings. But I've already secured this bargain."

"Then let us bargain with you for him." Taran straightened shoulders that appeared as if they would someday be broad, once he finished growing.

"No. I have no wish for another bargain. I already have a use in mind for him." Damig turned, his shoulders moving, as if shrugging away the annoyance of the other two dragons. "Besides, aren't the two of you a little young to be bargaining at this assembly? Shouldn't your parents keep you better in line? Go back to your eyrie, Clawstones. Now, Golbet, as you were saying..."

Golbet glared at the two young dragons before he faced Damig again. "Yes, it's a bargain. He's all yours. I'm ready for a good soak in a lava pool after all that waiting around in the cold for him to arrive."

With that, Golbet jumped from the raised walkway, turning into a dragon and spreading his wings on the way down.

The two young dragons who'd lost the bargaining shared a look, but they didn't protest again.

Val's stomach sank, and she couldn't look at Harm. It would have been far better for him if the young Clawstones had won the bargaining. Their Flight was rumored to be good to humans—freeing them, even.

But she didn't know Damig, and Flight Thunderwing had a reputation as a hard lot, even among dragons.

Damig gestured to Harm and Val. "Come."

Val tried to motion to the cord without dropping Daisy. "Damig of Flight Thunderwing, I'm the mercenary who was tasked with retrieving this human from the Human Realm. If you would please accept his delivery, I'll be on my way."

Harm made a noise in the back of his throat, as if he couldn't believe Val was just abandoning him now.

But she couldn't do anything else. This was her job. They'd both known it would come to this, in the end. No matter how much her heart hurt. Or how much the guilt squirmed through her chest.

She was a free mercenary, and she couldn't let herself get caught in a binding with him. Her throat tightened at the thought, her heart pumping harder in her ears. That was the whole point of being a part of the Wild Hunt. The freedom it gave her.

She had to get out of here. Get out of here and...and...

Would she return to the Realm of Monsters as if nothing had happened? Report to Diego that her mission was complete and wash her hands of it? Of *him*?

Or she could do what she could to try to free Harm. Perhaps if she contacted the Primrose League, the Wild Fae Primrose—that fae nobleman who rescued humans —would step in or send one of his men to rescue Harm.

Or she could figure out a way to rescue Harm herself. She was a mercenary. Being sneaky was part of her job.

Assuming Diego let her out of the Wild Hunt ride he was planning.

Damig spared her a single glance before he gripped the center of the cord and began leading both her and Harm. "I'm afraid I can't accept the delivery any more than Golbet could. I already bargained whatever human I could secure at the Dragon Moot to Warlord Zaya in the Court of Sand. I'll be taking both of you to her in the morning."

"What? No! That's not how this is supposed to work!" Val gritted her teeth as she staggered forward under Daisy's weight.

The Court of Sand. She couldn't go to one of the warlords. She just…couldn't.

Why couldn't she just make one simple delivery? It wasn't supposed to be this hard. None of her past missions had gone like this. At this rate, she'd never get this dragon-cursed rope off and regain her freedom.

Chapter Seventeen

Harm sat on one of the beds in the stone room that dragon had shoved him, Val, and Daisy into. There weren't any windows, and the only light came from beneath the thick wooden door and from the single lantern sitting on a table beside his bed.

As soon as Val had set her down, Daisy had crawled beneath the far bed, tucking herself as far from the dragons as she could.

Val gave another inarticulate growl before she slammed her shoulder into the door. "I'm not part of this bargain! Just accept the blasted delivery and let me go!"

She banged her fist against the door before she leaned her forehead against it. If she'd been anyone else, he would have thought she was about to cry.

"I'm sorry." Harm gripped the edge of the bed. He shouldn't be hurt. He'd known all along that she was only here to deliver him and be on her way. Nothing more. None of those moments he'd thought they'd shared truly mattered in the end. She would do what it took to save herself.

He couldn't blame her. Who would want to get stuck in one of these bargains?

"It isn't your fault." Val banged her fist on the door again, then kicked it for good measure.

"Still, I'm sorry you're stuck here with me. I know how much you were counting on delivering me to Golbet and getting on your way." Harm swallowed, hating the harsh rasp to his voice. "Will your Wild Hunt leader be angry that you're late again?"

"No, he'll understand. He knows how dragons can get." Val slapped her palm on the door one last time before she leaned her back against it, facing him. Her expression remained tight, though he couldn't quite read the emotion deepening her brown eyes or puckering her forehead. "It isn't that I *want* to abandon you. It's just...I'm just not supposed to be here. If I'm stuck here, then I can't..." She hissed something almost like a suppressed scream through her teeth.

Harm waited. Staying quiet seemed like the better part of valor right now.

Val sucked in a shuddering breath, her shoulders slumping. When she spoke again, her voice was quiet, as if she couldn't believe she was saying this. "If I'm stuck here, then I can't do anything to free you."

She was planning to try to free him. She wasn't going to just abandon him. The elation lasted only as long as it took for him to remember how dire their situation was.

"I doubt there's anything even you can do to save me from this." Harm's shoulders hunched under the weight of those words, the truth sinking deep into his bones.

He was going to die here in the Fae Realm. He saw that now. He'd never see his father or brother again. Never return to Tulpenland and its brick streets, canals, and windmills. Never figure out why that mysterious *fee* had meddled by poisoning Gijs and arranging for Harm to be bargained away.

A bargain was just too unbreakable, and Harm was just too weak when compared to dragons and warlords and monarchs. He'd be bound by Bindings, drugged with faerie fruit, and endure the rest of his short life in torment. It was simply inevitable.

"I don't know. But I can't find out in here." Val pushed away from the door and paced at the far end of the ten-foot tether. "And I just can't...I can't go to a warlord in the Court of Sand."

The words seemed almost dragged out of her, as if she hadn't meant to say that out loud.

She hadn't seemed this reluctant to go through the Court of Sand before, back when they'd been deciding their route from the Court of Revels. But she was almost as frantic now as Daisy had been when facing the dragons. He didn't think she'd become that way because of all the monsters. She faced those without flinching.

"Did something happen in the Court of Sand?" Harm worked to keep his tone low as he regarded her.

Val huffed a breath and sank onto the bed across from him. She flexed her fingers on the blanket for a moment before she lifted her gaze to meet his. "I was born in the Court of Sand."

Harm kept his mouth shut, his gaze unwavering, as he waited for her to continue.

Daisy peeked her nose out from under the bed, giving Val's ankle a nudge.

Val's gaze went unfocused as she reached down to pet Daisy. "The local warlord accused my father of treason. Whether or not my father actually committed treason, I don't know. All I remember is being awakened in the middle of the night. My mother was screaming, my father begging, as we were dragged from our home and forced through a rift into the Realm of Monsters."

"That sounds terrifying." Harm had been taken from his own realm, but at least he had been a willing adult. She'd been a child.

"Terrifying." Val gave a laugh that was more scoff than mirth. "That wasn't the half of it. My parents weren't prepared for the starvation, the monsters, the death of that realm. Both of them were dead within days of our banishment. I would've died too, if a band of the Wild Hunt hadn't found me. I bound myself to them, and they raised me."

Made her who she was, though she didn't say as much. Being raised by the Wild Hunt certainly explained a lot.

"That sounds like a tough childhood." Harm scuffed his boots on the floor, resisting the urge to go to her.

Right now if he tried to offer the comfort of a hug, he wasn't sure if she'd fall into his arms or punch him.

Daisy fully wiggled out from under the bed and leaned her body against Val's legs. The dog was probably doing more to comfort Val than Harm could.

Val gave a shrug, some of the shattered look leaving her eyes. "It is what it is. It isn't like I can change it now."

Harm nodded, his gaze dropping. "My mother died when I was ten. It's been just my father, my brother, and me ever since. It was a good childhood, and I wouldn't change how close I am with them. But I still miss my mother."

Val leaned over as Daisy flopped onto her back for a belly rub. "I've gone through the Court of Sand plenty of times for missions—the rifts there are the most reliable way into the Realm of Monsters—but I've done my best to avoid the warlords. I will never go back to pledging myself to a warlord, noble, or monarch who could use me or banish me or own me like that ever again. The Wild Hunt gives me freedom from that."

After the things Harm had seen here in the Fae Realm, he could understand that, even if he wasn't sure the Wild Hunt was the freedom she thought it was. She was here, after all, tied with the same rope he was and bound by the guilt of being complicit in transporting him to captivity.

Harm held up his wrist with the end of the cord. Better to steer the conversation on to a less emotional footing. "It isn't how I'd like to see the Court of Sand either. But the Court of Sand should be easier to escape from than the dragons, right?"

"Yes and no." Val's tone steadied, her face smoothing, as if she too were calmed by their usual discussion about his eventual escape. "The dragons are obsessive about things they consider theirs. Once they have someone bound into their service, it's incredibly difficult to leave."

That was what Harm had gathered, based on previous discussions. Escaping a dragon had sounded impossible.

"But they usually don't find pleasure in cruelty for the sake of cruelty the way many of the other fae do. Human captivity is more business for them than it is about dominating others." Val's mouth tipped in a wry line, though it wasn't a smile. "They're dragons. They already dominate everyone around them. Few of them feel the need to prove it."

"In other words, the dragons would have been harder to escape, but I would have likely endured less torture while serving them for the rest of my life." Harm waved toward the door, his other hand drifting toward the sword still buckled at his hip. That would explain why the dragons hadn't felt the need to disarm him.

"Correct. The warlords, though..." Val grimaced, her gaze going distant again.

Harm wasn't about to ask her how bad Warlord Zaya was. Based on his observations of the type of *feeën* who dealt in bargains for captive humans, she likely wasn't the honorable and kindhearted sort. Was she the type who shoved innocent children through rifts into the Realm of Monsters?

More cruel, but more possibility of escape. Harm tried to dredge up a shred of hope.

Nope, things still looked hopeless. He was absolutely going to die here in the Fae Realm. Should he be hopeful that at least a cruel *fee* would mean he'd likely die sooner rather than later?

"Harm." That note of steel returned to Val's voice. Her posture straightened as she stopped petting Daisy, her eyes flinty again in that warrior-look. "I won't abandon you here in the Fae Realm. As soon as I'm free of this"—she held up her arm with the tether—"I'll free you. I don't know how, or if I can. But I promise, I will return you to your home, no matter what it takes."

Harm opened his mouth. Closed it. He wasn't sure how to respond to such a big promise. "Thanks. I just… thanks. I don't think I'd even have a chance of getting home without your help."

For a moment, her gaze dropped away from his, the muscle at the corner of her jaw knotting as if she didn't know how to accept his gratitude.

Besides, he knew what neither of them wanted to acknowledge. Just because she'd promised didn't mean she'd succeed. There was every chance both of them would die in the attempt.

"Look. I should have told you this long before now." Val leaned backward as Daisy hopped onto the bed and snuggled into her lap. As much as a hefty, muscular dog could snuggle. "But there's this fae lord who goes by the moniker of the Wild Fae Primrose. He lives in the Court of Knowledge and rescues captive humans. I don't know how to contact him, but I've heard his League is spread over the entire Fae Realm. If I can't rescue you, then surely the Primrose League can."

Primrose. That was a flower, wasn't it?

Harm dug into his pocket, having to search for several moments before he found what he was looking for. He pulled out that small red flower the strange human had given him at the faerie market in the Court of Knowledge. He'd nearly forgotten about it after he'd stuffed it in the magical pocket once he'd changed into his new clothes.

The flower was a little wilted, but it didn't look as bad as he would've expected for having been riding around in his pocket for several days. He held it up for Val to see. "I think I might have met someone in the Primrose League."

Val's eyes widened, her gaze traveling from the flower to him. "That's a wild fae primrose. Where did you get that? When?"

"A man approached me while you were haggling for my sword at the faerie market. He couldn't have been the Primrose himself since he was human, but he gave me this and told me to trust someone if they gave me another one." Harm studied the little red flower. Such a small, unassuming thing.

"Good. Then you've already come to the attention of the Primrose League." Val returned to petting Daisy. "They might even be plotting your rescue as we speak."

Harm dropped his gaze from Val's. "I'm sorry I didn't tell you back then."

"No, you were absolutely right not to tell me." Val gave a shrug, as if she wasn't angry in the slightest that he'd kept something like this from her. Instead, her tone was almost...pleased. "You're a human in the Fae Realm doing what you need to do to survive. It's smart never to give information freely, and you should definitely keep as much as you can from your captor. You probably shouldn't even be telling this to me now."

"You aren't my captor." Harm closed his hand around the flower before he stuck it back in his pocket.

Val held up her arm and pointed at the tether running between them. "Yes, I am."

"No, you're not." Harm gestured at the door. "You're as stuck in this mess as I am right now."

"True." For the first time, Val's shoulders relaxed. She leaned against the wall behind her, though she had to keep her arm stretched in front of her because she was at the end of the cord. "At least there are two beds this time."

"Such luxury." Harm smoothed his hands over the blanket on his bed. Then he met and held Val's gaze. "I trust your promise, Val. Far more than I trust a random flower given by a stranger in a dark alley of a faerie market. I trust *you*. Whatever we'll face tomorrow in the Court of Sand, we'll do it together, all right? You won't have to face a warlord alone, and I know you won't abandon me there."

Val looked away from him, focusing on Daisy instead. "You're far too *good* for the Fae Realm."

"I don't know about that." Harm sighed and shook his head. "I used to think I was good. I lauded myself for just how good I was. But it was all a show. The proper dress. The proper cleanliness. The proper appearance of virtue. But acting good and *being* good all the way down to your soul are two different things. I was the former. But if I was the latter? I don't know."

He used to judge good as what someone did to put on the proper, societally accepted method of proving their goodness.

But all of that had been stripped away here in the Fae Realm. All the proprieties and rules he'd lived by were gone.

And yet when all the trappings were taken away and the world turned on its head, good and evil were still the same. Right from wrong still mattered. In the end, it was all a matter of the heart instead of the outward appearance. Why would it matter if he wore all the proper layers of clothing, spoke with due gravity, did all the things expected of him, if he didn't harbor a shred of love and kindness in his heart?

"You are good, Harm." Val stroked Daisy's ears, the dog wiggling on her lap. "I've seen plenty of evil here in the Fae Realm. Enough to see when someone is different. When that person is kind and loyal, even to the fae escorting him to his grim fate. Your family and your duchy in the Human Realm are fortunate to have you, and it would be a tragedy if someone like you were to die here in the Fae Realm."

Harm coughed, looking away from her as the back of his neck burned. That was by far the nicest thing anyone had ever said to him, and he wasn't sure how to handle it. "Thank you."

The moment hung between them for a moment before Val cleared her throat. "Don't let it go to your head. Now, we should get some sleep. It'll be a long day tomorrow."

"Aren't they all?" Harm shook his head, leaned over, and blew out the lamp.

Chapter Eighteen

The next morning, Harm found himself once again clutched in a dragon's talons, watching the world flash by below. This black dragon —Damig—held them the same way Golbet had, clasped in his front claws without squeezing. There wasn't any gentleness in the grip, but Harm didn't fear he was going to be squashed either, leaving him free to enjoy the ride and the view of the Court of Stone passing below.

In the dragon's other front claw, Val's dragon ride wasn't nearly as peaceful as his since she had her hands full with a panicking, flailing dog.

The beat of the dragon's wings provided a steady, almost soothing rhythm as they soared. The white mountains and dark evergreens blurred as they passed, their shadow keeping pace over the ground. Every once in a while, the shape of another dragon veered across the sky in the distance, glinting in jewel-tones from brightest reds to deepest purples.

Even after all this time in the Fae Realm, Harm couldn't get over the strangeness of everything. Would his world and life seem boring after all of this? Assuming he ever returned to the Human Realm.

As the sun rose higher in the sky, the dragon carried them over the border, the land beneath them instantly changing from white mountains and dark evergreens to burnt scrub brush, gravel, and sand unlike anything Harm had ever seen before. This high up, he couldn't feel the change in temperature that would signify crossing from the wintry landscape to the desert.

The occasional village of sandstone homes or a nomadic tribe with their airy tents flashed below. The small figures of people or animals moved between the homes or tents as they passed, a few halting and peering upward at the dragon flying overhead.

At last, a larger cluster of sandstone homes appeared on the horizon. A taller, castle-like fort of stone stood on the hill above the town.

The dragon swooped, banking toward the fort. Harm's stomach dropped, but his heart soared. He'd likely never experience flight again, and he wanted to savor every moment of the adventure. He climbed to his knees, gripped a talon, and peered between the talons to take in their landing.

The dragon folded in his wings and zipped from the sky at a dizzying speed. At what seemed the last moment, the dragon's wings flared with a *whump* from hitting the seemingly solid air. Only Harm's grip on the talon saved him from tumbling within the dragon's fist.

The dragon's rear legs landed with a *thump*. Then

without any warning, he spilled Harm, Val, and Daisy onto the sandy ground.

Harm rolled, the sand grinding into his skin and going down the back of his shirt. Bother. He already hated sand.

A few feet away, Val gave a wheeze as Daisy landed on her stomach, then a groan as Daisy shoved off her to scramble away. The dog clawed at the sand, trying to get away from the dragon.

Harm scrambled on his hands and knees to grab Daisy's leash along with Val, keeping the dog from dragging her again.

Once they had Daisy somewhat under control, Val pushed the rest of the way to her feet, her face hard and blank as she faced their surroundings.

Harm released Daisy's leash and stood. His leather jerkin and trousers were gritty with sand as he brushed at them, taking in the fort as he did so.

Stone towers marked out each corner with thick walls connecting them. *Feeën* warriors, dressed much like Val was in leather armor adorned with a breastplate, marched back and forth. At least they didn't seem too concerned by the appearance of a dragon in the middle of their fort. Harm wouldn't have wanted to find himself in the middle of a *feeën*-dragon battle.

In front of Harm, a squat, sandstone building loomed. Maybe the headquarters of this fort. Or perhaps the home of a *feeën* warlord.

The double doors opened, and two *feeën* warriors marched out of it. They stepped aside, and a *feeën* woman strode into view. She wore silken robes that swirled around her, yet she had a curved sword and dagger buckled at her sides. Her black hair was done in braids woven into an elaborate hairstyle that glinted with gems and gold strands.

In a blink like a shimmer on water, the black dragon shifted into his *feeën* form. "Zaya."

"Damig." The warlord's eyes glinted, her mouth tightening in something between a smirk and a sneer. "Is this the human you promised in your bargain?"

"Yes, it is." Damig gestured to Harm.

"The sand dragon venom, as bargained." The warlord gestueed, and four human men trundled from the building, carrying barrels on their backs. They set the barrels down before Damig and stepped back, though they kept their heads bowed.

Harm swallowed. That was a preview of what he'd endure once he was bound to this warlord. At least basic grunt labor was better than what Queen Titania had planned for him. Or Queen Mab.

Damig withdrew a large bag from the pocket of his jerkin. Even though the bag was much smaller than the barrels, he somehow lifted each barrel and stashed them inside until all four barrels disappeared into what must be a magical bag.

Once that was done, Damig transformed back into his black dragon form, the bag still hooked over one long talon. As he beat his wings, he kicked up clouds of sand.

Harm squeezed his eyes shut, shielding his face. When the swirling wind and scouring sand finally stopped, he cracked his eyes open to discover that the dragon was already high in the sky overhead.

Warlord Zaya stared down her nose, first at Harm, then at Val. "And who are you?"

Val stepped forward, straightening her shoulders as much as she could with Daisy yanking at the end of the leash. "I'm the fae mercenary tasked with delivering this human from his realm. If you would please accept the delivery, I'll be on my way."

Harm tried not to flinch at the cold tone to Val's voice. He had to trust what she'd said the night before. She was merely extricating herself so that she would be free to attempt to free him.

Warlord Zaya's gaze swept back to Harm, assessing him with the same cool indifference one might use when buying fruit in the market.

Harm lifted his chin. He'd been passed around like a piping hot oliebol from the moment he'd entered this realm. He wasn't going to cower now.

Warlord Zaya gave something almost like a sigh before she turned back to Val. "As much as I would wish to claim such a strapping specimen, I no longer hold his bargain. I lost it in a card game last evening."

"A card game? Really?" Harm thought he'd muttered it under his breath, but perhaps he'd been too loud because Val shot him a quelling look.

Harm snapped his mouth shut. Still, this was ridiculous. He understood being bargained away. Somewhat. But, seriously, lost in a card game?

Val spoke through gritted teeth, the muscle at the

corner of her jaw flexing. Perhaps she was just as frustrated by this happening yet again as he was, even if she was trying hard not to show it. "Then who holds his bargain?"

"I lost his bargain to the leader of Wild Hunt Grimbrand." Warlord Zaya waved her hand, as if losing a card game was a small thing.

Val's whole body stiffened. Was something wrong? Was her band at war with this Wild Hunt Grimbrand or something like that?

"I suppose you'll wish hospitality for the night." Warlord Zaya's eyes glinted, the expression more sneer than smirk now. "As you are now employed by a courtless fae, you'll have to bargain for it. The Law of Hospitality doesn't demand it."

"No, we won't need hospitality. We're leaving." Val spun on her heel and marched toward the gates of the fort.

Daisy trotted at Val's side, calm now that the dragon had left.

Harm hurried to fall into step on her other side, working to keep his questions firmly behind his teeth rather than voice them in front of the warlord.

Val strode with such a bristling, dangerous edge to her that the *feeën* guards jumped to open one of the gates. Not even the warlord tried to stop them as they walked from the fort and onto the gravel path that ran from the fort to the village below.

Instead of following the path, Val turned and headed out into the trackless sands of the desert, leaving Harm with no choice but to trot along at her side.

VAL CLENCHED HER TEETH, her veins burning as she pounded her feet against the sand. She set a relentless pace, needing to put as much distance between them and that smirking warlord as possible.

This was all so wrong. So much worse than what Harm realized.

He was looking at her now with those big blue eyes of his. So very trusting. So very good. And she was going to have to face him and tell him the truth. A truth she hadn't known until that warlord had spoken the name of the Wild Hunt band.

The village and fort disappeared behind them as Val tromped farther into the desert. The gravel crunched satisfyingly beneath her boots while lizards scattered to hide in the rocks at her approach. The scrubby brush and cacti spread out in all directions, something almost like twisting paths winding between them. The occasional wash or canyon cut through the landscape.

It didn't matter what direction she walked. They just needed to be away. Far away.

Harm sucked in a breath, opened his mouth, shut his mouth, and released the breath. After a moment, he straightened his shoulders and opened his mouth again. "Is this Wild Hunt Grimbrand at war with your band or something?"

"No." Val flexed her fingers on the hilt of her dagger.

"Then...what's wrong?" Harm strode a hurried step forward, pivoted, and halted in front of her, forcing her to stop. "We agreed we'd face whatever came together."

Val couldn't make herself meet his eyes. She hunched under the force of the tumult inside her.

He gripped her shoulders with gentle fingers. "Val? What is it? Is it that bad?"

"Worse." Val forced her gaze up. She had to be stronger than this. "Wild Hunt Grimbrand isn't at war with my band. It *is* my band. Diego is the Wild Hunt leader you've been bargained to."

"Then…did he see me at that faerie market and decide he wanted to bargain for me? Why?" Harm's blue gaze still held far too much trust and confusion.

"No. Diego never does anything on a whim." Val found herself leaning into his grip on her shoulders. He was so steady in this moment when she was falling apart. "If he bargained for you, it means he always intended to bargain for you. Seeing us in the faerie market? He wasn't just picking up a weapons order. He was checking on us, finding out where he had to go to head us off."

"But how would he have known…oh…" Harm's eyes widened and went distant, thoughts flashing.

"Exactly. Diego is the mysterious fae who bargained with Queen Mab. He must be." Val clenched her teeth around those words, the fury burning in her chest again. "He told Mab to send someone to bargain with your father. He named you as the price for that bargain. He even sent me there so that I would be conveniently available when Mab needed someone to retrieve you."

"Then he poisoned my brother. Or bargained with the human who did." Harm's jaw worked, his blue eyes flashing sharper than she'd ever seen. "But why? Why does he want me?"

"I don't know." A partial lie. Val's stomach churned. She didn't know why Diego would target Harm so specifically. But in general? She had a pretty good idea.

"Why not just bargain with my father himself? Or stay in the Court of Dreams and snag me from Queen Mab?" Harm shook his head, as if more bewildered than afraid.

"Diego doesn't speak your duchy's language. He needed Mab to do the initial bargaining." Val shuddered, and Harm rubbed her upper arms, as if he thought she needed warming. With the scorching sun beaming down on them, she was plenty warm. "Perhaps he planned to bargain with Queen Mab for you but was called away or delayed. I don't know. But the result has worked in his favor. He used me. He's been using me this entire time to gain your trust to set you up for an eventual betrayal."

And that was the worst of it. All these years, she'd congratulated herself on being a part of the Wild Hunt where she was free and treated as a worthwhile member instead of a pawn to be used and discarded on a whim the way the fae monarchs treated their people.

But in the end, Diego had done just that to her, manipulating her in order to manipulate Harm.

"What do you mean?" Harm still didn't seem to fully understand.

Of course he didn't. When she'd told him about bindings, she'd skimmed over this part. She hadn't thought he'd ever need to know.

Val swallowed and rested her hands on his chest over his heart. "There's only one reason a courtless fae living in the Realm of Monsters would want a human. For forbidden blood rites."

"Are blood rites as bloody as they sound?" Harm's grip tightened on her shoulders, his heart beating harder beneath her hands.

"More bloody than you can possibly imagine." Val fisted her hands in his leather jerkin. "There's power in the blood of a human, especially when it's shed in painful and bloody ways. The darkness that can be unleashed is even more potent when the human has recently experienced a deep betrayal or great terror."

Harm remained silent, his expression going blank, as if he couldn't quite comprehend what she was telling him.

She shook him slightly by her grip on his shirt, the heart she hadn't even realized she had dying inside her. "He's going to kill you, Harm. You're going to die, and there's nothing I can do but deliver you for slaughter."

"Val…" Harm rested a hand over hers on his chest. "I'm bound by the bargain. I have to go, whether you deliver me or not. And if I have to go, I'd rather have you by my side."

"But it's *wrong*. And for once in my life, I want to do what is *right*." Val clutched his jerkin, her body shaking with the force of her emotion.

Her freedom, it turned out, wasn't freedom at all. Instead, she was bound to evil. To guilt. To the consequences of a life lived ignoring that true freedom was found in what was right and good and noble.

A part of her wanted to lean into him, rest her head on his shoulder, and gain strength from someone other than herself for a change.

He wasn't at all the type of man she'd thought she'd find herself falling for. He wasn't the strong, fierce type like the members of her Wild Hunt.

But he had something even better than strength of muscle or skill with a sword. He had a moral compass that pointed true toward goodness and kindness. No matter what the Fae Realm put him through, he'd never wavered from that.

"I don't want to play Diego's game. I don't want to be the means he uses to manipulate you before he kills you. I don't want to go back to delivering people like packages and not caring and not being good and…and…" Val half-screamed through her teeth as she released his jerkin.

She would have pushed away from him, but his hand still rested over hers. Somehow in the last few moments, his other hand had skimmed down her arm and ended up on the small of her back, holding her without trapping her.

Unlike what she was doing to him. Her gaze caught on the glimmer of the tether strung between them. And she hated it. Without it, she would at least have a choice. He wouldn't be her captive but a friend.

"If only I could take this thing off." Val dug her fingers beneath the cord around his wrist and yanked.

Instead of resisting, the cord slipped off his wrist as easily as if it had never been magically bound there.

What...Val froze, then lifted her gaze from the cord to meet Harm's eyes.

His gaze held hers for a moment, his mouth dropping partly open in his surprise, before he looked down at the cord again. With gentle, slow movements, he reached out and eased his fingers beneath the end of the cord still on her arm.

The cord slid off her wrist just as easily as it had his.

Chapter Nineteen

Harm dropped the cord, and it fell into a sparkling heap at their feet. He couldn't help but stare at it. After all this time, the cord had simply…come off. He was free.

"You said love could override bindings." Harm lifted his gaze back to Val's, searching the equally dumbfounded look on her face. "I would think wanting to do what is right—what is good—would have the same effect. Especially combined with…"

He couldn't finish that last bit. He couldn't be sure she felt the same pull to him that he did to her.

She was so attractively capable. Confident. Deadly. And yet so desperately in need of a chance to relax and smile.

"Yes…that might explain it." Val rubbed her thumb over his wrist, as if she couldn't quite believe that the tether was gone.

"Do you think that…" Harm's heart beat harder. He hardly dared to hope or voice the thought. "Is my bargain still in place? Or does the cord coming off signify that the bargain is ended?"

Val's wondering expression dropped into hopeless lines again. "No, your bargain is still in place. The cord was simply the binding of my mission to bring you to your new master, but that was something outside of the bargain, not truly a part of it."

"Right." He knew it had been too much to hope. "Then I still I have to go to the Realm of Monsters. Diego still has a claim on my life."

"Yes, but maybe we don't have to go. Maybe we can figure something else out. A way to end the bargain without breaking it." Val's dark brown eyes met his, liquid with desperation and pain.

"You said it yourself. I can't risk breaking the bargain and bringing down the fury of a broken bargain on my duchy." Harm eased his arms around Val again.

Despite the grim topic, something in him warmed when she didn't shove away or indicate that she disliked being encircled in his arms. More than that, she leaned into him.

"Besides, if Diego is the mysterious fae who started all of this, then he has information I need." Harm's chest squeezed, the warmth disappearing. "Something else is going on, endangering my father, my brother, and my duchy, and Diego is the only one who can tell me what it is."

He'd started this whole journey through the Fae Realm to save his brother. He had to keep going—no matter the risk—to make sure his family stayed safe. Even if it meant he wouldn't see them ever again.

"He won't tell you." Val shook her head, her mouth pressing into a tight line. "And bargaining with a few pieces of pottery isn't going to work with him."

"No, but he will tell you." Harm tugged her slightly closer, the toes of his boots digging deeper into the sandy gravel. "He thinks you're still his loyal mercenary. He might not monologue to gloat to the human he plans to kill, but he might show off to the mercenary he used to pull this off."

"He might." Val toyed with the ties of his jerkin. "But he will still kill you."

"He can try." Harm attempted a grin, but it faded a moment later. He slowly lifted a hand and eased a strand of her black hair behind her tapered ear. "I'll have you. And I know you won't let anything happen to me."

"I'll do my best, but it won't be that simple." Val tilted her head, leaning into his hand as if she didn't even realize she was doing it. "The Wild Hunt leader becomes the leader by being the strongest, the fastest, the best. More than that, he will have the might of the whole Wild Hunt band at his back. It's no easy thing to defy one's Hunt leader."

"Then we'll need a good plan." Harm traced his thumb over her cheek. "We have a *feeën* mercenary, a human prince, a sometimes three-headed dog"—who was currently rolling on what looked like the desiccated body of a dead lizard—"and..."

He caught himself before he mentioned the iron knife out loud. Even now, he couldn't confirm it to Val.

Not when she still needed her deniability for facing Diego.

The iron knife. *Feeënvolk* were susceptible to iron. Even *feeënvolk* like Diego. It was the one thing he couldn't counteract.

And if…Harm couldn't help but grin. "I have a plan. Or, well, the beginning of a plan."

"Then let's hear it." Val started to pull away from him, the look in her eyes returning to cold calculation.

"In a moment. There's something I'd like to do first." Harm tugged her closer still until she was flush against him. "Would you stab me if I kissed you?"

Val blinked at him for a long moment, as if kissing hadn't even crossed her mind. Understandable, given they'd been talking about death and hopeless battles. Hardly talk that inspired thoughts of kissing. Perhaps he shouldn't have mentioned it.

But she didn't yank out of his arms or pull her dagger either. Surely that was a good sign.

"You want to kiss me?" She rested her hands on his jerkin again, as if she wasn't quite sure where to put them.

"Yes. But I wanted to make sure you wouldn't stab me if I did. You were quite insistent about the whole stabbing thing previously and…"

She stretched onto her tiptoes and pressed her lips to his.

He dug his fingers into the silken strands of her hair as he kissed her. Her hands worked their way up his chest to wrap around the back of his neck, pulling him in tighter as if she was desperate to keep him close. That desperation lent an intensity to the kiss Harm hadn't expected, but he responded in kind.

Something slammed into Harm's side, claws pawing at his arm.

Val pulled away from him as that same muscular body wiggled between them, licking and jumping. "Daisy!"

Harm laughed, shook his head, and scratched one of Daisy's heads behind the ears. "Feeling left out, were you, girl?"

All three of Daisy's heads had their tongues lolling, eyes slightly crazy as she licked their hands.

"I, uh, guess we should keep moving while you tell me this plan of yours." Val bent, picked up the cord, and stuffed it into her pocket, too pointedly not looking at him. Though her cheeks still seemed a bit more pink beneath her bronzed skin tone than normal.

Not necessarily with discomfort. More with the stiff posture of someone who didn't quite know how to handle the emotions she was feeling.

As Val marched into the desert as if she was trying to outwalk her feelings, Harm grinned and fell into step beside her, even though he wasn't bound by the cord to stick close any longer. Daisy loped along before she broke off to chase a lizard, which scurried under a rock before the dog could chomp it.

Harm swung his arms at his sides, feeling lighter than he had in a long time. Perhaps it was the kissing haze, but he wasn't even all that terrified of the painful bloodshed and possible death in his future.

"So. The plan?" Val kept marching forward with that same ruthless pace.

Harm's grin widened until his cheeks hurt, though that could have been the sun burning his far-too-pale skin. "Well, I'm not sure if you're going to like it. It involves more kissing. And being stuck together. And it's rather permanent."

Val shot him a quelling look, reaching for her knife as if she was contemplating stabbing him after all. "Then why do you look so happy about it?"

"Because *I* rather like this plan." Harm resisted the urge to pull her close and kiss her again.

Though, he probably should do it now, before he told her his idea. Afterwards, she was just as likely to stab him as she was to kiss him.

"That is what has me worried."

"You will probably get to stab someone. Likely not me."

Val raised her eyebrows. "You should have led with that."

"I'd be hurt that stabbing people rates higher than kissing me, but I suppose I'll just have to kiss you until that changes." Harm walked close enough that their shoulders brushed. "Or just accept that your stabbiness is one of the things I love about you."

Val halted in her tracks before she whirled on him. "You...what..."

"I love you. Or, at least, I'm falling in love with you." Maybe it was that kiss, but Harm wasn't going to hesitate. Now was a time to be bold. "And I'm pretty sure you're falling in love with me too. You kissed me without stabbing me, and the tether came off."

Val huffed, flapped her hands, and made a noise in the back of her throat. She whirled away from him and set out into the desert again. "Fine. Whatever. Yes, I'm falling for you. Don't let it go to your head."

Harm's grin still tugged at his beard as he kept up with her fast pace.

Val shot him a glare. "Don't keep grinning like that. Clearly it *is* going to your head. We're about to face certain death, you're grinning like your brain just fell out of your head, and I have yet to hear this plan of yours."

Ah, right. Harm drifted a little farther away from her. Getting out of stabbing range. He might be in a kissing haze, but he hadn't completely lost his mind.

HARM PROPPED his boots on a rock as he sat on the larger rock next to their firepit.

The fire crackled and popped, a bright light against the blue darkness of the desert around them. Shadows of the cacti and brush danced on the side of the tent. Overhead, a riot of stars blazed across the sky.

Daisy lay next to his feet, though her head was up as she watched Val.

Val stalked around the fire, light and shadows dancing across her face. She kept drawing and sheathing her dagger, as if wishing she had something to fight.

As she stepped over Daisy and past Harm yet again, he reached out and grabbed her arm, halting her. "Val. Why don't you sit?"

"How are you so calm?" Val turned to him. She didn't sit, but she also didn't tug her arm free.

"We've already talked over the plan for hours while we walked. There's nothing more we can plan." Harm stared up into her eyes, trying to read her expression. "Tomorrow's troubles will keep until tomorrow. We don't need to add them to today."

Val huffed through her clenched teeth, shifting as if torn between sitting and tugging away from him. "But if there's something more we can take into account or if we missed something in our planning…Harm, if we lose tomorrow, you'll die."

"And if we succeed, you'll lose everything." Harm tugged her closer. This time, she finally sat on the boulder next to him, so close their shoulders and legs were pressed together.

Val shrugged, staring into the fire instead of looking at him. "Lose what? A life as a homeless mercenary taking missions that involve hurting innocents? There's not much to lose."

As there was a good chance he would die tomorrow, Harm dared to put his arm around Val's shoulders, tucking her close. She didn't exactly relax into him, but she leaned into him a little. "Still, I'm sorry."

She remained stiff beneath his arm, her shoulders hunched as she stared down at her hands in her lap. "There's something else that I should have told you long before now."

Harm stiffened. Nothing Val said in that tone of voice was ever good news.

"Time doesn't move the same way between the Fae Realm and the Human Realm." Val spoke slowly, her gaze looking everywhere but at him. "When we return to the Human Realm, there's no telling how much time might have passed there. It might have been ten minutes. Or ten years. There's no way to know until we get there."

Oh. *Oh*. Harm's breath caught in his throat. "My brother and father are in danger, and I might not get back for *years*?"

They'd think he was dead. Or perhaps they'd be dead, killed by whoever had poisoned Gijs in the first place.

"I'm sorry. I should have told you but..." Val shrugged, shaking her head. "It's not something I've had to think about before. I never return my packages. Only deliver them."

Harm tightened his grip on her shoulders at the note in her voice. "It isn't something you could've helped, even if you'd told me. You're attractively competent, but even you can't control time."

Val rolled her eyes, the stiffness to her spine unbending slightly. "No. But I've heard there are those who can. Sort of. For most of us, walking through a faerie circle or a rift is like stepping through a door. A wibbly-wobbly, whirling door that tries to tear you apart for a moment before you get put back together and spit out the other side. But for others, it feels more like a path. They can navigate between the realms to somewhat control where and when they end up in the Human Realm. Supposedly the Wild Fae Primrose is one such fae."

"Would it be worth trying to track down the Wild Fae Primrose or a fae like him for our return?" Harm's legs ached at the thought of more hiking through the wilds of the Fae Realm. They already had enough of a journey trying to get back to the Court of Dreams and the particular faerie circle that connected to Tulpenland.

"I don't think so." Val sighed and shook her head again. "While the Fae Realm itself runs on the same time, all of the courts interact differently with the Human Realm. If you'd remained in the same faerie court, you would've stayed somewhat tied to your own place and time. But now that you've journeyed all across the Fae Realm, you're thoroughly unmoored. I doubt even the Wild Fae Primrose himself could return you exactly to the time in which you left. I just hope you aren't so untethered that we end up a century out of time in your realm."

A century. His father and brother would be long dead by then. What would he even do if he returned to the Human Realm, only to find he had no family left and no home to return to? He and Val wouldn't even have a home here in the Fae Realm to fall back on. They'd belong to neither realm.

Val's shoulders heaved with a deep breath beneath his grip. "As you said, tomorrow will keep. There's nothing we can do about the time of our return now. Why don't you tell me about Tulpenland?"

A pang shot through him, but he forced a smile. "Tulpenwerf—that's the capital city where I live—is all brick roads, brick houses, and tiled roofs, lining the network of canals that we use more than the roads. The countryside is flat farm fields for as far as you can see, and you can spot all the little towns for miles around. Honestly, you'd consider it boring. There's nothing trying to eat me in Tulpenland."

"Nothing? Really?" Val nudged her elbow into his ribs, a hint of a smile curving her mouth. "It seems everything we've met wants to eat you."

"Well, pretty sure the grain sprites were trying to eat you."

"Only because I shoved you out of their way. They would have preferred to eat you." Val raised her eyebrows.

"Right..." Harm winced, just thinking about all the things that had tried to eat him in the Fae Realm. There was the wolf. The scarecrow. The crone. Queen Titania was certainly hungry for him. It would be quite the relief to get back to Tulpenland where everyone and everything he met wasn't trying to eat him. "Well, Tulpenland is a lot more peaceful. It's home."

"Home." Val spoke the word as if she was rolling it over her tongue, tasting it. "I've never had a home before. At least, not since my family was banished from the Court of Sand."

Harm hugged her tighter. "You'll have a home with me. It might be a little boring. Unless the other kingdoms decide to start sending assassins after me."

"It wouldn't surprise me." Val rested her hand on her dagger again.

"You don't have to sound so happy about the idea." Harm exaggerated his grumble.

Val smirked. But after a moment, the look faded. "Harm. Tomorrow, when we..."

"Stop thinking about it. We've planned enough for one day." Harm dug into his magical pocket with his free hand. He retrieved two of his remaining pottery plates, the last of his cheese, and the flask of cassis. "Tonight, we're going to feast."

Val took the things as he handed them to her, but she didn't start unwrapping the cheese. "Are you sure? If we succeed, we're going to have a long walk back to the Court of Dreams, and this time I won't have the protection of working for a fae court. We might need your bargaining goods more than ever."

"We can wash the plates. Aren't they more valuable here in the Fae Realm if they've been used by a prince?" Harm took the cheese, unwrapped it, and used a small knife to slice it. "But I think tonight of all nights is one for celebration, don't you think?"

Val huffed again, but she didn't refuse the cheese when he put it on her plate. She picked up a piece and took a large bite. "I rather like this cheese."

Daisy sat up, placed her nose on Val's knee, and gave her the big begging eyes.

"When we get to Tulpenland, you can have all the cheese and cassis you want." Harm reached toward Daisy, a piece of cheese in his hand.

Val caught his wrist. "Don't give Daisy anything until

we're done. We'll never have any peace if you give her something now."

He quickly stuffed the piece of cheese into his own mouth instead.

As he reached for another piece, Daisy's ears perked, and she looked into the darkness, a low growl rumbling in her chest.

Val set aside her plate. "Monsters. We're in the Court of Sand. We might not get a lot of sleep tonight."

Harm sighed, stuffed the rest of his cheese into his mouth, and shoved the plates and flask back into his magical pocket. "Great. I'll face near certain death tomorrow while sleep-deprived."

Val drew her sword out of her pocket, twirled it, and pulled her dagger from its sheath with her other hand. "Less talking, more arming yourself if you don't want to face tomorrow injured."

Harm faced the darkness where several pairs of red eyes had appeared and drew his sword. He was beyond ready to get this over with and return to Tulpenland. Not having stuff trying to eat him each and every minute would be such a luxury.

Chapter Twenty

Val faced the stretch of bare sand dunes ahead of them, the heat shimmer already dancing. She toyed with the new leather cuff around her wrist, her stomach churning more than she'd ever experienced.

One wrong move today, and Harm would die. Perhaps they'd both die.

Harm halted next to her. He, too, wore a leather cuff around one of his wrists while he wore the tattered shirt and bloodstained trousers from his first couple of days in the Fae Realm. Some of the leather of the jerkin he still wore beneath showed through the rips in his shirt, but that couldn't be helped. He'd need access to the magical pocket, and the ripped shirt worked better than his other, undamaged shirt.

Besides, they were counting on Diego focusing on the blood.

Harm held out his hand. "It'll be all right."

He was far too optimistic about that. And yet Val took his hand, willing to hope right along with him.

They'd survived the perils of the Fae Realm together. Perhaps, together, they could survive the confrontation waiting for them in the Realm of Monsters.

Standing between them wearing her harness and leash, Daisy licked their clasped hands, nuzzling their hands with her nose as she begged for a scratch.

"See? Daisy will take care of both of us. We'll be fine." Harm grinned and reached around to awkwardly scratch Daisy rather than let go of Val's hand.

Val gave Daisy a scratch with the hand that held the dog's leash, but she couldn't match Harm's smile.

Instead, she tugged her hand free of Harm's, reached into her pocket, and pulled out the threefold cord. She held out one end to Harm. "We'll need to put this back on."

"I've missed being tied to you with a magical rope." His grin never wavering, Harm took the end of the offered cord.

"Well, I certainly haven't trusted you farther than ten feet from me here in the Fae Realm." Val held up her own end of the cord. "You're liable to be eaten by a giant sand crab or something the moment my back is turned."

"Too true." Harm loosened his end of the cord. "Together?"

"Together." Val slid the cord over the wrist with the cuff at the same time as Harm did his. She tried to remind herself that they, most likely, could get the cord off again as easily as they had the day before.

But she still couldn't stop the tightness in her stomach, a guilt she'd never felt before at placing that cord on another's wrist. Even if he'd placed it on himself this time.

She was done with all of this. Done with holding another person captive. Done with squashing the niggling feeling in her chest that what she was doing was wrong.

It was time she did something right for a change.

"So what happens now?" Harm gestured at the sand dunes stretching before them.

While it wasn't necessary with the cord stretching between them again, Val clasped his hand again, tightened her grip on Daisy's leash, and set out down the ridge toward the shimmers and shadows that moved in ripples across the dunes before them. "Now we step through one of those patches of shadows into the Realm of Monsters. The barrier between the realms is thin here. Those shimmers lead to the Human Realm while the shadows are rifts into the Realm of Monsters. It's why we had such a problem with monsters last night."

Harm grimaced and sidestepped to avoid the edge of one of the shimmers. "Do the monsters ever get into the Human Realm here?"

"All the time." Val shrugged as she tugged him around another shimmer. "The desert human kingdoms aren't as peaceful and monster-free as Tulpenland."

"Remind me never to travel to a desert kingdom even in the Human Realm. Or, at least"—Harm grinned and swung their clasped hands—"not without you and Daisy to protect me."

Val would have come up with a quip back, but a black rift opened up before them. "Time to go. This will hurt a bit."

Then she dragged Harm into the rift.

———————

DARKNESS CLOSED AROUND HARM, shredding his skin, his mind, his deepest self, like the claws of some beast. He tried to stumble forward, but he felt as if he was somehow outside of his body, not sure what way to go or if directions even existed anymore in this nothingness of blackness and pain.

Then Val's grip on his hand tightened, and he was dragged from the darkness into a scorching, gray desert. He dropped to his knees in the dry sand of the Realm of Monsters, gasping and patting at his chest, half-expecting to have his hand come away bloody. But no, the only blood on his shirt was old and dried.

Daisy whined and pressed against Val's legs, the dog's tail tucked beneath her belly.

Val let go of Harm's hand, reached down, and scratched Daisy's head. "That will be the second to last time we do that, girl."

"That was...awful." Harm climbed to his feet and brushed off his trousers, pretending he wasn't shaken to his core. He touched his arm, checking that the sheath with the iron knife remained safely in place. Iron knives, it seemed, couldn't go in magical pockets, as iron countered *feeën* magic. "Is it like that every time?"

"Yes. There's a reason fae only live in the Realm of

Monsters if they are forced to do so." Val didn't reach for Harm's hand. At the moment, they could be nothing but captive and mercenary. "Come."

A desert similar to the one they'd left behind stretched before them. Except that here the landscape burned far hotter, even though there didn't appear to be a sun in the charcoal-gray sky.

At least the desert they'd left behind had sun-bleached green brush, deeper green cacti, and roadrunners dashing after skittering lizards, a place bursting with life despite the heat.

The desert before them was truly dead. Any plant life was black and rotting while the only movement was from the occasional monster scuttling through the shadows.

Val stalked into the dead desert, a hand on the hilt of her knife, her other hand gripping Daisy's leash. Harm stuck close to her side, swallowing back his unease.

After a short trek, they came to the edge of a canyon. Below, a cluster of huts constructed of random bits of wood and animal hides filled the canyon. Gray and black smoke wafted from the various fires while the figures of *feeën* mercenaries strode between the shelters.

Val didn't even seem to hesitate before she strolled down the winding path that zigzagged down the canyon's face to reach the bottom, her shoulders straight, her back stiff, in that deadly posture she'd worn so often at first. Daisy clambered over the rocks with ease, but Harm picked his way down, falling behind until he was nearly at the end of the ten-foot tether.

Just as well. He appeared more the unwilling captive that way. He tried to add a few extra staggers for good measure, keeping his head down and his shoulders hunched.

At the canyon's bottom, Val strode between the various shelters. Some of her fellow mercenaries stopped what they were doing to nod to her or offer a stilted wave. Those salutes turned to sneers when their gazes landed on him.

At one fire, a cluster of five mercenaries stood as Val neared, their faces breaking into smiles that seemed to hold more warmth than the others. Val's comrades, perhaps?

Val halted long enough to nod at them. But then she kept walking, turning her face away as if she were too focused on her task to speak with them.

Harm dropped his gaze back to his feet instead of studying them. But he could feel their gazes pinned on his shoulder blades as he kept walking.

At the far end of the canyon, a throne made of random bits of wood, animal hides, and bones rested among the fallen boulders.

Diego lounged on the throne, his black hair slicked back, the streaks of silver at his temples even more prominent. His thin beard and mustache were well groomed while the leathers he wore over his clothes were well-oiled. A sword rested at his hip while daggers glinted at his belt and in the bandoleer across his chest.

At Val and Harm's approach, a smile curved his mouth. He lifted a hand. "Valeria! You have returned at last! I see your charge is still in one piece."

"Of course. I never lose a package." Val halted before the throne, her hand on her hip near her dagger. "A package I'm told belongs to you."

Harm halted a few feet behind her, the picture of cowed submission, or so he hoped.

"Yes, quite convenient, isn't it." Diego's gaze swung from Val to Harm.

Val tugged on the cord, and Harm staggered as if she'd forced him with far more roughness than she had. When she shoved him forward, he made a show of resistance, digging in his heels and squirming in her grip. She halted him at the foot of the throne, as if presenting him to Diego. "Do you accept the delivery of this human?"

Diego's mouth twisted with even more of a smirk, his dark eyes glittering. "Yes, I do."

Harm had been so used to the squeezing pressure of the bargain that he hadn't realized it was there until it was gone, lifting from his heart.

Finally. They'd traveled across seven courts to hear those words. Harm could stop journeying away from his family and at last escape back to them.

If he didn't die in the next few minutes.

Harm clawed at the end of the rope, ripping it off as if he hadn't been free the night before, and threw it away from him. "I don't belong to you."

"Yes, you do. That was the bargain. Your life is now in my hands." Diego rose to his feet with all the grace of a hunting lion. He prowled down the rocks from his throne and stalked around Harm, taking him in with a hungry look that was almost reminiscent of Queen

Titania's, though with a different undertone. "You did well, Valeria, in bringing him to me. I knew I could count on you for this task."

Harm lifted his chin, glaring first at Diego, then at Val, trying to sound hurt and betrayed instead of like he was reciting his lines. "After all we've been through, you're just going to give me to him?"

"That is my job." Val divested herself of the end of the rope and coiled it with swift movements, her tone and expression so cold it sent a chill through Harm even though he knew better. "You could have saved me a lot of trouble, Diego, if you'd just claimed his bargain from the beginning rather than let me travel across half the Fae Realm with a useless human in tow."

"I do apologize for the length of your journey. I had intended to bargain with Mab for him but was delayed in doing so. Arranging for more weapons and recalling everyone not on a mission took time, even with traveling through the rifts." Diego continued to stalk around Harm as if he was prey and Diego the wolf. "It's just as well. His blood will be all the more potent for the length of time he was traveling with you. I see he's already shed some along the way."

Was it Harm's imagination, or did Diego's gaze linger on the bloodstains the way one might study a favorite painting?

"Then you intend to use him for blood rites. I wondered, once I realized that you must have arranged all this." Val tapped her fingers on the hilt of her dagger, all cool indifference and idle curiosity.

"What do you mean? What's going on?" Harm swung

wide eyes from her to Diego, as if realizing the true depth of his peril for the first time. "Blood rites?"

Diego ignored his question, as if he were nothing but a yappy puppy. Instead, the Wild Hunt leader gripped Harm's shoulder, kicked the back of his knees, and shoved him to his knees.

As Harm struck the rocky ground, pain flared up his legs. He couldn't help his grunt of pain, little as he wanted to give Diego the satisfaction. He struggled against Diego's unyielding grip on his shoulder even as he remained hunched on the ground to shield his hands and arm from view.

Diego grabbed a hunk of Harm's hair and yanked his head back, pain tearing across Harm's scalp.

Harm ceased struggling, but he inched his right hand up his left sleeve and closed his hand over the knobby hilt of his iron knife.

Diego turned Harm's head this way and that by his grip on his hair, as if inspecting his neck for the best place to slice. "Others here in the Realm of Monsters have begun experimenting with such things again, and if our Wild Hunt is to survive, we must keep up with the times. This human's blood will do just that."

"He's just one human." Val's voice rang with a detached skepticism. "The others attempting blood rites have done it with far more volume of blood."

Out of the corner of his eye, Harm caught movement as more of the mercenaries drifted their way, drawn by the unfolding drama. They gathered with their arrays of weapons, arms crossed, as they took in the scene.

Harm couldn't help but tense. At least Diego would chalk up his stiffness to terror. And perhaps it was, but not for himself. Or not only for himself. His breath caught at the sight of Val with so many potential enemies gathered at her back.

"Yes, but he's the heir to his duchy." Diego's smirk slicked even darker. "Even if his younger brother does survive and inherits the throne someday, this human will always be the True Heir. His blood holds sway over his duchy."

The muscle at the corner of Harm's jaw flexed as he glared up at Diego. "You'll never get your hands on Tulpenland."

Diego snorted and gave a rough tug on Harm's hair, yanking his head even farther back until Harm struggled to breathe. "You don't understand, human. Tulpenland is already in my hands because I have *you*."

Even more of the mercenaries crowded close, and Diego's gaze flicked away from Harm long enough to take them in.

Diego's smirk widened as he tightened his grip on Harm's shoulder as if to grind him into the stone. "I'm the reason you're here. When I learned that a human king was seeking a fae poison, I was the one who gave it to him. I bargained with him so that he would poison the younger son, promising him that I would see to it that the heir disappeared. I told Queen Mab to send a fae to bargain with your father, I outlined the terms of that bargain, and I sent my mercenary to bring you from the Human Realm and eventually to me. Your blood has been in my control from the moment your destiny with the Fae Realm was determined, and there is power in such control over another's life."

The mercenaries were murmuring now, caught up in their leader's unfolding performance.

"What king? What enemy of Tulpenland conspired with you?" Harm snarled the words, his neck aching from the angle he was held. His questions were perhaps a little too pointed, but Diego was preening for his audience now.

Diego shrugged, a slick sneer on his face. "Heinrich, Henry, something like that. He's hardly your concern. Or mine."

And there it was. The answer Harm had been waiting for. King Hendrik had coveted Tulpenland's farms and trade for years. He couldn't take Tulpenland by force thanks to the network of canals, but it seemed he thought he could take it by trickery instead.

Father and Gijs were still in grave danger. King Hendrik must have thought he could swoop in and take over the duchy once Gijs died and Harm disappeared, leaving the duchy without an heir.

What had he done once Gijs recovered? Had he attacked? What form had it taken? Another poisoning? A full-scale invasion? Were Harm's father and brother even still alive?

Harm needed to return home without any more delay.

Diego swung his gaze away from Harm to the mercenaries. He finally released Harm's hair so that he could gesture grandly, though he kept his painful grip on Harm's shoulder. "He will soon learn the perils of bargaining with the fae. He wanted Tulpenland for himself, but with this human's blood, Tulpenland will soon be mine. My Wild Hunt will ride on the duchy and ravage from border to border until the canals run red. It will be a golden age of glory and spoil for Wild Hunt Grimbrand!"

The mercenaries cheered. All except Val, who remained at the front with her arms crossed, her expression stony. She'd give them away if she remained so unenthusiastic for her leader's planned Wild Hunt ride.

Instead, she met Harm's gaze and gave a single small nod.

Harm tightened his grip on the iron knife hidden beneath his sleeve, eased his weight onto one knee, and struck without giving in to the urge to take a deep breath, which would only give away his intentions.

He swept out a leg, knocking Diego's legs out from under him, even as he reached up and gripped the hand that had been clutching his shoulder. As Val had drilled into him, he dragged Diego down, yanked his arm behind his back, and pinned him to the ground with a knee.

Diego's face mottled. Perhaps angry at being bested by a human. Or embarrassed to be so bested in front of his Wild Hunt. Harm had only succeeded because Diego hadn't been expecting an attack from his captive human.

In a blink, Harm drew the iron knife and had it

pressed to the Wild Hunt leader's throat. The scent of burning skin filled the air, and Harm gritted his teeth to resist the urge to stay his hand. Any sign of weakness or shirking from doing what needed to be done would be exploited.

A few of the mercenaries stepped forward, hands going to their weapons.

Harm pressed harder against Diego's throat with the iron knife, causing a louder sizzling sound. "Stay back, or your leader dies."

Beneath Harm's knee, Diego twisted to glare at Val. "Didn't you search him for weapons?"

"Yes. I'm not incompetent." Val huffed, as if it was all Diego's fault he was currently pinned beneath Harm. "He had no weapons on his person when I searched him."

Harm resisted the urge to grin at her very careful answer. Instead, he jabbed Diego in the throat again with the knife. "My father passed this knife to me after she searched me. I've kept it hidden ever since."

Diego's body shook as he chuckled, his face smoothing back into that controlled sneer. "What is your plan now, human?"

"A life for a life. That was the original bargain, and it's the bargain I offer you now." Harm refused to flinch at the blackened mark that spread beneath the Hunt leader's jaw. "I hold your life, and you hold mine. I'd prefer if we each held our own lives in our own hands."

"Very well. A life for a life. You are free of the binding to me." Diego spoke almost too lightly, as if releasing Harm didn't mean giving up all his plans. As if being pinned to the ground was all just a part of his plan after all.

Harm sucked in a breath as something twanged deep in his chest. The captive binding breaking as he was released.

He was free. No more bargain to be fulfilled. No more captive binding holding him here in the Realm of Monsters.

Harm stood and backed away from Diego, keeping his back to the canyon wall, the iron knife still gripped in his hand.

Diego pushed to his feet, brushing off his clothes with nonchalant flicks of his fingers. "What do you think you've accomplished by that little display, human? You're still stuck here in the Realm of Monsters. Even with that iron knife, do you think my Wild Hunt will let you simply pass through their ranks?"

Harm swallowed, taking in the horde of mercenaries crowding into the space before the throne, leers on their faces as they toyed with the hilts of their weapons. If he'd been alone, he never would have survived this escape.

But he wasn't alone, even if he didn't dare look at her.

"Perhaps we'll hold a Hunt. The fire of crushed hope and utter terror will add potency to your blood when I shed it to tear into your realm." Diego spread his hands wide, as if Harm's escape had been a part of the plan all along.

More cheering, accompanied by the shush of blades being drawn from their sheaths.

Then Val stepped forward, her dark brown eyes blazing, her hand on her knife's hilt. At her back, Daisy growled as she faced the crowd of mercenaries. When Val spoke, her voice rang strident and clear over the noise. "No. There will be no Hunt. Diego, I challenge you for the leadership of Wild Hunt Grimbrand."

Chapter Twenty-One

"You dare to challenge me?" Diego gave that scoff again.

Val held Diego's gaze, steel settling in her gut. This was it. Either she won, and she and Harm both lived. Or she failed, and they both died. "Yes. In all your plans, Diego, you neglected to take one thing into account. He wasn't in your hands. He was in *mine*."

"And here I thought I'd sent a *loyal* mercenary on that mission." Diego's jaw hardened as he drew his sword.

"Yes, well, I've discovered a loyalty to something greater than you." Val eased a step closer to Harm, her eyes still locked on Diego.

"Him?" Diego pointed toward Harm with another scoff.

"No." Val didn't elaborate more than that. Saying she now had a loyalty to all things right and good sounded even more cheesy than saying she was loyal to Harm.

Instead, she forced herself to put her back to Diego

as she faced Harm. He'd put his back to the canyon wall as she'd instructed, keeping himself as safe as he could for the coming fight.

With the mercenaries and Diego watching, they couldn't exchange anything too romantic. But she stood as close as she dared without fully embracing Harm.

"Take care of Daisy." Val held out the end of Daisy's leash.

Harm nodded, taking the leash and wrapping the leather around his hand. Then he reached out and clasped her forearm, tugging her even closer. "Take care of yourself."

As he did so, a weight settled in the hidden pocket she'd added along her thigh the night before, just as they'd practiced so that the move wasn't obvious. It wasn't in the magical pocket, and she could still feel the item pressing into her as she turned away, not meeting Harm's gaze. If she did, she might lose her edge.

She faced Diego and drew her sword from her pocket, then her dagger from the sheath at her side. This was the moment she was likely supposed to say something tough or snarky. Oh, well. She'd rather skip straight to the part where she stabbed that smirk off Diego's face.

Diego prowled closer and circled her, his movements liquid as a hunting chimera. Without even a flicker in his eyes to give away his intentions, Diego struck, his sword darting forward with all the speed of a snake's tongue.

Val parried the sword's blade, knocking it aside enough that it slid harmlessly past her shoulder. Even as she shoved his sword away, she stabbed at his chest with her dagger.

He knocked her dagger aside with his, and he twisted his sword away from hers. He pushed forward, pressing his advantage of height and reach.

Val danced backward and parried his rain of blows. She swiped at his chest, changing the trajectory of her sword to aim at his leg.

Diego jumped back, and the tip of Val's sword sliced through the fabric of his trousers, even if it didn't manage to touch his skin.

With a growl, Diego put even more force behind his next blow, forcing Val backward yet again. The back of her ankle struck one of the boulders, and she stumbled, nearly falling.

With her balance off, Diego struck, knocking her dagger from her hand. He kicked her, and she fell, her back crashing into the canyon wall. She caught a ledge with her hand and kept herself semi-upright.

Diego's sword swung at her head, and she barely managed to get her sword up in time to block his blow. Her arm ached from the impact, and she scrambled to dig another of her knives out of her pocket.

Diego pressed close and grabbed her wrist before she could get her knife out. He pinned her sword to the cliff's side with his own as he loomed over her. "Valeria. So foolish. You were never a match for me."

He dragged her forward by his grip on her wrist and tossed her away from him with such force that she tumbled to the ground. She rolled, keeping a hold of her sword. Her back slammed into a rock, and she halted, coughing to catch her breath and spitting the dust out of her mouth.

Diego remained standing near the cliffside instead of pressing his advantage. He shook his head. "All this, and you won't even save him."

Before Val could scramble to her feet, Diego whipped around. Their fight had taken him far too close to where Harm stood.

Harm's eyes widened, and he fumbled as he reached inside the tatters of his shirt for the sword stashed in his magical pocket.

Val rolled to her feet, lunging for Diego. But she was too far away, her movements too slow. She'd never get there in time.

Diego stabbed forward with his sword, aiming squarely for Harm's chest.

Dropping Daisy's leash, Harm gave a cry as he drew the sword out of the pocket, the hilt nearly catching on one of the tatters of his shirt. He just about dropped it as he whipped it up with both hands, his movement even more awkward in the confined space. Somehow his blade clanged against Diego's, directing it to the side just enough that it sliced a cut along Harm's upper arm instead of stabbing him through the heart.

Before Diego could bring his sword back for another strike, Daisy snarled and leapt, sinking her teeth into Diego's sword arm and clinging there. Another head appeared and clamped teeth on Diego's leg.

Diego howled and hopped backward, the dog tenaciously hanging on. He dropped his sword but lifted his dagger, preparing to stab Daisy.

Val yanked the iron knife from the hidden pocket, a burning filling her, though it wasn't the burn of iron. Perhaps killing wasn't the action of someone who was truly good. But Diego had hurt Harm, and he was about to stab her dog.

She'd become good another day. This was a day for death. Sometimes, the only way to deal with evil was to dispatch it with extreme prejudice.

Diego tried to turn. Tried to bring his dagger up to block her. But Daisy had him pinned by his arm and ankle.

Val batted his hand aside and stabbed the iron knife down into Diego's chest.

Diego's eyes widened, his gaze dropping to the knife in his chest, then up into her face, realization stealing the color from his skin and eyes.

She'd stabbed him with iron. He might have survived a wound made from faerie steel, if he took a healing potion in time. But not one caused by iron.

"Daisy, release." Val stepped back, yanking the iron knife from Diego's chest. At her command, Daisy released her hold, and she took up station in front of Harm once again, still growling.

Diego sagged to the ground, a hand pressed to his chest, though the gesture did little to stop the blood. He gasped out a single word. "How…"

Val shoved the leather cuff up her arm, revealing a thin golden line around her wrist. Harm did the same, showing the matching line around his wrist.

Holding Diego's gaze, Val brandished the iron dagger. "As I said, he was never yours. We freed each other, and in the end, we chose to bind ourselves to each other of our own free will. I'm married to a human, and thus I'm immune to iron."

Diego's last breath gurgled from him as he collapsed the rest of the way to the canyon floor.

Val stared at him for another long moment, ensuring that he was truly dead. Then she drew her gaze up to take in Harm where he still stood with his back pressed to the cliffside, a hand clapped over his upper arm, his sword still gripped in the other.

He gave a slight shrug. "I'm bleeding."

Val heaved an exaggerated sigh as she fished in her pocket for her cleaning cloth. "Again?"

"I didn't do it to myself this time. And I kept a hold of my sword." Harm held up the weapon as if presenting a trophy. A wrinkle accompanied his frown. "Though you lost hold of your knife."

"I was busy trying not to die." Val wiped down the blade of the iron knife.

"That's when it's generally considered a good idea to keep a firm grip on your knife." Harm's mouth curved with his grin. "And your sword. I know a certain mercenary who would chew you out and make you run through extra drills for that."

A cough came from somewhere behind her, accompanied by the clank of weapons. The rest of the mercenaries were getting restless.

"Don't think this gets you out of knife practice." Val huffed, stuffed the rag back into her pocket, and returned the iron knife to the hidden sheath she'd rigged up. She retrieved a bandage from her other magical pocket, crossed the remaining distance to Harm, and quickly bound it over the slice on his arm. "That will have to do for now. Don't want any of these clods getting ideas of blood binding you. It's a lot harder to do now that you're married to a fae, but if you keep bleeding all over the place like this, someone will figure out something."

Harm winced as she tied the bandage to hold it in place. He brushed his fingers over the back of her hand, giving her a slight nod.

He had her back as she tried to get both of them out of this mess once and for all.

Val turned and faced the Wild Hunt mercenaries arrayed before her. She planted her hands on her hips, ready to reach for the iron knife again if needed.

Several of the mercenaries sauntered forward, weapons already gripped in their hands. One—seemingly deemed the spokesman—stepped forward, an ax in one hand. "Do you really think we're going to take orders from you, now that you've married a human? You're a good warrior, Val, but not that good."

If he thought he'd rile her with insults, he was barking up the wrong canyon. Unlike him, her ego wasn't so easily bruised.

Val held his gaze, her hand easing toward the iron knife. "No, I don't expect you to. I release you from your binding to me. I abdicate as the leader of Wild Hunt Grimbrand. To the strongest go the spoils."

For a long moment, the mercenaries stared at her, as

if they couldn't believe what she'd just done. Then, with shouts and war cries, they lifted their weapons and turned on each other, blades flashing, dust rising.

Val gripped Harm's arm and tugged him after her. "We should go."

"Right behind you." Harm swiped Daisy's lead from the ground, though the dog remained pressed close to them, all three of her heads still out.

As they hurried to find a way around the melee, Val retrieved her sword and dagger where they lay discarded on the sandy canyon floor. No sense leaving behind good weapons, even if she was headed toward a new, likely very boring and weapon-free life in the Human Realm. She sheathed the dagger but kept a grip on her sword.

She and Harm edged along the canyon's side to avoid the fighting. She had to shove aside a few mercenaries when they tumbled toward them, but other than that, the Wild Hunt was too focused on brawling to pay attention to them.

At last, she and Harm stood at the end of the canyon, the twilight of coming night closing around them. Somehow during their escape, her grip had shifted from his arm to his hand.

Now he swung their clasped hands. "Ready to go home?"

"You know it won't be that simple. We need to hop through a rift, walk across a couple of Fae courts, find the right faerie circle, and hope we end up in your duchy in a relatively timely manner." Val rested her free hand on her dagger's hilt, her stomach churning.

What would his family think of her? And his duchy? Would she even be able to make a life in the Human Realm?

She'd already made this choice. That didn't mean she couldn't be somewhat frightened. Even if she wasn't about to show her fear.

"And once we get there, we'll still have to deal with the king who poisoned my brother." Harm grimaced, his hand straying toward the magical pocket where he'd stowed his sword.

Right. The conniving king. Val's nerves vanished. "An evil king to vanquish sounds promising."

"You won't be leaving without us." A deep baritone voice spoke from behind them.

Val whirled, tugging Harm behind her as she drew her sword. "Don't try to stop us."

Five mercenaries of her former Wild Hunt band stood before her, festooned with weapons, although none of them had them drawn. The three men and two women had nearly identical stances with their arms crossed, their feet braced.

Val's heart twisted. These five mercenaries were those who had been almost a small family within the larger band. They were the ones she'd actually trusted to watch her back. The ones she actually regretted leaving behind. When she'd passed them earlier, she couldn't bring herself to do more than glance at them, for fear they'd read her plan in her eyes.

Familiar as she was with them, Daisy's tail wagged.

Abelardo, the male fae who had spoken, stood in the lead with his small turquoise fleech dragon twining by his feet. "We're not trying to stop you. We want to go with you. We accept you as our Wild Hunt leader, and we will follow wherever you go."

"I'm going to the Human Realm. With him." Val jabbed a thumb over her shoulder at Harm.

"Yes, we gathered that." Abelardo gave a shrug without uncrossing his arms. "He's some kind of prince, right? Princes always need more mercenaries."

Harm made a strangled noise in the back of his throat, but she couldn't tell if he was protesting or laughing.

"Perhaps some princes. But I'm going to be following his moral compass." Val pointed at Harm yet again. "And his moral compass points rather true."

"Well, that's good." Abelardo made that shrug again. "Because clearly none of us have one."

"Yeah, it might be a nice change of pace to try being moral for once." Chela, one of the female mercenaries, relaxed out of her crossed arms stance.

"Harm?" Val sheathed her sword and half-turned so that she could face him and her fellow mercenaries. "It's your duchy."

They might be married, but she didn't feel right in speaking for him now. Perhaps she would one day, once they'd been married for more than a few hours and known each other for longer than a few weeks.

But right now, she held her breath as she waited for his verdict.

Chapter Twenty-Two

H arm couldn't tear his gaze away from the pleading in Val's deep brown eyes. The rest of her posture remained stiff, the hard expression frozen on her face.

But her eyes betrayed her. She was giving up everything—her home, her Wild Hunt band, her realm—to follow him to the Human Realm. He'd be an utter cad if he asked her to give up her friends as well.

Besides, friends who were loyal enough to follow her to a new realm were the kind they needed on their side. Even better if those friends were armed to the teeth. Especially for when they faced King Hendrik.

"Of course they can come. If"—Harm shot a stern glare at the five mercenaries—"they are willing to follow the laws of Tulpenland and listen to your orders."

He might be the prince of Tulpenland, but these were Val's mercenaries. She would be their leader, not him. And he was quite all right with that.

"Val's our Wild Hunt leader. Of course we'll follow her orders," one of the female *feeën* spoke up.

"But I can take Acurru, right? I can't leave him behind." The spokesman *fee* gestured toward the turquoise dragon at his feet.

Harm resisted the urge to sigh. "Yes. After all, we'll be taking a sometimes-three-headed dog with us."

He gestured to Daisy. The movement drew the dog's attention, and she promptly sat on his foot, peering up at him with her ears slicked back in that particularly cute way of hers. Harm reached down and ran a hand over those soft ears.

"And my pet giant snails?" One of the male *feeën* who hadn't spoken until then lifted a crate where two snails the size of large cats left green slime marks on the wood.

"The snails too." Harm pinched the bridge of his nose. The staid Tulpenlanders would have conniptions when he returned.

Oh, well. He'd made his choice when he married Val. If he had to abdicate and Gijs became the duke eventually, then so be it.

Assuming fifty years hadn't gone by, and Gijs wasn't already the duke.

"If that's settled, perhaps some introductions would be in order." Harm glanced from Val to the five mercenaries. "I'm Harm from Tulpenland."

He didn't give his full name nor his official title. They'd learn all of those eventually. But he was learning. Don't give more information than necessary when here in the Fae Realm. Or Realm of Monsters, as the case might be.

The spokesman *fee* picked up his dragon, strode forward, and halted before Harm. He gave a respectful nod. "I'm Abelardo."

The male *fee* with the snails was next. He grinned as he nodded. "Ignatius, but I go by Iggy."

"Chela." The first female mercenary stated. The second one nodded to him. "Jesenia."

The final mercenary trundled closer. Even as tall as he was, Harm had to peer way up at the bare-chested, broad-shouldered male *feeën* warrior. The massive sword the warrior held was over five feet tall.

Harm swallowed. "And who are you?"

The warrior stared down at him for a long moment, leather creaking in the silence. Then he spoke in a resonating bass. "I am Grutte."

"Nice to meet you." Harm forced the words out past a polite smile.

"We should leave." Val gestured back the way they'd come. "The sound of the fighting is dying down. I don't think we want to still be in the Realm of Monsters once a new Wild Hunt leader is chosen."

With that, she took Harm's hand again, and he found himself hauled across the desert. Rather willingly so.

He was less pleased about having to jump into a rift again. But at least this would be the last time.

As Val stepped into the rift, tugging him after her, he barely had time to suck in a deep breath before the squeezing, clawing, ripping feeling tore through him again.

Just when he thought the shreds of his being might disappear into the void between the realms, he was dragged out the other side. He coughed, releasing Val's hand as he fell to his hands and knees on the burning sand on the other side of the rift. "That was just as—"

With a *thump* that vibrated through the sand beneath him, two huge azure dragons landed before them. Before Harm could do more than scramble upright, a large, scaled tail lashed forward, knocking Val and the other *feeën* aside and curling around Harm's waist.

He was hauled through the air, then plunked back to the sand behind the dragon. His legs buckled at the impact, and he would have fallen again if he hadn't been held by the tail still wrapped around his torso. With the tail pinning him so thoroughly, he couldn't even reach the sword stuffed in the magical pocket of his leather jerkin.

In a blink, the second dragon transformed into a *feeën* woman with brown hair and blue eyes and wearing a blue woolen dress edged in white fur. Something about her seemed vaguely familiar, though Harm didn't have much of a chance to wrack his brain to remember.

The dragon holding him gave a low growl, fire licking around his jaws. Val drew her sword, standing at the front of her cluster of mercenaries, all of them dropping into fighting stances as if they thought they could fight off two dragons. Although, Grutte's massive broadsword looked big enough to whack the head off a dragon.

The female *fee*—dragon?—stepped closer to him,

placing her back to the others. She held out her hand to him, then uncurled her fingers to show him something small and red resting on her palm. "We're here to rescue you. How are you bound? If it's a captive binding, we can take off right now. If you're blood-bound, things will get more complicated."

"Uh, neither?" Harm stared at the little red flower she held. A wild fae primrose. Just like that flower the strange human man had given him at the faerie market.

These dragons were a part of the Primrose League. He could trust them.

If they didn't flambé his wife and her friends first.

Harm hurriedly shoved the leather cuff up his arm to show the gold line. "I have a marriage binding. That's my wife."

At the same time, Val pointed her sword at the other dragon's face and shouted, "Let my husband go!"

The dragon swung his huge head around, and his slitted eyes focused on Harm. When he spoke, his lips peeled back to reveal fangs nearly as long as Grutte's sword. "Is that true?"

"Yes!" Harm held up his arm to show the other dragon the golden line from the marriage binding. "I was fully willing. As was she."

When the dragon swung his head back to Val, she had stowed her sword in her pocket so that she, too, could shove the leather cuff out of the way to reveal the matching golden line around her wrist. She then drew the iron knife and held that up, pressing the flat of the blade to her forearm. "This is an iron knife. Clearly I'm immune."

The dragon stretched his head forward, and Harm tensed as the dragon's huge maw got far too close to Val. Yet Val remained unflinching as the dragon sniffed the blade in her hand.

With a puff of smoke into Val's face, the dragon withdrew and shook his head as if he'd just snorted pepper. "Yes, that's iron, all right." The dragon released his tail's grip on Harm.

Harm steadied himself and tugged at the now even more tattered remnants of his bloodstained shirt.

In a blur, the dragon shifted into a *feeën* male with brown hair and blue eyes that matched the female dragon-*fee*. He flashed a grin that was only mildly less toothy. "Sorry about that. The Wild Fae Primrose sent us to rescue you."

"I remember you now." Harm waved between the two dragons. "You were at the Dragon Moot. Taran and Tora, right? You bargained for me."

"Tried to bargain for you." The female, Tora, grimaced and gave a flick of her hair.

"We didn't succeed." The male, Taran, crossed his arms. "So we tracked you to Warlord Zaya."

"Then to the desert." Tora took up the thread the moment Taran stopped for a breath. "We've been flying overhead for an hour now."

"Trying to decide if we should follow through a rift."

"But we didn't know which rift would lead to the right Wild Hunt band."

"Not that we couldn't take on a Wild Hunt by ourselves."

"But we didn't want to miss you and risk that you'd be killed before we got there."

"Quite convenient that you popped out right where we were patrolling."

"Saved us a lot of trouble."

Harm coughed to interrupt. "Pardon the question, but are the two of you twins?"

"Yes." Tora smiled, flashing brilliantly white teeth. "How did you guess?"

"We are obvious about it." Taran elbowed his sister.

"Though we aren't quite up to finishing each other's sentences." Tora jabbed her brother in the ribs with a finger.

"Not for lack of trying."

"All right then." Val marched forward to Harm's side. Daisy stuck so close to Val's heels that she nearly tripped Val several times.

The rest of the mercenaries hung back, as if waiting for Val and Harm to finish the negotiations before they made a move.

When Val halted next to Harm, she laid a protective hand on his arm. "As you can see, he doesn't need rescuing. So we'll be on our way."

"We can help with that." Taran gestured from himself to his sister. "Unless you *want* to walk hours across the scorching hot desert."

As it was late afternoon, they had several hours of heat remaining before the desert cooled for the evening. Yet even if they walked the whole night through a monster-infested, rift-filled desert, they wouldn't cross the whole Court before morning.

"We're fine." Val's grip on Harm's arm tightened, as if she was preparing to drag him across the desert again. She'd gone all prickly and stiff in that way of hers.

"You're a mercenary. You don't have access to the Anywhere Doors. We do." Tora waved from herself to her brother. "That would save you a lot of time."

Harm stilled, meeting Val's eyes. "I need to return home as soon as possible. I've already been gone too long. And these dragons are with the Wild Fae Primrose. Maybe they can walk the faerie paths."

"I wouldn't get your hopes up there." Tora twirled a section of her hair around a finger.

Taran shrugged. "We don't know that we don't have that skill. We did well in training."

Tora's gaze swerved away from them. "This is our first mission for the Primrose."

"It's actually our parents' mission, but they got caught up at the Dragon Moot." Taran met Harm's gaze with an easy smile. "But we've passed all the Primrose's training."

Harm resisted the urge to drop his head into his hand. All right, so perhaps accepting help from these dragons wasn't such a good idea. But what other choice did they have?

He turned to Val. "I'm tired of walking."

Val heaved a sigh. "Fine. We'll take the dragons up on their offer." Her gaze dropped to Daisy, who was trying to curl up on top of Val's feet. "I suppose Daisy will survive one more dragon flight."

Without waiting another moment, the twins transformed back into their massive dragon forms. Daisy whined and pressed against Val as if trying to disappear.

Taran lowered his head to inspect first Harm and Val, then the other five mercenaries. "Are all of you coming?"

"Yes, they are." Harm dredged up the last shreds of his courage to face the dragon's large, slitted gaze. Even knowing these dragons were friendly, something inside him was shaking. "Val is married to me, and these fae are her Wild Hunt. They're all coming back to the Human Realm with me."

"That is…highly irregular." Tora puffed a cloud of gray smoke down at the cluster of mercenaries.

To their credit, none of them backed up, even as they coughed from the smoke.

"I'm not sure if we're allowed to turn a Wild Hunt loose on the Human Realm." Taran tilted his huge head, the horns running down his back winking in the far-too-hot afternoon sun.

"They're with me. I've given them permission to enter my duchy." Harm struggled to keep his knees from knocking together as both dragons focused on him. It would have been far less intimidating if they'd had this conversation while both of the dragons had been in their fae forms.

"I'm not sure you truly understand what you're doing." Taran snorted a cloud of smoke at Harm.

Harm coughed and waved a hand in front of his face. "Perhaps not. But I trust Val. She will keep her mercenaries in line."

Tora bumped Taran with her tail. "We can clear it

with the Primrose before we escort them all the way to the Human Realm."

"Good plan." Taran turned back to Harm, Val, and the mercenaries. "All right, everyone climb on. We'll be taking you home to our mountain for the night."

"Climb on? You aren't just going to grip us in your claws?" Harm shifted closer to Val. "That's what the other two dragons did."

"You're not prey. We'll at least give you the dignity of riding on our backs." Tora shrugged as she lowered herself to her belly in the sand, sticking out a leg.

"But don't ask about saddles. We aren't beasts of burden." Taran, too, lay in the sand and stretched out a leg.

Harm shared a look with Val before he bent and picked up a shaking Daisy. "One more adventure on our way home? At least they aren't trying to eat me."

"Not yet," Val muttered as she led the way climbing up Tora's leg.

With his arms full of terrified dog, Harm struggled to walk up the leg, and Val turned back several times to tug him up. He settled into a seat at the base of Tora's neck, wedging himself between two of her spikes. Val sat behind Harm and wrapped her arms around the spike and his waist, as if she planned to somehow hold Harm onto the dragon.

Chela and Abelardo with Acurru climbed onto Tora as well while Jesenia, Ignatius, and Grutte climbed onto Taran, though Taran gave a grunt when Grutte settled into a spot.

Once they were all on the dragons, the two dragons

spread their wings. With a short run, the two dragons hurled themselves into the air one after the other.

Harm gripped Tora's long, scaly neck with his legs while he clutched Daisy to his chest. The dog flailed and scratched at him, as if trying to climb up and over his shoulder, distracting him from the way his stomach remained somewhere buried in the sand rapidly disappearing below.

But at least he was finally headed home.

Chapter Twenty-Three

The journey to the dragon's mountain proved to be far more complicated than Harm had expected. First the dragons flew them over the desert until they reached an oasis, where they landed, transformed, and entered what the dragons called an outpost library. It was certainly filled with enough books to put any library Harm had ever seen to shame.

In the outpost library, the dragons greeted the librarians, then led Harm, Val, and the mercenaries to a door set in the back wall. An Anywhere Door, apparently. When Tora had opened it, the Door revealed a white marbled hall that bustled with people even at that hour of afternoon bleeding into evening.

No sooner had they stepped through the Door into the hall—holding tightly to each other since only the dragons could actually use the Doors—than Tora shut the door, opened it again, and suddenly the Door led to a cavern deep inside a mountain. Just like that with a few steps, Harm found himself back in the Court of Stone, no days of walking or long flights needed.

Now he understood why it was such a big deal that Val and the other mercenaries couldn't use the Anywhere Doors. He would have been delivered within a matter of minutes if Val had been able to go through the magical doorways.

They stood in a large cavern with the Door set into the rock wall behind them. A waterfall poured through a hole in the ceiling, sunlight casting rainbows through the mist. To their right, a large stairway led upward while to their left, an opening led to a long passageway. More doors and smaller openings ringed the cavern.

Beside the waterfall's pool, two statues formed of a white marble that contrasted with the gray stone of the mountain stood on either side of the creek that cut across the cavern and down one of the branching tunnels. One of the statues was of a dragon with its wings outspread and its mouth open to show rows of teeth. Across the creek, a statue of a human woman, her rounded ears visible, stood with her eyes looking upward and a crown on her head.

Tora must have seen where Harm was staring because she smiled and gestured at the statues. "Our great-grandmother was a human."

"I don't remember if our great-grandsire commissioned that statue of her or if her village in the Human Realm made it." Taran halted next to his sister. "I should have paid more attention when our grandsire talked about our history."

"I know our great-grandsire stole that statue of

himself from her village. Our great-grandmother teased him relentlessly about it." Tora gave a little sigh as she gestured toward the dragon statue. "An epic romance, or so we've always been told."

"Flight Clawstone already had a history of respecting humans." Taran nodded toward the statues.

"But thanks to her, we've been rescuing humans even before the Wild Fae Primrose founded the Primrose League." Tora grinned up at the visage of her human ancestor.

"Doesn't make us the most popular Flight among the dragons. Or in the rest of the Fae Realm, for that matter." Taran shrugged, then turned back to them. "Many of those who work here at the eyrie have human ancestors. If you're considering settling down here in the Fae Realm, you'd be welcome here."

Harm cleared his throat before the twins could keep speaking. "Thanks for the offer, but I must return to the Human Realm. My father and brother are still in danger."

But if he arrived in the Human Realm only to discover that a hundred years had passed and his father and brother were long dead, then maybe he'd consider it.

Though, Val was a summer fae. She didn't like the cold. Perhaps the Court of Knowledge would be a better option for a backup plan.

"Understandable. Although, we should..." Tora trailed off, meeting her brother's gaze for a long, speaking moment.

After returning his sister's look, Taran gave a nod. "Yes, I think we should."

Footsteps echoed down one of the passageways before a *feeën* man with dark, nearly black hair threaded with gray and skin a few shades lighter than Val's but darker than the dragon twins' strode out of the passageway into the light of the cavern. The man bowed to Tora and Taran. "Welcome back."

"Have our parents returned from the Dragon Moot yet?" Taran glanced from the man to the large stairway.

"No, not yet." The *feeën* man's gaze swept past the dragons to focus on Harm, Val, and the mercenaries. "I see we have guests."

"Yes. Could you please prepare…" Tora glanced from Harm to Val. "How many rooms?"

"Six," Harm said at the same time Val said, "Seven."

Harm raised his eyebrows and held up his hand, the golden line glinting around his wrist. "We *are* married. For the first time this trip, it's actually proper by Tulpenlander standards for us to share a room."

Val sighed, her look disconcertingly flat. "And here I was looking forward to finally having a room to myself again."

Harm's stomach sank, and he hurried to add, "But if you don't want to, we don't have to. Not here and not in Tulpenland. It's actually common practice for the consort to have her own suite."

"Sounds like a good way for you to be assassinated." Val's smile broke through with an edge of something dangerous and almost flirtatious. "I'm not letting you out of my sight."

"Then the seventh room?" Harm lowered his voice to change the timbre to something flirtatious back.

"For Daisy. So she doesn't hog the bed."

"Good point." Harm rested a hand on her waist, tugging her closer.

"Ahem." The *feeën* man gave a cough.

Harm leapt back, his neck heating. He'd forgotten they had an audience.

With another polite cough, the *feeën* man led the way down one of the passageways, pointing out rooms for each of them. He showed them to the kitchen and eating area, which had large windows giving sweeping views of the snowy, mountainous landscape outside.

Val grabbed a few items of food that the cook—a smiling *feeën* woman with brown curls—set out for them. Then she all but dragged Harm to their bedchamber with its adjoining room for Daisy.

Once there, Harm sank onto the edge of the bed. He twisted his arm and looked at the bandage, a hint of red seeping into the fabric. With all the busyness, they hadn't had a chance to tend his sword slice properly yet.

Val's gaze dropped to his arm as well, her expression going hard. "Shirt off."

Harm grinned at her, making no move to comply. "That does seem a little excessive, doesn't it? It's my arm. You can tend it with my shirt on."

"Is that so?" Val sauntered across the room, halting before him. She cradled his face with both of her hands, tipped his head up, and met his gaze.

Harm rested his hands on her waist and tugged her

even closer. "Yes. It seems like it might be gratuitous shirtlessness."

Val raised an eyebrow at him, smirked, and leaned down to capture his mouth with hers.

Harm leaned into the kiss, losing himself in the feel and taste of her.

She pulled away a breath. "About the shirt…"

"Coming off." Harm closed the distance and kissed her again. His wound had waited this long. It could wait a little longer.

This time when she pulled away, she stepped out of his reach and crossed her arms. "Stop stalling."

Harm sighed and scrubbed a hand over his face to try to clear the kissing haze. Stalling was much more pleasant than letting her tend his wound.

Bracing himself, Harm untied the knot holding the bandage in place and peeled it off. The dried blood yanked at the gash, ripping open the scab and sending a fresh trickle of blood down his arm.

He worked his way out of the tatters of his shirt. As he discarded it, he grinned at the consternation wrinkling Val's forehead. "What? Did you forget I was wearing more layers than an onion?"

Val huffed and dug into her pocket. "Whatever."

Harm worked his way out of his leather jerkin, then his fae shirt, which sadly now had a rip and a blood-stained sleeve. Would the tailor in Tulpenwerf be willing to mend it?

Val assembled her medical supplies once again, including placing her pot in the fireplace to heat water she'd retrieved from the pitcher and basin on a stand by the door.

As Harm set aside his fae-made shirt, Val sat beside him on the bed and held out a vial with that familiar glowing green sludge. "Drink."

"It's just a scratch." Harm took the vial, swirling the potion for a moment. "Is a high-grade healing potion really necessary?"

"You don't know what monsters Diego has been killing lately." Val poked at his arm as she inspected the sword slice. "Even clean, his sword wouldn't have been sanitized."

Right. Harm shuddered, thinking of the rotting desert and slavering monsters. He popped the cork out of the vial and downed the potion.

Val retrieved the now boiling pot, set it on the floor next to the bed, and took her seat beside him again. "I really need to get my hands on more healing potions. Now hold still."

Harm gripped the edge of the mattress and resisted the urge to lean away from her. "Can we go back to kissing? I liked that a lot more."

"No." Val dipped a rag into the water by their feet, wrung it out, and set to work scrubbing his wound. "Do you want to get an infection? Lose the arm? Die a horrible death thanks to some disease you picked up from contaminated monster blood? We've already delayed far too long on properly tending this."

"Uh, no." Harm sighed and submitted to her ministrations.

Earlier that morning...

Harm perched on the boulder beside the fire and faced Val, trying to pretend his stomach wasn't churning, his chest tight. This had been his idea, after all. He shouldn't be the one getting cold feet, if that was what this was.

Tulpenland marriages were particularly binding. As, it seemed, were fae marriages. This wasn't something to be done on a whim, even if it was the best plan. They'd have to live with the consequences for the rest of their lives.

But this was Val. He couldn't imagine returning to the Human Realm without her at his side. She forced him to change and grow in a way no one else ever had.

He cleared his throat and pasted on a smile. "How does this whole fae marriage thing work?"

Val paced back and forth across what was left of their camp, as if triple-checking that they hadn't left anything behind. With a sigh, she whirled and marched toward him, her face far too expressionless for someone about to get married. "Are you sure you want to do this?"

Was he sure? He took a moment to turn the thought over in his mind, thinking through the results, the alternatives, the future he could have with her versus the one without her.

That decided it. "Yes, I am. Are you?"

Val's expression cracked, letting through just a hint

of something warmer, as she sat next to him and took his hand.

As soon as her fingers touched his, both of their hands glowed with a golden light.

Harm stared at the sight. He'd nearly jumped out of his skin when their hands had brushed for the first time after they'd gotten the cord off the night before. "Still not used to that."

Val held their hands up. "We have the start of a binding. Completing the marriage binding would be the wisest course. It's never a good idea to leave unfinished bindings hanging."

Harm lifted his other hand and brushed her cheek. "I didn't ask if it was wise." They both knew it probably wasn't, but wisdom had jumped out of the canal barge the moment he'd turned himself over to her in that tulip field. "I asked if you're sure. If you want this. We can come up with another plan."

"And miss my chance to secure every mercenary's dream and become immune to iron? Not a chance." Now a smirk fully banished the blank expression, her hand not holding his dropping to her dagger.

"Ah, yes. Marrying me for my immunity. I see how it is." Harm brushed his thumb over her cheek as he cradled her face. "So much more scope for stabbing in the future."

"Exactly, assuming Tulpenland doesn't turn out to be as dead boring as you make it out to be." Val fished in her magic pocket a moment before she produced a long leather string. "Ready to tie the knot?"

If it meant getting to adventure the rest of his life at this warrior woman's side, then absolutely.

Harm grinned and dropped his hand from her face to take one end of the string from her. "Ready to spend the rest of your life keeping me from getting assassinated?"

"What am I getting myself into?" Val rolled her eyes, but her smile remained soft.

She positioned the middle of the string between their clasped palms, then wrapped their clasped hands with her end of the string while he did the same with his. They each repeated the fae vow of pledging themselves to each other, then they tied the ends of the string in a knot above their clasped hands.

As soon as the knot tightened, the string gave a brilliant flash so bright that Harm closed his eyes. When he blinked them open, the string had vanished. Instead, a golden line glinted around each of their wrists.

He scrubbed at the golden line with his free hand. It didn't so much as smudge, nor did his skin feel any different. "Does this fade? Go away?"

"I'm afraid not." Val frowned at her hand. "I'd forgotten about that part. Mercenaries so rarely marry."

"I doubt Diego has forgotten. He's going to know exactly what this means." Harm tugged at the end of his sleeve. Perhaps he could hide the line under his shirt cuff—as long as he remembered not to let his wrist show—but Val's sleeves ended on her upper arms.

"Here. This might work." Val dug into her pocket again, fishing around for a long moment before she withdrew a leather bracer. "If I cut this in half, I can fashion leather cuffs. We can wear them under the threefold cord, as if to prevent chafing."

Harm nodded. "I did get rather bruised from the grain sprites. Why weren't we wearing something like this the whole time?"

"I didn't plan to be tied by that cord more than a few hours." Val shot him a sour look, as if that was all his fault. "Diego saw us at the faerie market, and he will probably notice the difference. Hopefully he'll assume I got them at the faerie market before setting out on the long walk to the Court of Stone. I probably would have, if I hadn't been so busy procuring clothes and a sword."

While she set to work cutting the bracer, Harm turned his back to her to move the knife from his ankle to his arm. While they'd discussed the plan—and she even had a hidden sheath fashioned for the knife—she had yet to see it nor had he come right out and confirmed he had it. Just in case Diego questioned her.

Once the knife was secure, he tugged the tattered human shirt he'd worn during the scuffle with the wolf over the fae jerkin and shirt, hiding the knife before he turned back to Val.

She held out what looked like a leather bracelet with strings to tie it on. "Try this."

He took it and fumbled to tie it on his wrist over the golden line. She reached over and tied it for him, then he did the same for her.

She pushed to her feet, glancing one last time at their campsite, nothing but sand and a ring of stones around the coals now that she'd packed up the tent. "I think that's everything."

"Not everything." Harm stood as well, resting his hands on her waist. "Tulpenland weddings are sealed with a kiss."

"Are they now?" Val tilted her head as she wrapped her arms around him. "Then I suppose we should make it official."

Harm didn't wait for more of an invitation than that.

Chapter Twenty-Four

The next morning, Harm sat beside Val at one of the tables in the eyrie's dining hall, the rest of the mercenaries gathered around them. Breakfast wasn't pancakes, but the eggs and sausages were hot and filling.

As they were finishing, Taran entered the room, followed by a man dressed in green and brown, an unstrung bow across his back and a quiver of arrows at his side.

The man swept his cloak behind him as he sat on the bench across from Harm and Val, immediately claiming a plate of sausage and eggs.

Harm dropped his fork on his plate. "You're the stranger who gave me the flower at the faerie market."

Val rested her hand on the hilt of her dagger. "Are you the Primrose? I thought he was a fae."

Chewing a bite of the sausage, the man's gaze swept over Val in an assessing way. "I'm the Primrose's right-hand man, you might say."

"Then what are you doing here? Your League is well on its way to escorting my husband and me home." Val emphasized the word *husband*, as if she still resented that the dragons had nearly carried him off.

The man sliced off a bite of egg, popped it in his mouth, then waved his fork at Harm. "You're bringing these mercenaries back to the Human Realm."

"Yes." Harm resisted the urge to squirm under the man's gaze.

The man didn't cut all that much of an imposing figure with his stature that was several inches shorter than Harm's. But there was a confidence to his gaze and the way he carried his weapons. "And you truly believe your wife and her mercenaries will be no threat to humans?"

"I trust Val to keep them in line." Harm held the man's gaze without flinching.

The man gave Val one last, searching look before he nodded. "Then I have a proposal I wish to discuss with the two of you. The Primrose League is always looking for allies in the Human Realm, both to fight off incursions by rogue fae and to provide an end point for our network here in the Fae Realm. It isn't always safe or possible to return the rescued humans through the same faerie circle through which they were taken. Thus the need for people in the Human Realm to do the work of helping those who have been rescued to either return home safely or establish a new home elsewhere."

Harm leaned his elbows on the table as he considered, acceptance already on the tip of his tongue. After his experiences in the Fae Realm, he couldn't turn his back on others who'd been taken. Especially those who hadn't had the good fortune to have someone like Val fall in love with them.

Instead, he forced himself to voice the more practical consideration. "While I would accept, I'm afraid Tulpenland isn't very tied to the Fae Realm. The occasional faerie circle only appears in the spring when the tulips are blooming. We wouldn't be a very effective ally."

"You could still help our other allies by sending aid to fight off rogue fae or to provide a safe and peaceful home for rescued humans." The human man swirled a bit of egg through the running yolk as he flicked a glance from Val to Harm. "However, I think Tulpenland will be more tied to the Fae Realm than it has been before. You're taking six fae back with you. More, you will someday put a fae on the throne as your duchess."

Right. If his blood could hold such sway over the duchy that Diego would go to great lengths to claim it, then putting Val on the throne as his wife would also have consequences for Tulpenland's interactions with the Fae Realm.

Assuming Tulpenland still wanted him as their duke once he presented his *feeën* bride.

Even then, having *feeën* living in Tulpenland would still tie the land to the Fae Realm in a way it hadn't been before.

"I hadn't considered that." Harm scratched at his beard. "Good thing I'll have six former fae mercenaries to guard the duchy."

At his side, Val flexed her fingers on her dagger,

though she didn't join the conversation. Perhaps she felt this decision should be his.

"There's some risk to you and your duchy. Should your identity as part of the Primrose League become known, the more unscrupulous fae will attempt to harm you. And there may be times when the Primrose's agent is followed to your duchy when they bring a rescued human to you." The man grimaced, his hand dropping to his quiver. "That's not even taking into account the increased fae incursions due both to your ties to the Fae Realm and the additional travel back and forth through the circles."

"Fae incursions and assassination attempts are things we can handle." Val patted the hilt of her dagger, her tone almost too pleased. When Harm looked at her, she shot him a smirk. "This sounds a whole lot more fun than the boring Tulpenland you were describing."

"Then for the good of my marriage, I suppose I should accept." Harm grinned, clasped Val's hand, and lifted it to kiss her knuckles. Then he turned back to the Primrose's right-hand man, who was polishing off his breakfast with astonishing speed. "Yes, we're willing to help the Primrose League any way we can."

"Very good. Someone will be in contact soon." The man pushed to his feet, nodded to each of them, and turned to leave. Taran fell into step with him, the two of them talking quietly as they went.

Tora plopped into the seat the stranger had vacated and smiled. "So. You're joining the Primrose League."

"Looks like it." Harm smiled back. The expression faded after a moment. "I couldn't do otherwise. I just hope Tulpenland is accommodating of the changes I'll have to make."

"They'll come around one way or the other." Val's smirk was sharp as she caressed the hilt of her dagger.

"I don't think threatening people will make them more accommodating." Harm bumped their clasped hands against her knee. "We'll start with charm and patience."

"That'll be your job then. I'll save the stabbing for those who aren't won over." Val leaned her shoulder into his.

Tora pointed at Val but focused on Harm. "Are you sure you want to unleash her on your innocent duchy?"

"Yes." Harm squeezed Val's hand.

"Then we'll leave just after lunch to bring you to the Human Realm." Tora gestured from them to the rest of the mercenaries. "We'll take the Anywhere Door to the Court of Knowledge, then we'll have to fly to the Court of Dreams. I'm afraid we need to return to the same faerie circle you came through, and we don't want Queen Mab to know what we're doing."

Harm nodded. If they didn't fly over the faerie queen's arbor palace, they should escape notice.

"Since we're leaving, I'd like to bargain for as many healing potions as you can get your hands on." Val withdrew her hand from Harm's before she leaned both elbows on the table, facing Tora.

"Healing potions?" Harm eyed her.

"Yes, healing potions. Knowing you—and given the danger you're bringing on yourself by joining the Primrose League—you'll need them." Val raised her eyebrows at him before she focused on Tora again.

Tora's blue eyes had sharpened at the mention of a bargain. "What will you give me for the healing potions?"

Val pointed at Harm. "All of the pottery dishes my husband has in his magical pocket."

Harm must have started or made some kind of noise for Val turned to him. "It isn't like we'll need to make more bargains. The Primrose League is taking us right to the faerie circle tonight."

"That's true." Harm reached into his magical pocket and withdrew one of the pottery plates. Besides, he wouldn't mind acquiring more healing potions, and not just for himself. Val was the one who'd be throwing herself into danger, and he'd prefer they had magic on hand in case she got hurt.

At the sight of the pottery, Tora's nostrils flared, and her eyes gleamed with something almost feral. She snatched the plate from him, holding it up as she inspected it.

Harm dug into his pocket, taking out three more plates, three teacups, and the only teapot he'd brought and somehow hadn't broken through his travels. With each new item, that gleam in Tora's gaze grew.

As Tora reached for another item, Val smacked her hand. "Not without the bargain."

Tora's nostrils flared again, and a thin wisp of smoke wafted out.

Harm's stomach dropped, and he reached into his

pocket again, this time for his sword. Was Tora about to go all dragon on them?

Then Tora's gaze cleared, and she nodded. "Very well. I will collect as many healing potions as I can get my hands on before you leave in trade for these items."

As she spoke, Taran returned to the room. He halted next to Tora and sighed. "What's all this?"

"A bargain." That sharp glint returned to Tora's smile. "I hadn't decided on an item to hoard yet. I'm thinking pretty pottery. It calls to me."

Taran sighed and turned to Harm and Val. "I hope you know what you've done. Once a dragon decides what they'll hoard, they'll be obsessed with that item for life."

"I know." Val's smile was almost as sharp as Tora's. "I've been told Harm's kingdom has plenty more of that pottery, and I'm sure we'll need more healing potions eventually. Tora, you'll always be welcome to bargain for more fancy pottery if you bring healing potions."

Harm turned to his wife, gaping at her. Though, he shouldn't have been surprised. She was a *fee*. Setting up future bargains was in her nature.

Then again, such a propensity for bargains would serve her well in Tulpenland.

Harm swept a glance from her to the other five mercenaries sitting at a nearby table. Even when he returned home, life would never be the same.

But that wasn't a bad thing. His life back home in Tulpenland could use a little good adventure instead of mere keeping up appearances.

Chapter Twenty-Five

Moonlight bathed the canal, brick road, and brick buildings as Val, Harm, and her mercenaries stood in the shadows of an alley, peering toward the Tulpenland palace. Guards patrolled the street outside while a few of the windows remained lit, even at this time of night.

Val's stomach churned as she faced that picturesque street. She'd stepped into a world unlike anything she'd known before. Her life would change irrevocably.

Sure, she'd been in the Human Realm before. But usually only briefly when retrieving a captured human or on a Wild Hunt raid. She'd never stayed long.

Was this how Harm had felt when stepping through the faerie circle at her side the first time?

No, he would've been far more nervous. The life that waited for her on the other side might be new, but it would be good. There would be difficulties. There might be cruelties as some among the Tulpenland court refused to accept her. But it wouldn't be a fate of torture and death that Harm had faced back then.

She was a mercenary of the Wild Hunt. Surely she could face her new future with as much courage as Harm had.

Harm started forward. "I suppose I'll just march up to the guards and announce who I am. You can wait here until I signal it's all right."

Val caught his arm before he could leave the shadows. "Wait. Those guards might not recognize you."

They'd yet to determine how much time had passed here in the Human Realm. Harm had commented that things hadn't seemed to have changed all that much since he left, so surely it hadn't been hundreds of years. But they couldn't narrow it down more than that.

Harm turned back to her, his grimace tugging at the beard he'd yet to trim. "What do you suggest?"

"We should sneak through the gardens and go in through a window at the back." Val pointed in that direction. "Then we'll find your father. Surely he will recognize you."

"I think he might still be awake." Harm pointed toward one of the lit windows on the ground floor. "That's his study there."

"That will make things easier." Val motioned to her mercenaries. There was no need to give them more instructions.

She led the way through the shadows along the canal, then down an alley, until they reached a street along the back of the palace. Here, gardens stretched along the building's back and side. They weren't extensive, but they featured enough hedges and statuary to provide some cover.

The gardens were lit by moonlight and the occasional lantern while guards patrolled here, too. But their discipline seemed lax, and they barely even glanced at the shadows as they marched by.

Something Val would change as soon as Harm was restored to his position as heir of Tulpenland. She couldn't allow the guards to remain this unobservant.

Val crept through the darkness beside the hedges until she reached the even deeper shadows beside the back of the palace. Once there, Grutte worked his way along the building, testing each window until he found one that was unlocked. Then he boosted each of them inside, including Daisy and Acurru, before four of them hauled him inside after them.

Harm pointed down the hallway, and Val set off in that direction, pausing at each intersecting corridor to check that it was clear before continuing.

As they reached the hall before the duke's study, Val halted and peeked around the corner.

Two men stood before a door. They wore breastplates, helmets with plumes, and each carried a pike.

Val withdrew around the corner and murmured into Harm's ear, "There are two men guarding your father's study. Will these guards recognize you?"

Harm peeked around the corner and dodged back so fast he nearly smacked her chin with his head. He bent his head to whisper, "No. Those aren't even Tulpenland guards. I don't know what has been going on here, but those men are wearing King Hendrik's colors."

"Then do we have your permission to take them out?" Val dropped her hand to her dagger. Now this might be fun.

"Yes. Though do it quietly. And if you could refrain from killing them, that would be appreciated. It might be handy to question them." Harm pressed his back to the wall, as if getting himself out of the way.

Val motioned. "Grutte. Take them out. Don't kill them."

Grutte grinned and stalked around the corner. There was a stifled "Wha—" and two ringing *whacks*. The thuds of two heavy objects hitting the floor resounded down the corridor.

"All clear." After handing Daisy's leash to Jesenia, Val strode around the corner without looking first. She trusted Grutte to have handled it.

Besides, if he had been the one falling to the floor, the thump would have been *much* louder.

Harm followed so closely behind her that he trod on her heels. But she couldn't blame him for his eagerness. If she'd had a chance to return to her family, she would've run to them.

As they approached the door, Harm lunged past her, reaching for the doorknob. Val held out an arm, stopping him. She shook her head, then squeezed between him and the door. There might be more guards stationed inside the room.

Harm grimaced and took a step back to give her more room.

Val cracked the door open and peeked inside.

A large desk sat facing the broad windows, a lamp

flickering where it sat on the corner and splashing patterns onto the dark windows beyond. A man sat at the desk, his shoulders slumped, his head resting on his arms so that all she could see was his gray hair. He appeared to have fallen asleep.

She eased her stance to peer through the crack at different angles, trying to see if there was anyone else in the room. She couldn't see anyone, but someone could be lurking in a corner that she couldn't view from the door.

With a swift move, she whipped the door open, stepped inside, and placed her back to the wall next to the door. She scanned the room, searching the shadows. Unless there was a fae here behind an exceptionally powerful glamour, the room was empty except for the sleeping man at the desk.

She motioned for Harm to enter.

Harm rushed to the sleeping man's side and placed a hand on his shoulder, giving the man a gentle shake. "Father. Father, wake up."

The man stirred and lifted his head. He blinked and scrubbed a hand over his face, not yet looking up as he mumbled, "I'll seek my rest soon, Stijn."

"It's me. Harm." Harm gave his father's shoulder another small shake.

His father lifted his head, still blinking, first with bleariness, then with befuddlement, as if he couldn't comprehend what—or whom—he was seeing. "Harm?"

"Yes, it's me. I'm home." Harm's smile was caught somewhere between joy and apprehension.

"Harm!" His father finally shot to his feet, though he just stood there, gaping.

Harm stepped forward and embraced his father. For a moment, his father remained frozen, as if he wasn't sure what to do. Then, he wrapped his arms around his son, holding tight for a long moment.

Val remained where she was in the shadows next to the door. Harm's father hadn't turned around and had yet to see her. She'd keep it that way as long as possible. She wasn't sure how he'd react to seeing the fae he'd last seen hauling his son away, nor did she want to intrude on this reunion.

The man's shoulders shook as he murmured, "You're home. After all this time. I thought you must be dead."

Harm stiffened, his already pale face going even more white, and pushed away from his father's embrace. "How long has it been?"

Val hadn't gotten a good look at Duke Johannes—now or on that night when she'd taken Harm away—but his hair was all gray. His clothes hung on him while the glimpse she'd gotten of the side of his face showed deep lines in his forehead and dark bruises beneath his eyes.

"Five years. You've been gone for five years." The man's shoulders remained slumped and shaking as he gripped Harm's upper arms as if Harm's steadiness was the only thing keeping him upright.

"Five years?" Harm rested a hand behind him on the desk. At this rate, Val would have to intervene before everyone ended up in a heap on the floor.

Her heart ached, seeing how much time Harm had

lost in the Human Realm. Sure, it wasn't as much as they'd feared, but it was still far too long.

"Where's Gijs? He was healed, right?" Harm gripped his father's arms.

Val held her breath, a strange twisting filling her stomach. Gijs was the reason Harm had ended up in the Fae Realm, and the danger to Gijs and his father had been Harm's motivation to keep pushing forward. If something had happened to Gijs because she hadn't been able to return Harm quickly enough…would he forgive her? Or would he forever blame her for the captivity that had cost him his brother?

Duke Johannes collapsed into the chair again, weariness in every line of his face and posture. "The fae potion healed him, but within days King Hendrik's men kidnapped him from the palace. He's been held hostage ever since, a pawn to force me to be King Hendrik's vassal."

Harm swayed, then sat on the edge of the desk, bracing himself against it.

Val gritted her teeth, resting her hand on her dagger again. After everything Harm had gone through to protect his little brother, Gijs had been held captive as surely as Harm had been. Worse, his captivity had been for five whole years instead of the mere weeks Harm had been in the Fae Realm.

She pushed out of the shadows. "We'll rescue him, Harm."

Duke Johannes leapt out of the chair again with such force that the chair tipped over and fell to the floor with a sharp crack. He fumbled to draw the thin rapier sheathed at his waist even as he whirled. The sword's sheath whacked into the desk, jerking the sword's hilt out of his hand before he even got it partway out.

Well, that explained a lot about Harm's lack of sword skills. She could see where he got it from.

Harm snagged his father's wrist before he could reach for his sword again. "Father, I'd like to introduce you to my wife, Valeria of the Fae Realm."

"Your…but isn't she…" Harm's father swayed, as if to collapse into his chair again. He must have realized at the last moment that his chair lay on its back on the floor because he stumbled back a step to lean against the desk beside Harm.

"Yes, she's the *fee* who took me away. But everything's fine now. We fell in love and decided to get married." Harm straightened, that more confident edge he'd gained in the Fae Realm returning. "It's a long story. I'll tell it to you later. Right now, we need to leave to rescue Gijs."

"We?" Duke Johannes sounded even more overwhelmed.

As if taking that as their cue, Abelardo, Chela, Ignatius, and Jesenia peered around the doorframe. Daisy and Acurru squiggled between their legs while Grutte loomed over their heads.

Duke Johannes gave a wheeze as he collapsed even more fully against the desk.

"My wife brought a few friends along. These are her Wild Hunt. They're harmless, except to her enemies, and thus my enemies." Harm met Val's gaze and something of his grin returned to his face, though more sharp-edged and dangerous than anything she'd yet seen. "Are you up for another adventure?"

"Always. Especially one with a high probability of stabbing." Val grinned back and drummed her fingers on the hilt of her dagger. "And you promised me a quiet, boring life here in Tulpenland."

"Are you disappointed?"

"Not in the least." Val's grin hurt her face, her muscles unused to holding such an expression. But it felt strangely right, as if here in the Human Realm she was finally free to once again experience a full range of emotions.

Ignatius shouldered his way past the others. "Just point us in the direction of King Hendrik's castle, and we'll have your brother rescued before that dastardly king knows what hit him."

"Don't you mean *who* hit him?" Chela pointed over her shoulder at Grutte.

"I am Grutte." Grutte grinned and gave a small, friendly wave to Harm's father.

The wave did nothing to ease the white, about-to-pass-out look. Duke Johannes braced himself on the desk as if about to collapse.

"I'll commandeer one of the ships in the harbor. I'm assuming King Hendrik hasn't forced you to disband our navy yet?" Harm rested a hand on his father's shoulder.

"No…" Duke Johannes spoke as if in a trance. "But most of them have been recalled to port."

"Even better. I'll have my pick of ships." Harm patted his leather jerkin over his magical pocket. "As soon as I leave, you can kick out King Hendrik's men and take back Tulpenland. With a fast ship, we'll have Gijs rescued and be on our way home before word can reach King Hendrik."

Duke Johannes blinked yet again and shook himself, as if finally sloughing off the paralysis of the shocks he'd faced that night. His shoulders straightened as the weariness disappeared behind a hardness that was mirrored on Harm's face. "Yes, I can do it tonight. I've been preparing for this for years, gathering those still loyal to me. We'll have Tulpenland free by morning."

"Good. Then we'll be on our way. Hopefully the tide is in our favor so we can sneak a ship out under the cover of darkness." Harm started to cross the room.

Duke Johannes caught his arm. "You should know, I just received word that Gijs will soon marry King Hendrik's daughter. The wedding is less than two weeks away. I suspect that he plans to kill me as soon as my heir is safely married to his, effectively joining our lands under his control."

"With plans to kill off Gijs as soon as an heir is born, no doubt." Harm ground the words between his teeth. "Don't worry. We'll get there long before this planned wedding."

Val retrieved Daisy's leash from Jesenia, strolled across the room, and held it out to Harm's father. "Could you look after Daisy while we're gone? She's better for fighting monsters than sneaking, and she takes to ships even worse than she does to dragon flights."

Harm grimaced and motioned from his father to

Daisy. "Yes, Daisy can definitely stay here. Don't be alarmed, Father, if she occasionally has three heads. Just set her loose in the cellars, and she'll have the rodent problem cleared out in no time."

"Three heads…" Duke Johannes had that faint look to him again as he took the leash.

Val focused on Daisy and pointed at Harm's father. "Daisy, guard."

Daisy walked up to Duke Johannes and sat on his foot looking outward, her ears pricked and alert.

"Can you watch my snails too? They eat seaweed and leafy greens. Thanks." Ignatius shoved the crate with the snails at Duke Johannes.

"I…uh…" Harm's father grabbed the crate's handle with his free hand, gaping down at both the giant snails and the dog sitting on his foot.

"Does Acurru need to stay here too?" Harm eyed the dragon twining around Abelardo's legs.

Duke Johannes followed his son's gaze, then his eyes bugged. "Is that…"

"No. Since we won't have Daisy, Acurru will be our scent dragon." Abelardo bent down and picked up the dragon, stroking a hand down his head, long neck, and back. The dragon gave a growling purr. "While he's not quite as good as Daisy, if Acurru can smell something with your brother's scent, he'll be able to locate him inside a whole castle within minutes."

"That'll save us time." Harm nodded and strode to Val's side before he glanced over his shoulder at his father. "Is there something belonging to Gijs still here?"

"His room has remained untouched. There should

be something in there." Duke Johannes never lifted his gawking gaze from the dragon.

"Good." Harm reached down and clasped Val's hand. "Ready to stage a rescue?"

A rescue. Not a kidnapping. Not an assassination. Not a package delivery where the package happened to be a human she was taking to captivity and cruelty.

Once she would have considered something like this none of her business. She would have stayed out of it, unfeeling toward the young man's situation.

Being good and caring about other people wasn't so bad. Sure, it meant she needed to get involved and go out of her way to help. But at least that wasn't boring. Her life would be filled both with excitement and with actual meaning.

Val smiled at Harm and patted her dagger with her free hand. "More than ready."

Chapter Twenty-Six

Harm lit the last candle along the broad throne room and stepped around the guard sprawled on the floor.

While thoroughly bound and gagged, the man was still out after the little tap Grutte had given him. The poor man could probably use a fae healing potion for the head injury he had likely sustained. Harm resisted a wince. He didn't want to hurt the soldiers, who were just doing their job and loyally serving their king, but a few injuries couldn't be helped.

With the candles he'd lit casting orange light and deeper shadows across the room, Harm marched to the throne at the far end and perched on it.

Nope, too stiff. He slouched. No, now that was too low-class instead of powerful.

He swiveled on the throne and threw one leg over the armrest, attempting a languid sprawl.

If only he could ask Val for a second opinion. But she was somewhere in this castle with Abelardo and

Jesenia, retrieving Gijs. Ignatius, Grutte, and Chela were fetching King Hendrik.

That left Harm with the one job of lighting the candles and sitting on the throne looking powerful. He wore his *feeën* clothing, including the leather jerkin and mended shirt, with the *feeën* sword buckled at his waist.

The door gave a creak as it began to swing inward. He had just enough time to adjust his expression to something hard, leaning an elbow on the armrest in what he hoped was a confident sprawl, before the door opened the rest of the way.

Grutte had King Hendrik by the back of his night-shirt, the garment hiked to his knees as he was marched forward. It seemed the *fee* hadn't given him the chance to grab his dressing gown—or perhaps they hadn't known such a thing would be considered a courtesy.

Oh, well. Harm didn't mind that they'd denied King Hendrik that little scrap of dignity. King Hendrik certainly hadn't cared about such things when he'd bargained with Diego for the fae poison and Harm's captivity. And who knew what he'd done to Gijs in the last five years, even beyond taking him away from the one family member he'd had left.

Chela and Ignatius marched on either side of Grutte, their weapons still out. The door swung shut with a heavy *thunk* behind them.

King Hendrik's gaze lifted to the throne a moment before his face paled.

"Surprised to see me?" Harm smirked, the expression sharp-edged. "After you bargained with a *fee* to ensure I was taken into their realm, never to be seen again."

"That fae played me false," King Hendrik growled as he tried to wrench out of Grutte's grasp. He didn't manage it and instead flailed like a hooked fish. "First that brat recovers, and I have to come up with a new plan. Now you somehow return from what should have been certain death."

"He was a fae. What else did you expect?" Harm raised his eyebrows, trying to mirror Val's unimpressed look. "And before you get any ideas about bargaining with that fae again, he's dead. I witnessed his death myself."

"How inconvenient." King Hendrik tried to reach over his shoulder to pry at Grutte's hand. "Will you order your lackey to release me? Or will you continue to treat me with such disregard? I fear that will not win you any favors in our negotiations."

"No, I won't order him to release you. First, because he isn't *my* lackey. Second, these aren't negotiations." Harm tried to put a deeper growl to his voice. "This is quite hostile. I will make demands, and you will comply. Or else these lackeys will do worse than merely abduct you from your bedchamber."

Grutte lifted King Hendrik slightly higher off the ground, and the king made a choking noise.

He was still choking and clawing at his throat as the door creaked again.

This time, Val marched inside. She met Harm's gaze and gave a nod before she stepped aside, holding the door open for the person behind her.

A young man crept after her, carrying an orange-and-white dog. The young man's hair was a sandy blonde slightly darker than Harm's while his eyes were the same blue as their father's.

Gijs and his dog Vlek.

Harm gripped the throne's armrest, his stomach churning. Despite being told five years had passed, Harm had still envisioned his brother as the fifteen-year-old boy he'd been when Harm had left. He'd seen the changes in his father. But the gray hair and weary lines could have been chalked up to the grief he'd suffered. Seeing Gijs as a fully grown man hit the reality home with far more force.

Gijs halted, gaping. "Harm?"

Harm would have leapt up and embraced his brother, but he had to maintain his intimidating pose for a few more minutes.

A young woman with golden-blonde hair followed behind Gijs, one hand gripping Gijs by the arm and the other clutching the handles of a carpet bag. Jesenia and Abelardo followed her with Acurru perched on Abelardo's shoulder.

Grutte set King Hendrik back onto his tiptoes, and the king twisted around, trying to get a glimpse of the newcomers. His face was suffused red from the choking, but somehow it turned even more mottled. "Saskia?"

The young woman raised her chin. "Father."

Harm met Val's gaze across the length of the throne room. Val gave a shrug and a wry smile.

King Hendrik whirled to glare at Harm. "So this is

your plan. Kidnap my daughter in retaliation for kidnapping your brother."

"I'm not being kidnapped. I'm going willingly, Father." Saskia stepped even closer to Gijs. "What you have done to Gijs in holding him captive and threatening his father these past five years is wrong. More than that, I love him, Father. Because I love him, I want what is best for him. I'm going with him to Tulpenland where he will be free."

"But you will be a captive! Don't you see? He's just using you! They're all using you." King Hendrik clawed at Grutte again. He might as well have been trying to move a boulder uphill.

Val crossed her arms and glared at King Hendrik. "No one is being taken against their will or hauled off to captivity. We don't do that."

At least not anymore. Harm worked to suppress his proud smile.

"Who are you?" King Hendrik's sneer curled his mouth. As if he had any right to sneer at anyone, held by the scruff with his nightshirt hiking up his thighs.

Harm couldn't resist any longer. He let the swelling pride break into a smile across his face and fill his voice. "King Hendrik, I don't believe you've met my wife."

"Your...wife?" King Hendrik made that choking noise again, even though Grutte wasn't hoisting him off his feet. "She's..."

"A *fee*. Yes." Harm gestured to the other five *feeën*. "And this is her Wild Hunt. She will be calling them off. Or not."

"Don't you control your wife?" King Hendrik spat the words.

And he wondered why his daughter was running off with Gijs back to Tulpenland rather than stay here.

"We're allies. I don't *control* her. Instead, I'm honored that she fights at my side, as I will fight at hers." Harm would like to see the man who would try to control Val.

Oh, wait, he had. That man's body was rotting in the Realm of Monsters. Or, perhaps, consumed by the Realm of Monsters, if that realm ate bodies the way the Fae Realm did.

Saskia leaned closer to Gijs, whispering something to him that had both of them smiling as they gazed into each other's eyes.

King Hendrik snorted. "I won't even have to do anything to your kingdom. I can just sit back and watch it fall apart. Your people will never accept a *fee* as a duchess. Nor will they allow such...attitudes. Your kingdom will dissolve into chaos and ruin. Once it finishes burning, I will step in to take it."

Perhaps it would. Maybe Harm would find himself tossed out and Gijs put on the throne. But he wasn't going to debate King Hendrik about it.

Harm met Val's gaze again, and she tipped her head to Jesenia.

Jesenia grinned and opened the door. A wrinkle appeared on her brow, the only indication she gave of her concentration.

Moments later, rank after rank of *feeën* warriors dressed in leather and festooned with weapons marched into the room and arranged themselves along the walls in the shadows, which would keep their faces indistinct.

Considering they were merely a glamour created by Jesenia, that was for the best. She was particularly skilled at glamour, but creating an army of people was difficult. It wouldn't fool a *fee*. Luckily, the only *feeën* in the room were on Harm's side.

With the army of glamoured warriors to add weight to her words, Val sauntered closer to King Hendrik, whipped out her knife, and pressed it to the man's throat. "Listen well, *Your Majesty*. My husband might be inclined to grant you and your pathetic kingdom mercy, but I am not. So don't push me. We will be leaving, and you won't stop us. If you try to hurt my husband, his brother, his father, or his duchy again, I will return, and I will kill you. If you try to negotiate with a fae again, I will find out, and I will kill you. If you send your army to invade Tulpenland…"

"You'll kill me." King Hendrik's tone didn't waver, but he couldn't hide his gulp, which bobbed his throat against Grutte's tight grip.

"Glad we understand each other." Val tapped King Hendrik's chin with the flat of her blade.

How Harm wanted to march across the room and kiss her. He shouldn't be this attracted to her as she was threatening his enemy with death, but she was particularly gorgeous when she went all deadly and dangerous. Especially now that she was no longer threatening him with her knife.

But kissing would have to wait until they were safely

back on board the Tulpenlander ship anchored in a bay up the coast.

Right now, it was time to wrap this up and get out of here before King Hendrik realized there were only seven of them—well seven plus Gijs, Saskia, Vlek, and a mini dragon—and called out his entire army and navy to go after them.

Val leaned in even closer and whispered something into King Hendrik's ear that had the king turning white as his nightshirt. She stepped away, waving a contemptuous hand at the king. "Ignatius, bind him."

That was Harm's cue. Val had deemed King Hendrik sufficiently intimidated, and it was time to leave.

Harm pushed off the throne and did his best to saunter down the length of the throne room. He halted at Val's side, resisting the urge to pull her in close for that kiss.

As soon as King Hendrik was bound, gagged, and dumped in the shadows beneath one of the long drapes where it would take his guards a while to find him, the rest of them hustled from the room. Jesenia directed her glamour warriors to march out the door, only dissipating them once they were out of sight of the king, should he manage to peer past both the blindfold and the drapes. Abelardo had Acurru fly around the room and snuff all the candles so that the throne room was plunged into darkness once again.

Within minutes, they had crept through the castle, out the postern gate, and into the shrouding night.

Gijs halted and turned, still holding Vlek in both arms. "Harm, is that really you? I thought…you were…"

"I'm fine. Really." Harm stepped forward and slung an arm around his brother's shoulders, careful not to squish the dog. "But look at you. You're all grown up."

"You haven't changed a bit." Gijs was still gaping, his shoulders hunched as if he wasn't sure what to do with Harm's half-hug.

"It was only a little over two weeks for me. Time moves differently in the Fae Realm." Harm released his brother. "We came to save you from a wedding, but it seems that isn't necessary."

"No, it isn't." Gijs edged closer to Saskia, sharing a smile with her. "Over the past five years, Saskia and I fell in love. We were actually sneaking out to run away together when your...*fee* found us."

He'd hesitated, as if he wasn't quite sure what to call Val.

Val raised her eyebrows, even as she gave Harm a gentle shove. "It was quite convenient they were already packed and ready to leave. Which is what we should be doing."

Harm resumed walking, and after a moment, Gijs and Saskia fell into step with the group, even if they kept eyeing the *feeën* around them.

After a moment of silence, Gijs cast a glance from Val to Harm. "Wife? But you said you'd only been in the Fae Realm for two weeks?"

"It's a long story. Things are different in the Fae Realm." Harm wasn't sure he could explain it. For some reason, marrying Val after knowing her only two weeks seemed like a perfectly normal thing to do in the Fae Realm.

Yet now that he was in the Human Realm, he didn't regret it one bit.

"We fell in love, and we decided to return to the Human Realm together." Harm reached for Val's hand, his heart lifting when she clasped his. "Just to warn you, I plan to abdicate my position as heir to you if Tulpenland isn't ready for a *feeën* duchess just yet."

Gijs sighed. "And here I thought I'd finally been released from that. But you might be surprised. After nearly getting subsumed into Suskeny, Tulpenland might be willing to take any alternative, especially since I intend to marry Saskia. Someday, she will be the queen of Suskeny, and I will be her consort. If I'm also heir to Tulpenland, that will mean Tulpenland and Suskeny would be united, as King Hendrik wished. If a *feeën* duchess is the price of their continued independence, Tulpenland will accept her gladly."

Harm studied the stranger who was his brother. "When did you get to be so wise and diplomatically canny?"

"I've done a lot of growing up in the past five years." Gijs grinned with a wry tilt to his mouth. "I'm not the only one who has changed. You're..."

"Less staid and stuffy?" Harm swung the hand he had clasped with Val's.

"I was going to say more...sharp-edged? Dangerous? Wild, even. And not just because of the *feeën* around you." Gijs gestured from Val to the others. "A bit *feeën*-mad, perhaps."

Harm just shrugged. If he went down in history as Duke Harmen the *Feeën*-Mad, he could live with that.

As long as it meant he was free to be genuine as he fought to help others, then he didn't care what he was called.

"Oh, good. Then all my hard work in training you has made a difference." Val bumped into Harm with her shoulder. "I wasn't sure for a while there if it would stick."

"Yes, the whole wolf incident didn't inspire confidence." Harm lowered his voice so that his words were only for her.

"No. Nor did the screeching as I tended your scratches." Val raised her eyebrows, her smirk definitely flirtatious.

"They were far more than mere scratches." Harm leaned closer to her. "And I wasn't screeching."

Val made an unimpressed humming noise in the back of her throat.

Gijs smirked and hurried to fall into step with Saskia. She wrapped her hands around his arm again, giving a small laugh when Vlek licked her face.

Harm would have to get used to having a brother so close to his own age instead of a decade younger. The Fae Realm might have stolen five years, but perhaps it had given him what could be a closer relationship with his brother.

His hand in Val's, Harm slowed his pace still further until the two of them were trailing behind the others. "Do I want to know what you whispered to King Hendrik there at the end?"

"Probably not." Val's mouth pressed into a line, as if she wasn't repentant but thought she should be. "I just reminded him that we'll have his daughter in our care the way Gijs was in his for the past five years. Sure, we won't harm her or use her that way, but King Hendrik doesn't know that."

No, he didn't. He'd likely assume she was being used as a hostage, given that was the way he thought and acted.

"As long as the threat leaves Gijs and Saskia free to live their lives happily, I don't mind." Harm shot a glance to the others, but no one seemed to have noticed yet that he and Val were lagging behind. Harm leaned his head closer to Val's, murmuring, "Have I told you lately how much I love it when you're being all deadly?"

"Yes, but I don't mind hearing it again." Val halted, tipping her face up toward him.

There was no reason to hold back now. Harm lifted his hand to cradle the side of Val's face, the moonlight trailing blue and silver highlights in her hair. "Will you stab me if I kiss you?"

"I'll stab you if you *don't* kiss me." Val's dark eyes sparkled as she released his hand, only to clasp her hands in the collar of his shirt, tugging him closer.

"In that case..." Harm pressed his mouth to hers, gently cradling her close even as a fire lit deep inside him.

When he'd stepped into the Fae Realm, he'd expected cruelty and torment. He'd never imagined he'd fall in love, especially not with the prickly *feeën* warrior woman who had hauled him through the realm with a magical tether.

But he couldn't imagine returning to Tulpenland with anyone else at his side.

When the two of them finally pulled back a hair's breadth from each other, Val murmured against his cheek, "We should keep moving. King Hendrik's men might come after us at any moment."

"I suppose." Harm pressed little kisses to her nose.

"And you promised me all the cheese and cassis I could eat and drink." Val swayed slightly farther away from him, though she didn't let go of her grip on his collar.

"Don't forget the stroopwafels, pancakes, and oliebollen." Harm trailed his fingers through her hair, reluctant to let her go to keep walking.

"Of course not." Val stepped out of his reach, giving him that eyebrow look, before she turned her back and kept walking. "Besides, your father has been left with Daisy and a crate full of giant snails for a week now. We really ought to rescue him."

That might as well have been a bucket of sea water tossed over his head. Harm hurried to catch up with her. "Right. We'd better rescue him before Daisy destroys the entire palace."

They couldn't return to Tulpenland soon enough.

"Come on!" Harm tugged Val down the palace steps and onto the brick street beside the canal. At their feet, Vlek and Daisy bounded on their leashes. The dogs had become inseparable, and Harm was beginning to wonder what their puppies might look like. Although, he wasn't sure Tulpenland was ready for even more sometimes-three-headed dogs running around.

"Are these pancakes really that much better than the ones the palace serves?" Val shook her head at him, even as she hurried to keep up with his long strides. She wore her *feeën* leathers, causing more than a few people to stop and gape.

Though if they had negative comments, they didn't voice them. If that was because of Harm's presence or because Val sported enough weapons to take on a small army, including a sword, two daggers, four smaller knives, and a blunderbuss, he didn't know. All of her new iron weapons couldn't go into her magical pocket. And she had a lot of new weapons.

"You'll have to assess that for yourself." Harm grinned even as he tugged her down the street, taking the time to nod and smile at those they passed.

This was the first time he and Val were going out and about in Tulpenwerf since he'd returned nearly three months ago. They'd been caught up in endless court events as his father celebrated the return of both of his sons, tedious soirees as both he and Gijs were reintroduced to Tulpenland society with Val and Saskia at their sides, and finally the grand celebrations for the weddings. First of Harm and Val in the Tulpenland tradition so that no one would question the validity of their *feeën* marriage and second of Gijs and Saskia, done with as much pomp and circumstance as possible so that her father couldn't undo it.

All of that had left little time for wandering Tulpenwerf and introducing Val to the wonders of the canals, cheeses, stroopwafels, cassis, and other foods and sights to be found.

But the time to schmooze the Tulpenland nobility and rich merchants had been worth it. As Gijs had predicted, Harm hadn't been forced out of his position as heir. He'd been deemed odd. Eccentric. His new ties to the *feeënvolk* questioned. But when it came down to it, Tulpenlanders would prefer to have him on the throne with a *fee* at his side than lose their duchy's autonomy.

Beyond that, the Tulpenland merchants were already rubbing their hands together, discussing the ways they could capitalize on trade with the Fae Realm. It seemed business outweighed the dangers of bargaining with the *feeënvolk*.

Val laughed, a broad, joyful smile on her face, as he dragged her down the street. She'd put up with all the parties, events, and celebrations, even if she hadn't enjoyed them.

At least going out for lunch was something Harm could give her that she would enjoy almost as much as she'd enjoyed whipping the palace guards into shape.

Harm found a table at one of his favorite spots along the canal. When the proprietor hurried to their table, Harm ordered cassis and a pancake with plenty of strawberry jam.

A few people stopped by their table, bowed, welcomed Harm home, and congratulated him on his marriage. The braver ones worked up the courage to give Val a welcome and congratulations of her own.

When their food arrived, Val followed his example and liberally smeared her side of the pancake with jam. After she dug into her first bite, she closed her eyes. "This is really good."

Harm sliced off his first bite. "Told you."

"Here you are!" The dragon girl Tora, in her fae form, appeared out of the bustle on the street beside them. She grabbed a chair from beside a nearby table, plunked it beside theirs, and plopped into it.

"Uh, good morning." Harm managed a smile for Tora before he shared a look with Val. So much for their first meal out on the town. "What are you doing here? How did you get here? The tulips are done blooming."

"Oh, that. Turns out the basement of the windmill next to that tulip field has become a faerie circle. It's more or less round, after all, and it seems the turning blades give the magic a bit of a boost." Tora tore off a hunk of the pancake with her fingers and popped it in her mouth. "Ooh, this is really good."

Val scowled at Tora before she met Harm's gaze. "I'll send Abelardo to investigate the windmill. We'll likely need a guard stationed there to keep a watch for fae."

Harm mentally added arranging a guard rotation to his day's list of things to accomplish. "Tora, you didn't answer my first question. What are you doing here?"

"Besides trying Tulpenland food and acquiring more of that blue-and-white pottery?" Even in her fae form, Tora's teeth flashed white and a hint sharp. "The Primrose League has its first task for you. We rescued a human boy from the Court of Dreams, and it was easiest to get away by hopping through the faerie circle to Tulpenland instead of sneaking him out of the court. But as far as we can tell, the boy is from one of the islands off the coast somewhere. Not sure where. I'm bad at Human Realm geography."

"Returning him shouldn't be a problem. Tulpenland's ships travel all over the world." Harm glanced past Tora. "Where is he?"

"He and Taran are hiding just outside of town. We weren't sure how hard it would be to locate you." Tora tore off another bite of pancake. At this rate, Harm would have to order another pancake for himself and Val.

"And you volunteered to be the one to search us out." Val crossed her arms as she stared at Tora.

"Of course." Tora reached for the pancake again.

"We'll have to fetch him and see to his safety." Harm sighed and sliced off one last bite of pancake before he was forced to abandon it.

No matter. The rescued boy would be hungry. Harm would just order several more pancakes when they returned.

Val pushed to her feet, the leashes for both of the dogs in one hand, her other hand resting on the hilt of one of her new, iron daggers. "Let's go."

Harm grinned, plunked coins on the table to pay for their food, and climbed to his feet.

His life had changed beyond his wildest dreams since the last time he'd sat at this table. But he wouldn't trade this life for anything in the Human Realm, Fae Realm, or Realm of Monsters.

Ties of Death

A cursed king. A stolen bride. A desperate quest.

Emana hasn't seen her best friend Daenn since she left their gryphon rider clan for an arranged marriage eight years ago. She doesn't believe the rumors that he's become a ruthless tyrant since ascending the throne…not until the warm, kind boy she once knew hunts her down, kills her husband, and steals her back to the clan.

This new Daenn is cold, driven, and harder than the steel he wields with bloody efficiency, yet he claims to need her. Or at least, he needs her magic to temper his own chaotic, deadly power—through the shackles of marriage. But when Emana tampers with the new bond between them, their magic begins lashing out on its own, striking down innocents in alarming numbers.

Now, to save her clan and free herself from Daenn, Emana must journey deep into the heart of the jungle with him in search of a way to destroy his magic for good. But the more they are together, the more she sees echoes of warmth beneath his icy exterior that hint that maybe he hasn't changed as much as she thought. Except the search to sever their bond is filled with horrors, and destroying Daenn's magic might require a heavy cost—his very life.

Ties of Death is book 5 in Tethered Hearts, a multi-author series of no spice fantasy romances. Each stand-alone story features a magical bond that forces the couple to discover how much they're willing to sacrifice for the sake of love.

Read Ties of Death here!

TETHERED HEARTS

Ties of Legacy by Melanie Cellier
Ties of Starlight by Celeste Baxendell
Ties of Deception by Alice Ivinya
Ties of Bargains by Tara Grayce
Ties of Death by Constance Lopez
Ties of Shadow by Alora Carter
Ties of Frost by Selina R. Gonzalez
Ties of Dust by Deborah Grace White

The fictional Tulpenland was inspired by my trip to the Netherlands this past summer (2024) and by my own Dutch and Frisian heritage. While I drew a lot on Dutch culture, architecture, and language, Tulpenland is by no means meant to be an accurate representation of the Netherlands. Tulpenland is fully fictional and fully fantasy.

But here are a few of the fun historical tidbits I drew on when crafting Tulpenland:

It might surprise you to learn that tulips aren't native to the Netherlands, despite how much they are associated with the country. They arrived in the Netherlands in the late 15oos, and by the 17th century the flower's popularity sparked "Tulip Mania," an economic boom and bust all centered around tulips. Seriously, look it up. It's fascinating.

For Tulpenland, I fudged things a bit and moved up the arrival of tulips by a few centuries. Not that Tulpenland is particularly grounded in any one historical century. It's a fantasy duchy, after all.

Delft Blue pottery is also something the Netherlands is famous for. I went to their museum on my trip to the Netherlands and own a Delft tea set handed down from my great-grandmother. The method for making Delft

Blue came about around the same time as the arrival of tulips. I couldn't call it Delft Blue for my fictional Tulpenland, but Delft Blue was the inspiration for the pottery Harm hauls around.

Since Tulpenland is fictional, I really fudged things when it came to cassis. The cassis carbonated drink that I fell in love with while in the Netherlands wasn't invented until 1938. Cassis is now ubiquitous at restaurants, gas stations, and vending machines in the Netherlands, and I highly recommend that you have some if you ever go there. Cassis was such a big part of my trip that I couldn't *not* feature it, so Tulpenland got a fantasy version (more juice than soft drink).

On my final day in the Netherlands, we stopped at the Fries Museum in Leeuwarden, Friesland. There, amid artwork and beautiful historical pieces, was a truly massive sword. It is nearly 7 feet long. Just the blade is 5 feet long (as tall as I am). So of course I had to take a picture, read the plaque, and learn more about the history of that sword once I got home.

That sword is said to have been wielded by Grutte Pier (or Big Pier), a Friesian freedom fighter (or rebel, depending on which side one was on) who lived in the late 1400s and early 15oos. He became something of a folk hero in Friesland. Contestants on Season 9 Episode 22 of the TV show *Forged in Fire* created replicas of Grutte Pier's sword for the final challenge. These replicas were fully functional and wieldable, despite the massive size of the blade.

After seeing such an impressive sword, I had to include a nod to it in the character of Grutte with his sword. Once I had the character of Grutte, I couldn't resist the additional "I am Grutte" Easter Egg (though in Friesian, the "e" isn't silent and thus the name doesn't sound the same). But the nod to history came first, the Easter egg a secondary bonus.

I hope you enjoyed the fictional Tulpenland, and I hope you have the chance to visit the real Netherlands some day. Or if you live in the United States and a flight overseas is out of your reach, take a trip to Holland, Michigan (near where I live) to get a small taste of tulips, windmills, and a Dutch village.

Want More Books Set in this World?

Thanks so much for reading *Ties of Bargains*! I hope this zany story made you laugh and the characters stole your heart (especially Daisy).

If you would like to read more books set in the same Fae Realm as Ties of Bargains, pick up Stolen Midsummer Bride and the rest of the Court of Midsummer Mayhem series!

Stolen Midsummer Bride

Steal a bride. Save the library. Try not to die.

Basil, a rather scholarly fae, works as an assistant librarian at the Great Library of the Court of Knowledge. Lonely and unwilling to join the yearly Midsummer Revel to find a mate, Basil takes the advice of his talking horse companion and decides to steal a human bride instead.

A downloadable map of the Fae Realm is available on the Extras page of my website.

If you ever find typos in my books, feel free to

message me on social media or send me an email through the Contact Me page of my website.

If you want to learn about all my upcoming releases, get great book recommendations, and see a behind-the-scenes glimpse into the writing process, join my newsletter at www.taragrayce.com.

Did you know that if you sign up for my newsletter, you'll receive lots of free goodies? You will receive the free novella *Steal a Swordmaiden's Heart*, which is set in the same world as *Ties of Bargains*. This novella tells the story of how King Theseus of the Court of Knowledge won the hand of Hippolyta, Queen of the Swordmaidens.

If you don't wish to sign up for my newsletter, *Steal a Swordmaiden's Heart* is available on Amazon, though it isn't in KU.

Sign up for my newsletter now

Acknowledgments

Thanks first of all to the lovely ladies of Tethered Hearts: Melanie, Celeste, Alice, Constance, Alora, Selina, and Deborah. It was such a great time putting this series together with you all! A special thanks to Constance and Alora for organizing the series and all the hard work you put into it behind the scenes.

Thank you to Kim and Mara for an amazing trip to the Netherlands. This book would have been a completely different story without that inspiration.

A very special shout out to Nathanya, a reader from the Netherlands who read over a draft of this book. Thank you for helping me with the final tweaks! All mistakes and stumbles left are purely my own.

Thank you to my parents and grandparents for passing along the stories about my Dutch and Frisian immigrant ancestors. Those tales of stubbornness, perseverance, and love filled my childhood.

Thank you to my brothers, sisters-in-law, nieces, and nephews. All of you make life special and filled with family.

Thanks to my friends: Bri, Paula, Jill. Thank you for all the encouragement and evenings spent with laughter and chocolate.

Thanks to my writer group. Your feedback really

helped polish the beginning of this book (even if we are always more distracted by tangents than we are focused).

To my writing friends: Molly, Morgan, Addy, Savannah, Sierra, and many others: thank you for being there every step of the way on this crazy writing life.

For my proofreaders: Deborah and Bethany: thank you so much for finding time out of your busy lives to polish up my books so I don't completely embarrass myself (any mistakes that make it past you are totally my fault).

Most of all, thanks to my Heavenly Father for His generosity in all things and all times.

9 781943 442706